What the reviewers are saying:

"Stunning prose. In *Kiti*, Manning transports us with high drama to the High Arctic. This breathtaking and chilling chronicle of life in another time and place is a special story that no reader will forget."
—Claire Braz-Valentine, Playwright and Poet

"Amazing stuff! *Kiti* is a unique addition to the small-but-growing pantheon of real woman heroes—forced by necessity and empowered by innate talents. . . . Manning has carved an astonishing new character out of what hardly seems promising source material: the perpetual ice and cold of the far frozen north. *Kiti* is cool."
—Kent Lee Brisby, Director of Asian Story Theater (San Diego)

"Rare and delicious! Here's a quest adventure with a strong female protagonist, a tale that grabs readers and holds them in icy thrall."
—Walter Mayes, Librarian and Co-author of *Valerie & Walter's Best Books . . . a Lively, Opinionated Guide*

"My laughter was out loud, and my tears were in awe of the universal qualities we humans share. Anxiety and pain and determination anneal a woman powerful and inspiring. Although this Inupiat dwells in a culture, time and place alien to most, *Kiti* is all of us—a new literary heroine."
—Jenny Kay, Editor and Teacher

"Using characters that walk off the page, *Kiti* lets us feel the warm breath of a seal, whiff the aroma of whale blubber, shiver in frigid temperatures. . . . Manning weaves her reader into the icy fabric of the Arctic."
—Chicki Mallan, Travel Writer and Author of *Moon Handbooks: Yucatan Peninsula, Belize, Colonial Cities*, et. al

Also by Phyl Manning:

Arctic Circles
Phyl's Books, 2013

Here, There and Otherwhere, Volume 1
An Ordinary Woman in Extraordinary Places
Kalana Press, 2013

Here, There and Otherwhere, Volume 2
An Ordinary Woman at Extraordinary Times
Kalana Press, 2013

Here is the African Jungle
Illustrated by Steve Ferchaud
Wizard Graphics, 2006

KITI

Phyl Manning

Phyl's bOOks

Wilton, New Hampshire

KITI
by
Phyl Manning

Paperback: ISBN: 978-1-62742-006-8
Kindle: ISBN: 978-1-62742-007-5
e-Pub: ISBN: 978-1-62742-008-2

Cover and Interior Design by Pam Marin-Kingsley

Phyl's bOOks   an imprint of
Kalana Press
PO Box 377
Wilton, NH 03086
www.phylsbooks.com
www.kalanapress.com

To the memory of Ivan L. Manning,
who supported his wife in more ways than she knew.

Characters
(in order of appearance or mention)

Original Family and Village(Inland)
SUKITILAN: Only daughter of Pichikut and Narluk (almost seventeen winters in age)
PICHIKUT: Mother of seven; spirit of one
MAQ: Village Midwife and Pichikut's Friend
NARLUK: Much respected *angakok* of inland people; Sukitilan's father
NUNA: A dog to die for
AJAK: Nuna's pup
PALUNGA: Youngest of the five brothers older than Sukitilan; disappeared on tundra
OOJULIT: Eldest son of Pichikut and Narluk
PAJUK: Next-eldest son of Pichikut and Narluk
Characters mentioned, but not shown:
    (KARIKIT): One of two middle sons, lost on floating ice
    (MAMAK):Other of two middle sons, lost on floating ice
    IYARPOK: Lead dog ("The Laughing One") in contention with Nuna

On the Trail
KITI: Young woman on a dangerous mission (Inlander)
ARAJIK: Baby of unusual circumstance (Born Inland)
TUK: Young man who has recently lost his family (Coastal)
TONRATU: One of two who visit Kiti (Inlander)
ODLERK: Other one of two who visit Kiti (Inlander)
IYARPOK: Lead dog ("The Laughing One") in contention with Nuna

Tuk's Village (Coastal)

PUSIK: Woman who nurses and befriends Kiti
ITOK: Village hunter and husband of Pusik
ANJUK: Old man who is self-appointed leader
KANERK: Storyteller who reveals the tale of Chikut
Characters from Tale
    (CHIKUT) Heroine of Kanerk's tale at the Walrus Feast
    (MUNKUT) Chikut's father in the tale
    (KOLOKI) Water serpent in tale of Chikut

The Ice Village (Coastal)

ERTOK: Spry old woman who remembers Pichikut and is now Kiti's closest friend
POMAKUT: Husband to Ertok
ISUMAK: Popular child among villagers
ADLA: The stranger who wanders in from barren grounds
SAGAK: The wise but not so old man whose counsel is sought

Prologue

Below, south, in the place its inhabitants call civilization, great optimism ushers in the Twentieth Century. The United States goes onto the gold standard. Six cities there agree to form baseball's American League. That *Tramp Abroad* Mark Twain returns after nine years overseas. Klondike gold continues to gild the dreams of young adventurers. Hawaii becomes a U.S. Territory. The so-called "World Expo" draws many to Paris. Near-septuagenarian Field Marshal Roberts, having been thrust into the Boer War, is noisily "Marching to Pretoria," and Arthur Evans excavating on Crete reveals the remnants of a stunning Minoan Culture unknown heretofore.

More, French Impressionist Renoir unveils his Nude in the Sun—a dual concept inconceivable to those of the High Arctic. Sigmund Freud publishes The Interpretation of Dreams—whereas people of the far north have translated their "sleep memories" for centuries. But never mind, for none here will see any of Renoir's miracles of form and light or read Freud's book.

The high Arctic is untouched by events occurring to the south. Not in this featureless land where human time is measured as a book with infinite chapters—some long, some short; and each the life of one individual body. And where a spirit's time is endless. The place where Lesser Time is figured by the number of sleeps during which a person removes outer furs and crawls between thick pelts of bear and fox and wolverine laid out in time of snow upon the ledge of ice called *iglerk* built within each igloo . . . or in summer, lightened and laid upon the ground—two unequal seasons and the moons within them.

The better of these seasons is the long and lightless winter with wax but only partial wane of ten moons. Then, people pursue activities required to sustain and embellish lives richly infused with encounter, episode, expression and experience . . . but few "belong-ings" needed or desired.

The lesser season is the two-moon summer with light perpetual. Giant and relentless tides push coastal populations inland. Great swarms of ravenous insects demand blood from every living creature. Fledgling fowl rise from ground nests (for no trees are in this place) to try their wings. And over ancient permafrost, rivulets of ice-melt twist through dells that wind among low verdure on the endless inland prairie.

It is the summertime when people must travel without sleds and teams for hauling, must endure the dripping skies, and when coastal peoples must search for unaccustomed game in unfamiliar places—and wait, wait for the longer, friendlier and more familiar season when they return to the Sunrise Sea.

Chapter 1.
Beginning

In this winter world, a pastel shimmer in the near sky flares briefly to reveal tundra plains that otherwise roll smoothly out to invisible horizons. And on the billowing flats lie seven pale blisters of life. They bubble up from snow fields on this black mid-morning of a polar winter day. Six flicker with a pale glow while one more brightly lit shows shadows indistinct, distorted on the curved ice wall where wicks burn brightly and people move within.

The mother died when the baby was born. Actually, the body of the woman named Pichikut ceased to breathe before the birth. Her bright spirit, of course, would ascend to join other spirits and await opportunity to enter another newborn.

Near the end, Pichikut's only daughter Sukitilan stood over her above the special birthing ledge of ice within the arching walls of the snowhouse. Can a healthy infant arrive after labor of two sleeptimes and now a third day starting? the girl wondered silently. Can it happen that a child comes after all this toil? And if the mother dies as Pichikut herself has predicted, and when it happens that no woman of the village can provide milk . . . will the infant then be laid out naked in the wind to freeze?

No. Surely not. Our father Narluk—all-wise *angakok*, a shaman honored widely among inland Inupiat of the Caribou—would never commit this terrible act his wife foresaw. Not when he knew that a snow-death was against her express wish. And especially not after he learned that arrangements for feeding a motherless child had been so carefully planned.

The left hand of Sukitilan lay buried in folds of the blanket that warmed her mother, her *ananak*, this laboring Pichikut. The white sea bear fur made soft and malleable with human saliva, urine and great effort. The girl's right hand reached up to lightly tug scar tissue at the gnarled lobe of her ear as she watched her mother snatch shallow breaths raggedly . . . over . . . once again . . . again?

"Someone must push!" Sukitilan scolded softly through tight lips. "A woman needs to help the babe be born."

So warm. Condensation rolled down the circling wall to make runnels underfoot. Sukitilan used both hands to lift the neckline of her *illupak*, the light pelt undergarment worn uncovered inside shelter. Air reached her skin, and she exhaled slowly in relief. Her lungs wheezed from breathing the stale breath of village women who suffered along with the revered wife of their shaman: present pain along with their own still-remembered childbirth labors.

Too hot! Sukitilan thought now. She pushed straggling strands of black hair behind both ears, once more allowing the middle fingers of her right hand to rest against the scarred lobe. She bent low above Pichikut's face, but no longer sensed upon her eyelid any hint of breath.

Two sleeps ago, when Pichikut's compressions signaled a baby soon to arrive, it was Sukitilan who went out to summon Maq the midwife—wizened and tattooed, with red-rimmed eyes and skillful hands. The other five women of the village came—were loyally assembled still. And each providing heat.

Supplying sound, too, Sukitilan realized when most of it suddenly ceased. She looked around. Somehow, the women seemed to know that the critical time had arrived. Chatter faded, and laughter stopped entirely.

That early sound was now replaced by earnest chant and the snapping *click-er-click* of amulets. Rhythmically, one voice and then another called out the names of good Inuit men and women now gone to the spirit world. Identified aloud were free shades no doubt eager to live again by entering an infant newly born.

The child would emerge when it heard the proper name, and that last name called was likely to be the spirit that controlled. It would protect and guide the early breaths, the first precarious days until it proved itself, prevailed over other minor specters as guardian of the new being throughout its life. The Way of the People, Sukitilan reflected: *peeusinga*.

Pichikut had told her daughter what to expect. She said also that her own coastal people on ice islands far north at the top of the world secured a guardian spirit at the time of birth in the same manner.

"And does it happen that those upon your frozen islands also leave a motherless child alone on ice to die?" Sukitilan had wanted to know. She could still ask such direct questions of her mother, her *ananak*, but only with no one else nearby. Others? Them Sukitilan was far too old to query—not her brothers, certainly not her father Narluk. Nor could she question villagers and violate their privacy—or she would receive for her answer a softly exhaled "Hoo-oo" of censure or at least a disapproving look—head tilted sideways with a long stare from eyes black as wet berries. She must not intrude on the delicate inner spirit of another.

"Perhaps yes," Pichikut had answered directly as was her way. "A newborn can be set out to die—if the small one is doomed otherwise to suffer a lingering death from lack of food and care."

That would be a kindness, the daughter admitted, for a snow death is without pain. "But if provision has been arranged?"

"Then perhaps no, for all Inuit love their babies."

This Sukitilan now beginning her seventeenth winter was long-legged, lean by nature—and would therefore not ever be considered beautiful. Too, her right ear lobe was notched and glossy with a scar. She took comfort in the disfigurement, though, and her bare right hand touched it for reassurance. Here was a legacy from a sled dog puppy's attack when she herself was a toddler scampering from her mother's hood. And this was proof that good luck rode her shoulder. Too, this was a permanent bond with the great white sled dog Nuna—the very one whose great-sire as a youngster had leapt upon the child to savage her ear.

No, the only daughter of Pichikut would not even consider a double death of mother and infant, she reminded herself now, despite *Ananak's* prophecy. And no need to. She looked down at the now-motionless woman before her and swallowed. Of course a vigorous child would soon arrive; and naturally Pichikut would live; and all would be in harmony as before except that Sukitilan would no longer be youngest in her family and her village. A strange, choking sound came from her throat.

Maq the midwife clasped Sukitilan's shoulder, squeezed in sympathy, but the young woman shrugged her hand away, then bent to test for her mother's breath once more upon the tender skin of her own eyelid. Nothing.

"*Ananak!*" Mother! she hissed without regard for the great discourtesy committed by addressing another person so directly. "Pichikut!" Perhaps she could shock the woman into seizing back her departing life spirit. Surely no fate more harsh than present circumstance could come from such offense.

Her *ananak* had commanded so much.... Here was Pichikut's Plan, now in effect. A healthy newborn—male or female—is to be kept alive, she told her daughter often; for she herself never did expect her body to withstand the birth of this seventh child so late in her own life. Pichikut welcomed death, Sukitilan knew, to slough her worn body as a quiet finish to this existence, perhaps followed by a small rest before her spirit commenced the next?

And the daughter would not wish to take this well-earned interlude from Pichikut—even though the girl quaked at the thought of continuing without the strong woman who had guided her in ways no other mother could. At least, not any that Sukitilan had ever known or heard about.

But the beloved form before Sukitilan on the high birthing ledge lay motionless, and the girl despaired.

Suddenly, Maq reached deeply into the birth channel and brought forth a red, squirming mass that clenched as air struck flesh. A weak bubbling sound from the infant became a lusty protest even as the old woman nipped the cord and tied the ends. She pushed the squalling child into the hands of Sukitilan without a word, then turned away and scuttled out through the hide baffle before others in the snowhouse knew what had happened—before they realized that all their utterances and amulets were not enough to anchor the spirit of this mother. Before they themselves dived into the tunnel and disappeared.

"Someone needs help—" Sukitilan protested as she watched the village women go so hastily. She fell silent as she saw the hide flap stop its swinging, glanced around the empty igloo that was home. She understood their haste, of course, for Pichikut had predicted this very panic. She would die in an unsealed place, she explained to her daughter. Villagers would believe that the woman's spirit, angry at having to depart, would now be loosed upon the community. And although people honored and respected the wife of *angakok* in life, they were likely to fear her deeply in death because all knew her spirit to be uncommonly strong.

But Pichikut had reassured her daughter that neither she nor anyone had anything to fear. "No logic lies in thinking that a spirit who protects someone throughout life becomes suddenly sinister when death occurs."

Now alone in the igloo with the spiritless body of her mother and the fretting baby brother . . . "*Aa-gii-ii!*" No! Pichikut, a daughter trembles with misgiving about everything except her mother's spirit—which is most welcome in this place!

As she had been drilled, the young woman automatically bathed the child in snowmelt, long ready as it warmed above the seal oil lamp. Here was of course the first and likely the last bath he would ever have. Yet another boy, she saw, and sighed. Six brothers for Sukitilan? The baby quieted as she wrapped a soft hare skin around him, then sucked mucus from his nostrils.

Feeling helpless, she studied the hiccuping newborn in her arms. The next steps were to arrange for feeding and then present the vigorous babe to their father Narluk. And the result of that meeting would control the child's future . . . and that of Sukitilan as well.

Chapter 2.
Preparation

Sukitilan slipped into the snowhouse where the sinew wick burned low. She laid her baby brother in robes atop the *iglerk*, the family sleep ledge built up to cover nearly half the snowhouse interior. This new Inuk was perfect, she decided. All parts husky and well formed, intact, bright eyes trying hard to focus. When chill wind struck the boy, he howled, tiny fists beating air, body pink with resentment and getting pinker as his ire increased. How much easier would her own life likely be, she reflected, if this infant were not so robust. She quickly tucked the wrap around him. The lusty shouts ceased, and the two regarded each other.

"Eh," the sister said softly, "a babe knows what he wails for, stops crying when he gets it." A good quality in any person, she decided. This seventh child of Pichikut was hefty, bound to become a mighty hunter like his father and his brothers. She did not dare to dwell fully on the question, but wondered at the crisp edges of her mind: Who will someday be the ones to teach this child the secrets of the trail? If not his father or brothers, could it then be his big sister?

She hurried to put outdoor clothing over her *illupak*, tucked each furry pants leg into a waterproof *kamik*, that snow- and waterproof warm boot that clung to the foot like skin. Then she plucked up the newborn and placed him deep inside her parka front where he would rest warm supported by the taut drawstring.

Cradling the little one, Sukitilan crawled past the baffle and through the tunnel until she came up into the darkness of the winter morning. She listened, heard nothing—the sled dogs except for Nuna were gone with hunters on the trail. No one would see her movements—good! Except for her father the *angakok*, village men were somewhere on the trail to find food—her two remaining brothers also, despite their mother's circumstance.

And right now, village women were inside their igloos packing, busily preparing for a move by sled to flee as soon as possible the detached spirit of Pichikut. Narluk and his two grown sons still living—at home, anyway—would seal this snowhouse when they returned today, would build a small new shelter for the single night of sleep—but everyone including the family of Sukitilan would be gone before this time tomorrow. No one would grumble, for moving was a part of life for every Inuit—if not to escape an unbound spirit as in this instance, then to find a better region for the hunt or else to elude a troublesome predator or more likely an angry trail spirit. *Pirtok*, no one can undo that which has already happened.

"Nuna." Sukitilan crawled into the small igloo built for the dog and her six whelps. "The time has come." The girl gathered up five of the pups, reassuring their mother. She left one little female. This was "Ajak," Sukitilan's favorite among the three-moon-old offspring left overlong with their mother to assure continued lactation. "It is not a good thing to relinquish all of one's litter and replace with an alien," she explained.

Nuna gave a short pule of inquiry, then rose to follow the person now backing through the entry and carrying most of the dog's family.

With an intermittent whine, the canine parent padded behind her as Sukitilan walked out into the village with her burden. "These great hulking creatures should have stopped taking their mother's milk long ago," the girl explained to the anxious dog. "It happens that someone got extra meat for extra time so that she would produce ever more milk for the strapping pups."

Now she coughed delicately to call the people in the first snowhouse. Then she added softly to Nuna as they waited, "For them and for their mother's coming task."

This first woman along with the next four expressed delight over receipt of the canine gifts—the offspring of Nuna?! Intelligent and healthy sled dogs to train!

Nuna cocked her head and quieted, but an occasional whine still escaped.

"You enjoyed them longer than the normal period," Sukitilan told the bitch as they made their way back to Nuna's tunnel, "and your lovely little Ajak is retained." A moment later, "Plus a newcomer, so a great responsibility."

Inside, Sukitilan put Ajak to her mother's teat, then removed the bundled human baby from the front of her *illupak*. She held him near Nuna's nose while she softly explained, then laid him beside Ajak and worked his mouth around a separate teat. Within a few moments, the now-hungry infant got the idea.

Nuna was startled, true, and Kiti kept reassuring her until the big white dog relaxed. After all, a baby is a baby is a baby. . . .

"It is not a good thing," Sukitilan admonished her, "to care so strongly that some cranky spirit is challenged to take away that which is beloved." The young woman drew breath on a sob, wondered where those words came from. Not from Pichikut, who always loved without restraint. From the immature Sukitilan, then. The girl who had lost three brothers and her mother—and now might lose her home.

She left the bundled infant with Nuna, returned to the igloo, started sorting. She separated what she would need if she had to go alone, including Pichikut's Big Feed. This large hide container was filled with extra robes and precious *apvik* fur, that waterproof and cozy coat of the unloved wolverine. Also here with seal oil were well-bagged "emergency" food—spirits bless her mother for this forethought! And the odd sewing sinews and bone needles, a few "surplus" tools and weapons. This treasure plus, stacked open in the igloo, some food and a few more robes, she hauled up to and then secured on Palunga's sled.

Irk! Stop! Do each task in order, one by one, as you were taught. Sukitilan piled melted permafrost clay along the sliding surface of each whalebone runner on Palunga's sled. It froze immediately. Using her sharp snow knife of fire-hardened bone, she sculpted the mud to make a reasonably even coating two fingers deep along the length of each runner, then carefully with a trembling hand carved off each bump and nubbin. Next came melted snow warmed in her mouth, spit along the sliding surface layer by layer, each coat freezing on contact and polished with a scrap of cured caribou hide until the shallow crescents gleamed in starlight.

The sled had been placed a full moon ago out of sight in a gully invisible to the village. If she could accompany her family after the sleep, she was now already packed. But she was also ready to go if she had to escape in the sleep time. All that would be necessary was to select and harness dogs for her team. And except for the addition of Ajak—all was as planned previously with Pichikut.

The village hunters including her brothers Oojulit and Pajuk would be home soon, she thought. And those two would be grateful that she had emptied and then sealed the igloo where their mother's body lay. They would build a small trail igloo to shelter them through the sleep, then abandon it forever after waking.

Narluk would appear late on this night, she supposed, as was his wont when troubled. And then would come those critical moments when he would make his decision about his new son.

Chapter 3.
The Plan

Sukitilan reviewed her mother's scheme. The woman's predictions were unfolding as truth—*Ananak's* death, desertion by fearful villagers, vigor in the newborn baby. Before this dark day was finished—eh, soon!—the daughter would surely know whether she must actually carry out her mother's desperate design: Pichikut's Plan. . . . Rescue the newborn from a tradition-bound Narluk. Take the trail north and east alone with the baby and Nuna, a small sled and the best dogs as her team. Keep the infant safe and healthy while eluding any who might follow. Finally seek asylum at the ice island village of Pichikut's own origin. The design seemed almost simple as the girl reviewed it now. But it wasn't, and it would not be, she knew.

Secretly, *Ananak* had been training her daughter over numerous moons, developing and practicing the necessary skills despite the girl's protests. The pregnant woman had drilled her on what were likely to become essential, life-protecting capabilities. Above all, Pichikut insisted, were patience and perseverance.

To teach these qualities, Ananak had Sukitilan fidgeting as she hovered above a spear-drilled hole in lake ice which her mother insisted must be considered the breathing hole for a seal.

"It happens that the hunter must make no sound and cast no shadow moving on the ice," Pichikut whispered.

After long hours of surveillance, Sukitilan thought that she would explode like a carcass on tundra heated by summer sun. "No seal will ever rise in mere lake ice!" Sukitilan complained. "This time of great discomfort is for nothing."

"*Nipjarnok!*" Hush! her mother commanded. And not until two days around one full sleep had passed, Ananak leaving and returning silently as she managed family matters at the igloo, was the girl free to go home to rest upon the warm *iglerk*.

"And if *nathek*—that small, oily, delicious but most wary seal—rises in such small time as this," her mother said as she dismissed her, "then the hunter is indeed fortunate."

"It happens," Sukitilan retorted, "that this girl will not ever be so hungry as to hunt for seal."

Pichikut tilted her head and considered her daughter for some moments. Then she snorted. "It is at least hoped that the person will not expect seal through freshwater ice." Then she laughed aloud, a joyful, unrestrained sound that echoed off icy mounds and boulders nearby.

Skills considered crucial included ice fishing, even though Sukitilan like most Inupiat (and their dogs) did not much like the taste of fish. Also necessary was use of the sturdy little killing spear designed by *Ananak* to be light and manageable. And more complex but still essential were ways to rapidly assemble and use the compact harpoon crafted with much skill long ago by the maternal grandfather called Munkut to fit the hand of then-young Pichikut herself.

A unique aspect for the requisite training of a daughter included practice in how to dilute the too-rich lactation of a sled dog—for the anticipated trip was meaningless unless the baby remained hearty.

How could her mother know such things? Also, the girl must find the killing spot on every food creature that might present itself along the trail inland or at the Sunrise Sea. Sukitilan used the spear and the harpoon to slay many a snowdrift bear and caribou. She loved being out with her mother for most of the play-games they enjoyed.

But surely all of this instruction and practice were pointless where pertaining to the care of a baby and assuring that the infant with its sister and a sled team could survive alone on the trail. Her mother would not perish in the coming childbirth. And if she did—which of course she would not!—then certainly the family must continue as a unit. So Sukitilan told herself. Often.

"How is it," the daughter demanded of her mother, "that *Ananak* knows so much about the trail?"

"It happens that Pichikut beginning as a child was sole huntress for parents overripe—"

"—Hoo-oo . . . No brothers!" Such a household was unimaginable to someone who had a surfeit of these siblings.

"Not even one, for the child fruited from the old womb of an aging mother who with her husband had despaired long before of ever having children."

"And Pichikut's father found no food?"

"An artisan, as the harpoon can prove. But then, most men can make weapons with some skill when the need arises," Ananak laughed. "It was said among the villagers that old Munkut always met with disaster when he took the trail. Even as a youth, so the story went, his step was heavy, his arm unsteady, the mercy of his heart usually overriding the rumble of his gut."

Sukitilan was silent as she considered these words. Such men normally became *angakok*—her own father being an exception. For Narluk was highly honored for possessing prowess on the hunt as well as celebrated shaman skills.

Her mother went on. "The loving husband and father, this Munkut, possessed an always-hungry family." Pichikut smiled. "So even while young, the daughter blest with fortune on the hunt found food for her family and team until her parents died."

"—And after that—?"

"—Provided for herself and some few needy widows and their children until still-young Pichikut married and left the village."

"*Ananak* uses the words 'fortune on the hunt—'"

"—Yes. She knew herself to possess great good luck on the trail—as does her daughter."

Sukitilan said nothing. All know that skill and courage have little meaning without fortuity as well. Did *Ananak* truly believe that her female child possessed this luck? This untried and unsure creature who quaked daily beneath the burden of her mother's demands?

But Pichikut only concluded her tale. She was a young woman alone when she met and married the mighty shaman Narluk. They went west and mostly south to live among his inland folk on landlocked tundra, she never again to make the long journey to her home at the frozen sea.

Her mother's differing origin would account, Sukitilan reflected, for the disparities in thought and practice between Pichikut and villagers here. Her mother reasoned a situation instead of always blindly following *peeusinga*, The Way of the People. She expected the same of her children. More like Narluk, though, all but the younger son Palunga leaned toward local custom. Pichikut must have wondered, would the daughter also disappoint? Never mind, Sukitilan was too young—at least too untried to know.

Sukitilan snorted. Her brothers' sister would not provide— not ever provide them the domestic ease they presently took for granted. For now and probably forever, Sukitilan would lack her mother's speed and grace and expertise within the home. The brothers might soon wish to find themselves women of their own to take over the hard work of managing the food supply, of preparing skins, of making and later mending all apparel.

And the brothers had recently demonstrated their desire to distance themselves from household crises. Both had gone out especially early and with grim resolution on these three mornings of travail for their mother. Like *angakok*, the intrepid warriors fled the snowhouse to escape the pain and waiting. The sister smiled inside the tightly drawn parka opening. Bravery manifests itself in settings other than the hunt.

She loved the two remaining brothers, but wished that they were here and useful right now. Oojulit so serious and Pajuk the joker—not serious at all. Yes, she was quite sure. . . . Her growing up with six men in the family probably explained why she had no wish to marry. The male of her human species held for Sukitilan no wonder and small potential for romance.

23

Several men, some still young, had come to the village to seek her father's counsel, then stayed on to meet and talk with *angakok's* daughter. But although she agreed to bed them when they asked, and although she thoroughly enjoyed those nights in the furs, her parents observing and making suggestions, her brothers joking and teasing, she found no one she would want to marry. Nor was she so charming that they stayed to pursue their cause. Tall and narrow were not qualities sought for in a woman. Being cuddlesome and having strong teeth were favored.

Five brothers until this day. The middle two, Karikit and Mamak had been away, now commencing the second winter, too long to expect their return. They had been with villagers on an ocean hunting trip about this time twelve moons ago—perhaps too early in the season and before sea ice was stable. A crashing blow came up, according to those who witnessed the catastrophe, and the grounded ice on which they camped broke off to become *situ*, a loose floe traveling southeast before the wind. Still, they had with them robes and hunting bags and trail packs with food and extra clothing. Also, their sled and team. On the same *situ* were three more experienced men and several dogs separated from their sleds. Some hope remained, therefore. Karikit and Mamak might yet return.

And then young Palunga, only a couple of winters older than his sister, had walked out to search for his brothers when they were not back by winter's end. In the thaw of late spring, he had left dogs and sled behind as useless on bare ground. Her favorite brother. Palunga, youngest of the five . . . funny and helpful, always troubling himself for others. Twenty winters old when he strode away, hunting spear in hand and trail gear rolled up into a sleep robe across his shoulders and steadied by a strap across his forehead.

He never did return to the village, and hope dwindled as summer bloomed briefly and faded. No one could survive winter here alone without sled and team. Next to Pichikut, her *ananak*, the sister had loved Palunga best.

24

Chapter 4.
Discovery

Nestling between robes on the *iglerk* with her family, but still fully clothed except for *kamik* (boots), Sukitilan came from a light doze into heavy dismay. The baby was awake and crying. She patted him, but he only wailed louder.

Narluk stirred.

She removed the baby from her parka and thrust him deeply into the blanket furs. He continued to squall.

The long sleep breaths of her brothers Oojulit and Pajuk shortened. Both shifted restlessly. She heard no sound at all from where her father lay.

Sukitilan dug into the robes and turned sideways to muffle sound with her body. She wanted to disappear with the child into one of the furry wrinkles, pull the cover after her. She addressed the infant with a whisper in his ear: "It happens, silence is needed here," she told him severely.

But his cries escalated. Could he be hungry or in pain? Yet, he did not seem distressed. His stomach was soft, his muscles relaxed. What he was doing, she decided as the weeping continued, was exercising his lungs.

She whispered, "*Nipjarnak!*" Be silent!

At that moment, the sleep furs that covered her were pulled up and away. From the corner of her eye, she saw in flickering lampglow that her father towered above. Quickly, she stuffed the howling child once more into her own clothing.

Narluk had not returned until well into the sleep time. He did not awaken anyone, did not speak at all, only beat and folded his *silipak*, removed his *kamik*, and crawled into the blankets.

Why had his daughter not spoken up? But then, why had he not asked? Doubtless, he thought all were asleep. He knew that his wife was not there, that they were in a temporary shelter—and he would have been sad but not surprised.

But for how long had Sukitilan thought to keep the child's existence a secret? What a fool she was, what a *soospuk*! She dragged a fur across her, hoping to dim the baby's cries.

"Trim the lamp wick," Narluk said.

Sukitilan came off the ledge reluctantly, the baby still in full voice. *Pirtok*. What's already happened cannot be undone.

Although she kept her head down, her eyes on the lamp, ministering to the wick as the snow hut brightened, she knew that her father stood by her once again. She sensed his turning away to get his furs from the bladder, heard him shake them and then put them on over his *illupak*. Sukitilan felt like some outlandish creature—herself now directly from the sleep ledge and betrayed by still wearing outdoor furs—standing gap-mouthed before her fully-awakened family with a sustained howl arising from her bosom. Adding to the bizarre effect, she saw her every motion as the lamp cast shadows onto walls and arcing roof.

On impulse, she withdrew the infant in his furry bunting, held him out. Now the father could behold his new son—could see how sturdy the child was. Narluk knew certainly that the baby had healthy lungs. The cries ceased immediately as the eldest and youngest members of the family studied each other.

The big man cleared his throat, started to speak, cleared again. "This babe was born of Pichikut."

"*Ee-ee,*" Sukitilan said softly.

Silence. Then, "Emerging before or after the spirits left her?"

"After." Sukitilan stood before him fully clothed, hide-slippered feet on ice, the baby howling again, but now replaced within the bosom of her *silipak*, his sound muffled.

Narluk stood motionless for so long that the icy terror of foreboding once again crept up to chill the girl. She felt such agitation that it was difficult to stand on her shuddering legs. Pichikut had described what the Caribou Inupiats, at least, the inland people consider to be kindness for a motherless child.

Sukitilan might blame this little one for their mother's death. She might blame him also for unwanted changes in her comfortable life. But the babe did not mean to make trouble. And unlike other little ones who could not go suckle at their mother's breast, this infant would not waste away and starve. He would be saved by Pichikut's Plan. By his sister and by Nuna. So to kill this healthy child—even quickly and without pain—would be no kindness.

"Give me the baby," Narluk repeated and reached out. He now wore his mitts, Sukitilan saw. He had finished drawing on his furs and *kamik* while she had stood in that frosty fog of fear. He was ready to go outside. Sukitilan raised her head slowly and saw the terrible resolve flickering in his eyes.

Narluk also had a Plan. Once again, Pichikut's prediction would prove accurate.

"*Pinnak!*" Don't! She turned away, but the baby's bellows resumed. She had seen before she turned her back to them that both Oojulit and Pajuk now sat cross-legged on the *iglerk*, atop the sleep ledge, furs clutched around them for warmth. Neither said a word.

"Give the baby to me!" Narluk's voice was hard, without inflection.

Sukitilan trembled—not with fear of what her father would do to her but of what she knew he planned for this tiny brother. She would not turn around. She would stay forever with her face peering across the *iglerk* to the wall—stay until she awoke to find that the whole family was still living in the large snowhouse no longer sealed. Pichikut alive. The baby born normally. All would be as it should be . . . and this dreadful, endless day and night would be only her bad dream to be picked over and analyzed and finally told aloud and laughed about as a trail tale.

Narluk's hand touched her shoulder gently. "The daughter must deliver the babe to its father."

"*Sog?*" Why? she demanded. She knew the reason. Could he say the terrible words?

"So that the father can do with it—"

"—Not it. A boy!" she blurted, once more producing the child, but cradling him with both arms so that he could not be snatched away. "Narluk's son!" She turned to the man slowly, arms locked around the baby now withdrawn and visible. Here he was, for full view. "A hearty, healthy child." If she had a name for him, he would seem more permanent. It would help also if she could name the spirit most likely to be protecting him.

Again she tried to remember—what was that last name called before Maq took the baby from the body of his dead parent?

Narluk glanced at the infant, then looked away, his decision clearly unchanged.

"He is well-fed," she told him, "and will continue to be so."

"That is impossible." The man stretched out his arms once more.

"*Owka!*" No! She pivoted once more, replaced the baby in her *silipak* bosom with wildly shaking hands. Miraculously, the little boy ceased his cries.

"A daughter must obey her father," the man urged quietly, then added, "and her mother would wish it."

"*Aa-gii-ii!*" NO! She looked at Narluk. Dark shadows around his eyes were emphasized by flickering light that came from the lamp. She knew he was saddened by the loss of his wife. Also by what he planned for the infant. And by his daughter's resistance, too. Sympathy for her father glimmered, but she snuffed it out.

"Pichikut planned ways to keep her last child alive."
Narluk answered nothing, but his arms lowered slowly.
"Nuna is gentled for her task."
"Nuna . . . ?!" His voice trailed off.
"Already, she accepts him, and he suckles her."
More silence, and then, "No . . . Not possible—Hoo-oo! . . . A human fed by *kringmerk*? By a dog? Ai-ee!!" His face reflected his dismay and disbelief.

"He'll be healthy—he's already healthy! Cared for by his sister. The father will see!" Sukitilan glared at her two brothers still motionless in their robes, eyes large with shock.

"The brothers will see, as will the whole village!"
Her voice broke into sobs. Then she swallowed, resumed her plea, repeating former words and adding gradually, amid hiccups of strain, the special provisions Pichikut had made. The leaving of Nuna's last litter with her to suckle for nearly three moons so that the dog's milk would last until the baby's birth and still would be sufficient. The girl described the woman's love for her unborn child, the sustained effort to train her daughter in caring for an infant, the daughter's reluctant efforts to learn.

What she did not tell Narluk was Pichikut's Plan. Her silence on that subject was not by design but by instinct, for then the whole scheme would have been exposed as pleas and promises bubbled like a spring freshet from her mouth into Narluk's deaf ears.

She did not tell him that she was packed and ready to go. That if necessary to save the baby she had promised to leave the family forever. That she would run fast and far with the child if her father insisted on heeding tradition without regard for special circumstance.

Finally, the words ran dry in her parched mouth, and she stood sobbing across from Narluk. Later, she thanked the spirits for restraining her loose tongue.

But now, he moved toward her, his voice soothing and deep. "If a woman in the village could suckle the child . . ." he began, then stopped. A hopeless possibility. No woman here had born a child in twenty-five winters.

"—Nuna can suckle—" she gasped for the twentieth time.

"—*Owka!*" No, she cannot. "Certainly, the babe will die—if not soon, then late—!" His voice broke off, and Sukitilan realized that he had put one hand inside her tunic from below while the other fumbled with the outer drawstring. She had allowed herself to be cornered at the end of the sleep ledge by the lamp, and she felt violated.

She flung both hands under the child and tried once more to turn away, but too late. Narluk's nimble shaman fingers released the string as he forced her arms up.

"Far better," he continued in the chanting tone his voice had assumed, "that the infant find death before he learns to savor life."

"*Aa-gii-ii!*" NO! she implored, trying but failing to sound like Pichikut. She felt her little brother taken from her. Narluk eased him away from under her parka with one of his huge hands while with the other he caught and held both of hers.

She stood shaking and sobbing afterwards, as her father stooped down to the old hide baffle which guarded the doorway of this small and temporary igloo. She heard her own voice continue to protest. But he and the baby were gone. Her big brothers, she saw, had dug beneath the furs to feign sleep.

"Someone sees the two brave hunters hiding from someone less than half their size!" she spat, her bare hand grasping at her ear. These two would never deny their father, regardless of personal feelings, they supported him out of fear?

She sighed. No, out of respect. And did she then not respect Narluk? Never before had she defied him. Nor did she want to now. But in this matter, his blind following of tradition made no sense. Pichikut had explained often the reason for leaving a motherless babe to freeze. Ice death was rapid, painless . . . final.

Not for this child, though. . . . And here was cowardly Sukitilan once again imagining when she should be doing. She leaped across the ice floor to where she could pull the warm *kamik* over her slippers. That she still wore the outdoor furs—her *silipak*—when she came from the sleeping ledge must have startled her father, certainly the brothers.

She dived into the tunnel, crawled from the igloo. She did not go for a weapon. Instead, she made her way around to Nuna's snowhouse. Why was everyone in this village so old, she raged. Why was no woman young enough to put this baby brother to her breast? She would be glad to leave this place!

Chapter 5.
Search

Nuna met her with a short whine of friendly greeting when the girl stuck her head past the baffle into the tiny ice room. "Come!" The pup Ajak asleep in the ragged fur covering the floor, the dog joined Sukitilan readily. The dark night snapped with cold but was at this moment without wind and lighted once more by greens and pinks and blues swirling above.

"It happens," Sukitilan told the bitch as they followed tracks across the tundra, "that we must find where he put the child, then hide ourselves until we're certain he is gone." If they arrived too soon, her father would see them coming. And this—absolutely!—*must* not occur. A second opportunity to save the child would not present itself. He would dash the baby on a rock, if pressed, just as she had seen him and other hunters out of kindness end a baby seal or bear whose mother was taken in error.

Nor must they be too late, she warned Nuna, or the child would be stiff and spiritless. She focused ahead on her father's big *kamik* prints. She did not worry overmuch about meeting Narluk coming back, for she knew that he was more than likely to walk over to some rocks above the frozen lake and there quiet his distressed spirit. For this drama tonight would trouble him greatly.

Once more, she pushed back her nagging sympathy.

The man should have considered. He should have respected the memory of his wife enough to honor her wish. He was closely tied to local ways, Pichikut had warned. And now his own Narluk's son must be set out to die because the babe was motherless and no village woman could suckle him? So it was done always. *Peeusinga.* That another arrangement was made did not matter, even if it was viable. Narluk could not project himself beyond the custom of his people, and his wife had known this to be true.

Up to the right ear went the young woman's mitt. Tears fell and trickled slowly on her face. Stifled sobs and hiccups broke the silence until Nuna returned across the tundra to walk beside her and stare up curiously from time to time.

The girl patted the dog's head, and the two kept going. Nuna kept her nose pointed upward in the air, probably scenting her foster child. But Sukitilan picked out tracks, occasionally glancing up to keep a lookout for Narluk, just in case.

It was of course Nuna who found the boy. As they started up a long rise, the dog suddenly raced ahead.

"*Nipjarnok*!" Silence! Sukitilan called softly, then stumbled along behind, unable to keep up. Where was her father? He must not see or hear them. She at last spied the dog on the crest, hunkered full length on the ground, pale coat on pale snow but shaggy fur in silhouette under the roiling lights above. To give warmth? Sukitilan scrabbled beneath the big creature to find her brother. He had lain naked upon his white hare bunting. Cold, yes, but not yet frozen. His arms moved slowly but his head twisted from side to side, lips puckered and sucking.

She had disturbed his feeding. Sukitilan plucked him up, tucked him into her parka, secured the drawstring. She shook the bunting, rolled it up and put it beneath her arm to warm.

"Now we go for team and sled," she told Nuna as they started the long walk back. Pichikut's Plan.

Halfway to the village, the baby once again began to cry. No weak whimpering, either, but lusty shouts of outrage. He wanted his meal. When Sukitilan had taken him out from under Nuna to place him inside her parka, he had in silence accepted the change for welcome warmth. Now, though, he made great noise. She sighed. No sound must awaken the people when she returned to the igloos deep in the sleep time. Especially, no alien sound of a babe.

Nor must her family stir as Sukitilan entered and left the village silent as the shadow of a red-throat loon.

She clicked her tongue to bring Nuna back, then laid herself down on the tundra, spreading the folds of her parka and trousers as wide as possible after she withdrew the child. Onto spare fur, she placed her brother newly rewrapped in the bunting. Nuna understood her own function immediately and lay beside them.

What an eater, this little boy . . . *Kargolarpok!* What a great smacking of lips, what noisy satisfaction. . . . Sukitilan smiled as she skimmed clean snow to warm in her mouth for thinning the too-rich canine milk. She listened with pleasure to the sound of feeding, and she delighted in the sight of Nuna nosing down to lick the child affectionately.

Here was a time to think without other action required, and she savored the moments, turned her thoughts forward to make final selection on which among the dogs of her father and brothers she should take for her team. Nuna would always be her choice for lead—but Nuna now had other responsibilities.

What of Iyarpok, the Laughing One? The one which had been Palunga's lead dog was now claimed by Oojulit. The creature would feel comfortable with his former master's sled. He was large enough to command respect from other dogs, reasonably intelligent . . . and with fierce views. Never mind, a lead dog needs strong will. Iyarpok was aggressive but not vicious. He might do well. She grinned in the dark, glancing up at the one star still visible, beyond the crest of—what was that?

A shadow bobbed at the top of the rise they had just descended. An animal? Some predator—no, she made out fur trim on a smoothly rounded sphere. A person? Not Narluk, for he would come striding down on them directly. Perhaps some spirit wandering in the sleep time—not malicious, or Pichikut's Plan could not be working so well. Here might be a helpful guardian—oh, she would consider the matter at some other time.

Identity other than *angakok* did not concern her, and she turned her eyes away. Sukitilan's bowl for now was full to overflowing. Only three lumpy morsels remained to chew. . . . She must get home, get harnessed, get away.

Chapter 6.
Sled

The girl's eyes burned as moisture collected at the corners. Poor, pathetic child, she mocked herself—tears? . . . She had no time to be a *kussuyok*, a coward—not now. Later, perhaps.

Her chin still shuddered as she tightened her jaw. She knew exactly what remained to do. She had rehearsed each act of preparation with Pichikut as many times as she had toes and fingers. More deliberation—let alone tears of useless self-pity—would only delay her; and speed or its lack could mean success or failure.

Regardless of these obscuring clouds that were her feelings, she must move automatically as the moon and stars.

On impulse, Sukitilan lugged from the harness porch of the abandoned igloo two more bladders of permafrost—iced dirt. In the summer season with warmer temperatures and occasional sunshine, frozen upper layers of earth warmed and softened.

She remembered digging the mucky stuff from beneath shallow-rooted grasses on the tundra. She would now take what she could carry to thaw above the travel lamp and pack sled runners as needed. She would have to mud and ice the runners several times each run while they made a bumpy winter trail inland, all depending on snow cover, so Pichikut had warned.

But then her mother promised that when Sukitilan got onto the smoother saltwater ice, one packing each day could be enough. On the trail when she ran out of permafrost, as was inevitable, she would with great difficulty hack more out from under the snow and heat it. She dragged the bladders up the rise. These would insure her having no delay along the trail for half a moon at least.

Her mind at ease temporarily, knowing that she was accomplishing what must be done, before she relaxed. A certain possibility floated into her head softly as wind-borne gossamer—a possibility which her imagination soon made a comforting probability. Here was an idea that brought energy and a brightening spirit. . . . Could Pichikut's spirit here and now account for present progress?

She tested every lashing on the sled, then rechecked the runners prepared hours ago. She jerked up and sideways on the loaded frame, tried to topple it. The cargo was balanced. Good. She laid out on the snow nine separate harnesses she had attached to the sled earlier. They made a rainbow arc with the longest lines at center for Iyarpok. She went down to the silent village for *kring-merk*, her choice among the sled dogs of her family.

The advantage of having no team of her own was that she knew the temperament as well as each dog's working style from having driven every team at various times. All the dogs knew and accepted her.

Oojulit would not be pleased to lose his lead dog. Yet, her muddling all three teams by selecting the best from each meant more confusion if anyone in her family tried to pursue her. The best dogs would be gone, and creatures mostly unaccustomed to each other would suddenly be forced to work together.

She must take only the one lead, though, or she would create within her own team a chaos unlikely to resolve itself for many moons.

Nuna would hate having Iyarpok in her place; but she should be preoccupied with her family—the one remaining dog, Ajak, and the human infant. . . . Still, Sukitilan would tie Nuna to the sled nest for the first few runs.

The girl selected two more good dogs from the team of her eldest brother, dug them from their warm drifts, bought their silence and cooperation in following her to the sled in the same manner that she had wooed the others—by offering frozen parts from a haunch of caribou. Delectable pickings for anyone, a banquet for a dog.

The creatures were unlikely to eat well on the trail, not at first. In the next days, Sukitilan planned to feed them and herself at every rest break only frozen char—no one's favorite—fish caught last summer, dried and cached secretly for this purpose under Pichikut's supervision. Freshwater fish were small, lean fare normally consumed in summer when neither Inuit nor dogs were working hard or fighting frigid temperatures; or else it was bagged for emergency rations in time of winter famine at home or on the trail.

She would have no chance to hunt during the early runs while she used speed and cunning to lay a false trail for any followers.

The dogs were nervous, unaccustomed to the new sled and to each other. One by one, she hitched and reassured them, talking soft nonsense in a soothing voice. She fought back her own shudders of anxiety that rose up once again to shake her at departure time.

Think carefully. Review what is loaded to go and what is left behind, she told herself. It will not be possible to return if a mistake is made. She balanced the inner churn by allowing herself to consider the possibily—no, the probability!—of identifying the guardian spirit for her small brother. She worked to control a rising excitement.

At last, she took her snow knife from the loaded hunting bag and went back to the village and the only snowhut she had ever built. "Nuna, come!" she commanded softly. The big white dog rose obediently but whined back at her sleeping pup when she got outside. How did she sense that Sukitilan now proposed more than a short walk on the tundra?

The girl crawled into the snow-hut, swooped up Ajak, then used the big bone knife to hack down the crawl door in back. Outside, she slashed the small igloo into an untidy drift. She caught Nuna's eye and raised her chin abruptly. Nuna was at her heel as she went up the hill with the baby in her tunic and Ajak wriggling beneath her arm.

Sukitilan finally felt calm. Very likely, *Ananak's* dispossessed spirits had found their new home immediately after her death. In this baby. Why not? Clearly, she remembered calling out her mother's name as the woman died. What she could not remember was whether the village women were still chanting other names. Probably—but even so, Sukitilan stood closer to Pichikut than the others.

Having the woman's life spirits within this child would account for much . . . Sukitilan's ease in the snowhouse with the lifeless shell of her *ananak*. The child's energy . . . his willingness to accept Nuna. His lusty shouts, too, would be Pichikut's contribution, Sukitilan decided with a grin. His survival of intense cold while he lay naked on the hilltop. Yes, she was convinced; the vigorous, lusty spirits of none other than Ananak protected this boy!

She arranged her passengers, Nuna first with a double lap of strapping to restrain her along with stern instruction to be quiet and stay put. The dog already disliked not being lead, or at least harnessed, her agitation obvious; but she obeyed. Then the girl placed Ajak beside his mother. Finally, she removed from her parka the babe in his bunting, laid him deep into the warm nest, the *upluk*, and studied the unlikely trio.

She covered all of them first with an old bear fur but permitted Nuna's head a peeking place. Then she loosely arranged the ragged fur salvaged from Nuna's snow-hut floor. She checked the food bags once again and counted six sleep robes beside those which made up the warm little *upluk*. Yes, the travel lamp. Pichikut's Big—no!—now Sukitilan's Big Feed. They were ready.

She ordered the dogs to their feet in the rainbow hitch. Huge Iyarpok was proud in front, wild to start, straining on his lines against the forked antler set deeply in ice to anchor the sled. The girl picked up the long whip of braided walrus hide.

"It is well that a mother accompanies us," she told them all softly. She felt new strength in the belief that she was not nearly so alone as she had thought. And that so far, she had followed The Plan reasonably well. She expected to hold the sled handles and lope behind the runners for a time, just to be certain that the load did not shift or slide and that her three passengers—no, four counting Pichikut—rode comfortably. Then she would take her spear and run forward with the dogs to leave behind her on the trail all the terrible events since her last sleep.

"*Pirtok*," she murmured, "none can change what has already happened."

She raised the anchor and lifted the long whip to let it lightly lash the surface of the snow beside the team. "And so it begins," she said aloud.

Chapter 7.
Seeking

From the crest of a hill, Tuk watched in the deep twilight of early afternoon as two young men not much older than himself moved around their camp. He seemed always to be an observer, these days, never a participant.

"Hoo-oo!" he complained softly. Had he missed great Narluk again? Only one remained of two sleds seen before the sleep. His own team staked at the sheltered gulch between two ridges invisible to the other camp, he trudged up the hill, icy wind scouring his face. He pulled on the strap to reduce the opening of his *nuilak*, the fur facing on his hood.

The snow cover was slick and treacherous. He fell, got up laughing at himself, moved on. "It happens that the man of nearly twenty winters is clumsy as a newborn seal."

Last night, he had located by their lampglow the very strangers he sought. The camp he made masked his presence. No need for a power battle among dogs. His own *kringmerk* no longer reacted to strangers. They were hungry. They were tired. So was he. The team seemed to share his anxiety. Alien scent was their fare at summer's start. As always, he with his family journeyed into mainland tundra from their coastal home to avoid the dangerous high tides of summer at the sunrise sea.

Barely two moons ago? A familiar sadness took his thought like sucking tide. He must separate himself from such feelings. Pirtok, none can change what has occurred.

When he got to the top of the north ridge, he looked back fondly at the furry creatures on which his life depended. The corners of his mouth turned up. The dogs would leap and sing to celebrate return to familiar scents and sounds, so long had they been gone from their familiar coastal shores.

Ah, the sea. He too would rejoice when—if—he could go home.

Even without his family. He must accept that they are gone. "*Inueruttyok*," the people are gone. Tuk heard his spoken syllables echo like a lonely cliff bird calling as it flew over wave-washed boulders. Fifteen sleeps since he had buried his parents and small sister under rocks above the frozen ground . . . and then awaited his own end.

Except that he did not die—did not even become ill, at least not yet. He had first moved northeast toward the now-thawed sunrise sea, his coastal home each winter. But his food would have to come from land while he awaited return of his village. No Inupiat kayak could withstand the vigorous summer shoreline.

But wait! When they returned, would he jeopardize these very villagers he knew and loved? Cause their sickness, death? He pondered the matter for three sleeps before making a hard decision. He turned back to stay on barren, unfamiliar tundra. To seek out *angakok*, find some shaman who could tell him whether a malignant spirit rode his shoulder.

Now Tuk studied each dog below him with affection. Too many to feed. His father's eight and his own six. He should pick out the best, butcher the rest—he had little to carry, and all who remained could use the food!—ah, but which to keep?

Originally, Tuk excused the lack of prudence by telling himself that he would observe them on the trail, see which worked best with others. So he harnessed all fourteen —but then they all pulled together in harmony!

They worked up spectacular appetites, as well. . . . But he knew soon after starting that all of them including himself would eat or starve together. These *kringmerk* were his only remaining family. Perhaps he would feel differently when the Hunger Beast gnawed deeply at his belly.

So he forced himself, last night, to be patient about contacting the strangers. He staked the big team and built a tiny trail house. Time enough tomorrow, when all were rested, for him to approach the shaman called Narluk whose trail he had followed now for eight sleeps.

Timing was important. The child inside him wanted to leap over the crest of the hill immediately. That youngster wished to shout his need at the top of his lungs, to stir up the strangers as well as their dogs at the very moment he found them. But the thoughtful Tuk-He-Was-Becoming remembered that the quick way to do a thing is rarely best.

A troubled young man needing information which only a shaman could give must present himself with dignity on a fresh day.

And here was that day, but no shaman could be seen. He snorted. So much for mature decisions. Or might such difficulties be sent him by phantoms of the trail to serve some strong purpose?

Narluk. He must find the shaman whose name was said first by many. He remembered his difficulty over inquiring of people without putting them in peril. He learned right away that it was impossible to keep physical distance between villagers and himself. In that sense, these inland Inupiat were like those he knew at home.

He tried entering a village only once—but then panicked as

first children, then men and women, came boiling from their summer soddies to welcome the visitor. Remembering the horror of his own family's sickening and death, the young man turned his team and raced away as far and fast as possible.

He must avoid villages until he knew himself to present no danger. He had better control with a small hunting group along the trail. So as winter began and he found sled tracks, he would follow until he encountered someone on the trail. Every hunter he found—Tuk ever careful to stay downwind at least a sled's length back—recommended Narluk.

What a powerful shaman he must be! By now, the young man pictured him tall as a kayak upended, wide as a muskox in full fur, age-wrinkled as a walrus and wise as the most venerable she-bear.

And now the man was surely nearby. Tuk walked alone toward the encampment. The two young men spotted him, came to meet him.

"A stranger is welcome!" greeted the smaller of the two. He was short, heavily muscled, but seemed to spring tall with energy at each step.

Tuk stopped, raised his arm and hand, palm out, fingers pointing up, to ward off the approach. "It happens that someone may carry sickness," he explained. He was downwind, but—who knew how far a malignant spirit might leap?

A rangy man who looked slightly older than his companion came to stand towering over the first. "This magnificent little fellow is called Pajuk, and the gangling collection of bones here beside him is his older and far wiser brother Oojulit." The soft voice belied his size. It is never good to draw the attention of trail spirits by speaking a name loudly.

The smaller man smiled broadly.

Tuk introduced himself, thinking as he spoke that angular Oojulit was too fleshless to withstand a famine. *Ai-ee*, too slim to miss a single meal. . . . Yet, he seemed hearty.

"Someone searches for Narluk," Tuk said.

"As do two others!" Pajuk laughed, his broad face folding inward to a grin. "It happens that a father went to hunt and left two lazy sons asleep rolled in their blankets."

Oojulit cleared his throat, features sobering. "These days, Angakok walks often while others snore and dream."

"Yes, and this worries an elder brother," Pajuk told Tuk, still smiling, "but the younger knows this to be his father's way, now that—"

"—A matter which holds no interest for the traveler," Oojulit interrupted smoothly.

Pajuk closed his mouth.

Tuk wanted to protest. He wanted to say that he was extremely interested in their father. But something private was here. He could sense pain tucked into the voices.

"It happens," Oojulit said then, "that Narluk's family has too much food for the lazy dogs to carry. It is necessary that a guest come help to eat a meal, poor fare though it will be.

Pajuk chimed in. "Eh, terrible stuff. . . . The family hunts but never finds, as someone is about to learn." He laughed easily, good spirit restored.

Tuk chuckled. It was pleasant to hear someone speak in the traditional manner, belittle himself and his hospitality—and then most likely produce a feast.

Tuk was intent on staying downwind of both brothers. He waited impatiently while the tall man studied the land to the south, the direction from which Tuk had come.

"If a visitor has dogs," Oojulit said—and who could be on a trail in winter without a team?—"it may be we can find a few old harness straps for them to chew."

Tuk got into the droll mood, even though he had fed his dogs their usual meager fare before leaving camp. "Someone's scrawny, mite-munched creatures would be pleased for a change to have a meal so substantial."

Actually, the response was barely understated. Tuk had fed them what he fed himself—fish almost exclusively, which they and he ate without gusto. It would keep them alive, but it offered too little fat to protect them from the frigid temperatures. He could give his team nothing but summer staples, for he was neither skilled nor fortunate at capturing prey inland.

Twice, he had sighted small groups of caribou stragglers at least half a moon behind a large herd. But he'd never managed to decrease their number or even the distance between them and himself. He had seen the occasional muskox, also, *oomingmak*, but was fearful of their speed and their ferocity described in fireside tales.

He remembered hearing of a villager who searched for muskox until the creatures found him. The hunter did not survive the encounter.

Oojulit returned to his camp while Pajuk trotted back with Tuk for sled and dogs. By the time runners were iced, sled loaded and team harnessed, the wind had shifted, now rising from southeast. The younger brother moved back to remain upwind on Tuk's request, but the two still visited. Pajuk turned everything into a joke, and Tuk enjoyed the jerky conversation, delighted in the rhythm of human speech.

Senseless prattle built amity between the two. Soon Tuk would get a shaman's answer to his question about infecting people. But meantime, here was welcome camaraderie.

Tuk's father always said someone's spirits behaved strangely after many sleeps alone on the trail. When an unsuccessful search for food is thought to be calamity directed at the hunter, he must seek companionship. At the time, Tuk could not imagine such a condition. He had never been lonely—for he was hardly ever alone. He had parents. He had a younger sister who never stopped chattering.

Now, though, he understood. A few sleeps back, he had convinced himself that moon and stars vanished deliberately behind clouds in order to blind him. That snow skittered wildly along the ground to obscure the land so that Tuk would lose the trail and be lost on featureless ground. He needed this Pajuk and his brother as much as he needed their father.

Tuk anticipated good food coming. He carried on his sled the remaining fish and berries saved by his family in summer, all before the terrible sickness. But here was early winter, and a person needed animal suet—not fish and berries—to meet increasing cold. So did dogs. Perhaps inlanders Narluk and his sons would serve caribou plump from summer's graze on tundra grass.

He wondered about their travel mostly east and all alone. He had the impression, as he spoke to hunters along the way, that Narluk had a large family. Where were the others? But of course he could not ask. One does not rudely pry thoughts from the private center of another.

What did Pajuk mean when he reported that his father now walked while others slept? Had something recently changed? Tuk thought back upon his search. After making the decision to find *angakok*, and while hearing time and again that Narluk was the person he should talk to, he had gone south and west to get to the man's village, taking direction from hunters along the way. All knew him. All recommended him.

Then when he finally neared the place late in a sleep time, he had to stop when he saw a young woman who looked to be suckling her baby while lying on the snow outdoors. She was accompanied by a huge white dog. He followed her on foot to a cluster of snow-houses glimmering in starlight.

In fact, he saw her silently leave the village soon after. Quick and confident of movement, capable with the team—an unusual sight, a woman alone with a sled. What was most peculiar was that she left with no one attending her. And she moved slowly, silently, until she got well away from the igloos. Then she vanished east at top speed. A curious matter but not his concern then or now.

He had gone back to his own double team, later found a rolling knoll where he could see the collection of glowing igloos and wait out the sleep time before approaching Narluk.

But Tuk had been weary, slept late, and the village was on the move when he awoke. Whole families together streamed north and west. He questioned a hunter driving a heavily-laden sled with one old woman perched in robes on top. Narluk's village? Yes. But the *angakok* was gone, the Inuk told him.

Their shaman with his family had left very early, perhaps even during the night. Odd, the villager conceded, but the shaman may have been called away by someone who reported urgent illness. The important man having just lost his wife, he may have decided to take his family with him.

Narluk would certainly seek out these villagers on return, the man said with pride, "for Angakok has lived among us for many years."

Now at Narluk's camp, both teams fed and staked well away from each other, the dogs were digging into drifts for shelter and sleep. Tuk's team was drugged silent by the unaccustomed feast. Tuk himself was relaxed for the first time in many days, his belly truly satisfied by good red meat. Narluk would surely arrive soon.

They put the two sleds in a wedge against the wind, draping both with heavy hides and robes to protect the lamp from a gale moaning up from the south. They sat on heavy robes, some belonging to their guest. Tuk thought it strange that inlanders he observed seemed to prefer a drafty tent or lean-to like this along the trail instead of troubling to make a cozy snowhouse. But of course he made no comment.

He detected Oojulit glancing anxiously to the northeast, the direction of Narluk's sled tracks which Tuk had noticed earlier. Once, Pajuk mentioned that his father would face a stiff wind on return. That was all. They spoke of other matters as they got to know each other without ever asking questions.

Chapter 8.
Finding

From the blackness of late winter afternoon appeared two dogs, one pale gray, the other rufous and brightly reflecting lamplight as he bounded to the brothers. Oojulit called each by name, and they devoured the food he offered.

"A father has loosed these to find us," he announced.

Pajuk was already on his feet, pulling the sled out from hides and robes, rolling up furs, icing runners.

Tuk got up also as Oojulit came to him.

"It is best to move the camp, since a father took only his sled and dogs with spear and hunting bag—"

"—No robes!?" Tuk exclaimed.

Pajuk shrugged. "Narluk is not one to plan deeply for the future," he grinned, but Tuk could see by lamplight that his eyes were narrow with concern.

No one would take a winter trail without robes, Tuk thought—ah! Except some powerful *angakok* who could burrow for warmth into the center of the earth. . . .

Oojulit walked over. "Does it happen that our visitor might plan to let the wind blow him as it will?" He pointed northeast, the direction of Narluk's trail.

Tuk flicked up his eyebrows, Yes. He picked up his water bladder, iced his runners.

"And can Tuk's team carry more than it brought?"

"Ee-ee-ee!" Certainly, Tuk said. Not only would he soon see Narluk; but by coming in the company of his sons, *angakok* would be more likely to take time to speak with him. "These dogs have eaten such good food—they could now pull sun and moon with all the stars behind." Even Oojulit laughed, for Sun and Moon, though brother and sister, are mortal enemies and can never be together in harmony.

Tuk unstaked and harnessed his dogs, spread on the sled his own robes and few remaining supplies, then stacked and tied additional packs brought over by Pajuk.

They cleared the camp.

Not long after Narluk's pair of dogs arrived, these same two on long lines raced back to lead the way. In full dark of clouded afternoon, the two pathfinding dogs stopped. Pajuk gently probed suspicious white mounds until he uncovered part of Narluk's team.

Five dogs staked apart came out reluctantly on lines from shallow nests in snow. The shaman probably helped dig the holes, Tuk realized, for drifts here had a thick ice crust. So Narluk was healthy enough.

"He took ten dogs this morning," Pajuk worried aloud. No rounded drifts remained.

Oojulit nodded. "It happens that three are still missing."

The young men probed in darkness as blasts of snow came horizontally on an escalating gale. A smoking ice fog spread along the ground.

Tuk unharnessed and staked his team, used his snow knife to break the crust so each could dig a shelter. But he held back Imana. He prized this yellow lead dog for his keen nose and good sense. It was he with snout raised to taste the air who had led him to Narluk's party after a snowstorm obliterated the trail. And now again Imana tested the snow cover, moving off toward a jumble of boulders.

Near a drift piled on the lee side of the stack, he stood and whined. Tuk followed but saw nothing before the dog sat down and sang, teeth bared, muzzle high, maw open, his eerie melody blending with the tempest.

Such was Tuk's faith in Imana that he called for Pajuk. He even forgot to stay downwind as the two excavated carefully with the flat of their snow knives.

Now came a faint wiggle from the other side. Pajuk drew back, transferred his snow knife to the other hand and grasped his spear from the ground at his feet. If they had disturbed a white sea bear with cubs, she would come whirling at them. Tuk, though, took comfort in knowing that they had not heard Imana's bear song. Nor were the dog's hackles high. Imana would know.

The head of a sled dog emerged at last, then another and one more. And now a man who must be the long-sought Narluk erupted from beneath the snow and stood up groaning. He was nearly as big as Tuk had pictured him—taller even than his elder son, very nearly tall as a kayak on end, and certainly thick as a young walrus. Tuk could see that he was younger than his reputation suggested.

"Eh . . . the sons arrive!!" Narluk squinted to look beyond Pajuk, only glancing at Tuk, until his eyes focused on his eldest. "It is good for a family to be together," he grunted.

"It is good also for a family to stay together—not wander off without a word," Oojulit responded.

Ignoring that response, Narluk walked up to Tuk. "A visitor!"

Stricken, for he had forgotten his problem in the excitement, and now may have endangered these people, Tuk moved downwind quickly. "It happens that someone needs wisdom from a great shaman," he said.

Narluk chuckled. But before Tuk could say more, Oojulit broke in. "A father is well?"

Again Narluk laughed. "The graceful hunter could not return to camp," he explained, "because it happens that he fell through lake ice warmed by a runnel. It became necessary to get dry."

That explained it, Tuk thought. Some dogs staked, some sent for help, then three holed up in a snow cave to share warmth and dry the man.

Oojulit nodded. "One has heard that such warm springs can thin lake ice invisibly and leave liquid in unexpected spots."

"Ee-ee," Narluk agreed, "and this eager old man ran before his team! His sled and dogs stayed comfortably dry."

"A father will someday remember to take at least robes at all times," Pajuk preached in a singsong voice, obviously an old sermon oft-repeated.

"*Kringmerk* is far warmer than a robe!" Narluk insisted.

Later, before anyone took advantage of the snug warmth in the lean-to they built in front of Narluk's ice cave, the man listened to Tuk's worries.

"How many sleeps since stones were placed above the empty vessels of a family?" he asked.

"Fifteen," Tuk said slowly, fighting tears brought by the memory.

Narluk looked over at his two sons. "It happens, a small igloo is needed now, nearby and downwind to the north. Our coastal cousin is bound to be more comfortable in such a trailhouse."

Tuk shuddered. Then *angakok* believed he still carried sickness? "Is it possible that a careless *inuk* has already contaminated his new friends?" He forgot to keep distance during those moments when he with Pajuk dug at the drift.

The man shrugged. "We shall soon know." He reassured Tuk by placing a mittened hand onto his arm. "In such instance, we shall also discover whether *angakok's* herbs and amulets have potency."

But of course the medicines were powerful. . . . Here was a strong shaman, and Tuk could sense his force. Unlike some *angakok* even among his own people who were noisy braggarts full of empty wind. Shaman whose magic beyond trickery was limited to sensing a time when a village had been especially lucky in the hunt and was planning a feast.

Narluk was soft-spoken with steady eyes. He had a family. He took part in the hunt . . . earned his own way and ministered to those who needed him.

Tuk relaxed and went to chink the seams on the small igloo now finished by Pajuk and Oojulit. Later, behind a protective wall of ice that enabled the big oil lamp to burn outside, Tuk stood up to tell his story.

"Late in summer, two strangers came. They arrived after the first heavy snowfall, as this man before you with his parents and small sister prepared to go back and join their winter village at the sea."

Tuk's movements as he spoke were first of drifting snow, then of wrapping and patting and tying packets on a sled, finally of people who approached.

"Must have been coastal Inupiat," Oojulit said, "not our caribou people."

"*Ee-ee*," Tuk responded. Yes. The son of Narluk could not have known where the visitors came from—but see how gracefully he got the information he sought without asking rude questions? Tuk placed the method in his memory for later use.

"When they returned at summer's end to build igloos near the sea, dog-people came to visit—the heavy-eyebrow *kalunait* from far south." Tuk drew himself up and stomped about, working his own brows.

"*Ee-ma!*" Oh yes! said the three rapt listeners. All knew about these exiled dog-sons of their sea-queen Sedna.

"It is likely that they came on land from their giant floating *kamik* which chases whales," the shaman added.

Tuk shrugged. He did not know. "Besides food and skins—" supplies *kalunait* were said always to want—"the men requested walrus ivory on which to make pictures with fine black marks— that's what the strangers told us."

Oojulit looked up with a thoughtful frown. "Called by them 'scrimshaw'?" he asked his father, and the man lifted his brows in agreement.

Tuk resumed, carefully tailoring his tale to the trail on which he had set himself, not veering off into his feelings of sadness for lost family or into resentment of lethal visitors.

"The Inupiat visitors told us that all in their ice village had sickened and died—all but our two guests. '*Tokoyok*,' they told us, 'a village is dead.' They said whole families died together in their igloos built on sea ice."

Narluk agreed. "One has heard before of savage spirits brought by *kalunait*, Sedna's heavy-eyebrowed pups. They come up from the south and sometimes bring sickness which strikes suddenly."

Tuk continued his story. The two survivors had sealed the village snowhouses and come inland to flee malignant spirits. "'Burning specters snarled within our people,' they told us. 'Within two sleeps came much coughing as the body attempted to expel them. Then nothing—all dead on their sleeping ledges, none left to nurture them, none left to be nurtured!'"

The strangers were invited to go hunting with Tuk and his family before moving on, and they spent time upon the trail together. "Then after they were gone, it happened that the sickness of their village people occurred as well within someone's parents and sister." Tuk's steady voice fastened on the sound of the words, not their meaning.

Narluk courteously waited for more. When Tuk simply sat down, the shaman spoke with sympathy, still fingering his amulets. "Someone needs to know how long the two survivors were on the trail before finding Tuk's family. Also how long they stayed to visit and to hunt."

"Twelve sleeps before they came upon us, so they said. Then at camp, and finally hunting on the tundra—" the young man thought back carefully—"four more sleeps, as is recalled."

Narluk cleared his throat. "To be fully safe, the visitor called Tuk should continue to stay downwind and separate, whenever he is with people—for yet one more half moon." The man smiled.

Relief flooded through Tuk. He could start home. . . . He would need more than half a moon to reach the coast from here.

And to meet anyone along the trail would be unusual—unless he deliberately followed tracks he crossed, as earlier, when he searched first for information and then for *angakok*.

"A wandering man has not caused sickness for others, then?" Tuk had to ask, even knowing such direct query to be discourteous.

The big man sighed. "These hot spirits are hard to understand. Still, if someone has taken all along his way the same precautions practiced here—"

Tuk raised his eyebrows and sucked in breath simultaneously, to communicate an emphatic Yes.

"—Then the cruel spirits which sat upon the two visitors, and which may be riding Tuk's shoulder now, could not easily spread."

The man looked over at his silent sons and back, cleared his throat. "Wiser men than this *angakok* have observed that these evil spirits are not great jumpers on an icy trail."

He stood up, plucked a couple of robes from a walrus hide packet and moved back from the fire more fully into the lean-to, and spoke no more.

That was it, then. Tuk would go due east in the darkness of a new day. He should proceed straight as possible to the coast, he thought. His experience with procuring food was based mainly on knowledge of sea creatures. Ai-ee! Only fish and berries until he reached the Sunrise Sea.

He looked over at Pajuk and chuckled. "Inland Inupiat would laugh to have seen someone's family from the coast chase caribou off the tundra, last summer." They had run a long time, his father and he, and had caught nothing but a weak calf already panicked by wolves.

"*Ee-ee*, and all would laugh to see our inland family clear every coastal rock of seals," Pajuk said.

Both burst out laughing as they took turns imitating themselves on the chase of unfamiliar prey. Each had honed special skills for capturing creatures well known to his own people. And neither knew much about the other's.

Oojulit grinned. "For this hunter to capture a seal, the creature would need to be tethered to a stake."

"—Or perhaps weak and dying," Pajuk agreed.

All three roared.

"It happens," Narluk rumbled from within his robes, "that an early start is needed after sleep."

The three got up. Tuk wondered about the purpose of this trip for *angakok* and his sons. Their destination was something he was not likely to learn, since none had so far volunteered information and of course he could not ask. Who would carry so much food on a mere hunting trip? How would animal spirits recognize a need and make themselves available? Would he ever meet these men again? *Ahmi*, who knows the future?

He walked over to his tiny snowhouse and, before crawling inside with his robes, took pleasure in its glow from the low flame lit within. Pajuk had just now given him a small bladder of seal oil to be used on the trail when Tuk departed after the sleep time.

Now he thrust the precious fat deep into his pocket. He would save it for a special time, he decided, not waste it on himself alone.

Chapter 9.
Decision

Sukitilan raced south and mostly east on hissing runners. She planned to mislead any pursuers until new snow hid her tracks completely. Then she would veer north along the coast. If fortune rode her trail, she would be near the sunrise seacoast by the time her tracks disappeared.

Pichikut had filled her with instruction about travel on *tuwak*, the coastal ice. About its advantages, how important it was to her goal. Saltwater ice was smoother, she told her daughter, more dependable, once frozen—necessary if the girl was to cover the vast distance to Pichikut's village in the moons of protective black winter which assured ground cover for a sled.

Sukitilan must not mind the booming of the ice, her mother said. Nor must she tremble at the great cracks and mighty splashes, for these were adjusting pressure ridges and the natural stress of labor as icebergs were born of parent glaciers. To ward off encroaching panic, Sukitilan now reviewed the lore as she raced before her sled beside the dogs.

In spite of Pichikut's instruction and obvious familiarity with and therefore preference for sea surface travel, Sukitilan dreaded it. That smooth ice her mother spoke of could also be treacherous. It could break away from the mainland in large pieces to float away forever—as it had done with her two brothers.

Or it could snap into smaller bits and tip its occupants into the black water—sled and contents, dogs, people—all pulled down by Sedna the Sea Queen to disappear beneath the surface.

And it could conceal with its whiteness and unending pressure ridges the great white bear in search of meat, a creature that hurtled out from a cave, a boulder or a drift of snow, even up from an open lead within the sea itself.

Eh, these were not good thoughts. . . . She must reach thickly frozen saltwater directly as possible after her tracks were covered. Before that, she must seem to be going elsewhere. But each hour of travel away from home and family had so far increased her foreboding and the sense of loss.

The trip was like stretching the loose end of a supple sinew firmly fastened to family and village: tension increased with distance. For a while, she feared that the band might pluck her up—twa-a-ang!—and plummet her back home to face disaster.

But then as time passed, she feared the band would not—that it would snap apart and leave her forever separated, solitary on a hopeless trail. Using Palunga's sled, as it turned out, imparted no great confidence. How fortunate had he been? As time passed on the lonely trail, she even began to doubt that her mother's spirit lay within the helpless child. A big sister's fantasy does not affect reality.

She had convinced herself by now that she fought not only her *angakok* father . . . but also *peeusinga*—the custom established by Inupiat. All very well for Pichikut, she supposed. Her mother had been so strong, a mature and experienced adult when she came from ice islands far north. Her differences were several, but long ago accepted in the village of her husband.

The woman could afford to be confident; also now dead. But here lay folly for a daughter who shared none of these advantages . . . . What a *soospuk* she was, what a nitwit. . . . All alone, hardly even a woman with only the sixteen full winters, who dares not only to tangle with tradition but also to invent a trail into unknown territory!? A senseless fool!

She backtrailed. She would return to the place where her village had been, then follow tracks from there to find the new location and join the group. She struck a trail back parallel to but distanced from her former path. Perhaps even now—and certainly by the time she found her people—Narluk would have put his grief behind him and thought the matter through.

He would have considered and agreed with his wife's wishes, would realize that his youngest son (and perhaps his only daughter?) need not die. He would in fact be relieved to have another chance. Would be grateful that Sukitilan had protected the infant. Would welcome the baby and Sukitilan into the family once again.

Throughout the return, though, especially during mealtimes and sleeps, the spirit of Pichikut peered out at her daughter accusingly through the great black eyes of her son . . . so it was, or so Sukitilan fancied it to be.

She avoided looking into the face of the baby as she cared for him. Then after the third sleep on the way home, something caused her to turn away once more, this time fury overriding fear—and now for the first time fully resolute.

She slept part of one night among sheltering rocks on a high embankment. A shrieking northeast wind awoke her, and low clouds hurtled in. She became anxious to get underway before gale and ground blizzard delayed her.

She attended her runners, packed up ready to continue her way home, a bit south by now and mostly west.

But from her sleep ridge, she heard the voices of Narluk and her brothers brought by the wind. She silenced her suddenly restless team, then spotted her family as it carefully followed her early trail.

"*Aa-gii-ii!*" she raged, No! . . . It cannot be. So determined, Narluk? So resolved to kill? How dare he be so strong against the wishes of his wife? All the trouble taken first by Pichikut and now by Sukitilan herself.

The target of her fury split itself in flight—as if two geese at the point of a single arrow cheat the aim as they separate and wing to different destinations. Those three below on her earlier trail, yes.

But also, how weak, this female. . . . So filled with fear and such sorrow for herself that she had given up and turned back despite her promise? Despite knowing what was most likely to be in store for the little one? Despite all the early planning and the effort to make sure that he survived? And despite her small brother's right to live!

The cold wind snapped at her cheeks as she watched the travelers disappear, three upright figures and two small teams—shadows south and east.

She lifted clenched fists to the sky. "Spirits, make time stop and roll backward!" the girl murmured. "Come, snow. . . . May the wind rise, bring swirling fog and blinding flake!" she chanted suddenly. . . .

> Let Ooangniktuk, the great north wind
> Meet in this place
> With Nigituk of the south!
> May they circle in a drumming duel,
> Well-matched, thumping through the tundra—
> Howling in their anger—
> Neither able to subdue the other . . .
> Let them come!
>
> May they wear their snowflake mantles,
> Thick to coat the rocks and prairies,
> Muffling a sled trail well.
> May their labored breath while dueling
> Fill the land with ice fog circling—
> And their groans from struggle

Pierce the air to frighten all who hear!
Let them come!

May the two Big Winds collide
With clashing power
To make a storm as violent
As the tempest
Raging on this ancient land
Beneath a distant ball of fire
When land first began. . . .
Let them come!

Never before had Sukitilan called up weather. Perhaps a mighty storm was fated to arrive on that day. Or possibly, the spirit of Pichikut lent its great influence to her plea. But halfway through this day's run, this time turned and heading due east and back again toward coastal ice, she had to feed and stake the dogs, help them dig their drifts for shelter.

Within Nuna's large snow cave, she made room for herself and of course both babies, too. The blizzard raged for three sleeps and rearranged the landscape.

Narluk's following her was not such a surprise, she realized after inner rage had settled as she nestled into heavy robes within the ice cave. But once again she felt violated. When she first saw her family below, her fury was without limit. She hated the thought of Narluk's chasing her like prey, the brothers blindly aiding—all moving slowly and with full confidence.

Well, in this hunt they would not find success!

Afterwards, as time on the trail passed and her outrage became a focused determination, she saw with greater clarity. What had she expected? *Angakok* is more closely tied to custom than most. In fact, *angakok* often himself directs *peeusinga*, the actual Way of the People.

And Pichikut had predicted Narluk's action, foreseen it

clearly despite the love she bore her husband. Narluk's tiny son was motherless. It is the father's responsibility among the caribou people, at least, to end the infant's life and thereby end its suffering. Was Narluk's honor at stake?

Eh, let him search. . . . The power of this recent storm now past would have covered her tracks completely. She had turned back, yes—and she was ashamed of her cowardice. But now she was committed absolutely to the proper course of action.

She would find her mother's people, find those villagers who lived throughout the winter upon ice islands in the far north. Her father and brothers would have no inkling of where she had gone. Not soon, at least, and perhaps not ever. . . .

East she went, and rapidly, half a moon and more until she reached the sea. She took only small time to hunt and fish. Sometimes, she was successful—others, not. But her brother and her dogs did not starve, and of this fact she was proud.

She moved cautiously, at first, making sure each night to camp in a draw surrounded by rocks or hills so that her presence was hidden from any who might search. And gradually, the childish rage directed at her father, the fury trained upon her brothers, turned to jaw-clenched strength that hardened her muscles and braced her resolution.

She still feared Narluk's power—as she should, for his influence spread far—but she no longer cried on the trail. Nor did she wake in her sleep time shaking uncontrollably. Sobs still came sometimes before she slept, and she occasionally trembled at the unknown land and alien conditions that came with each new day. But she now looked back with disbelief at the frightened child who had started this trip.

Most sleeps passed in the shadow of boulders or some shallow cave checked first to see that it was not home to some other creature. She trusted Nuna for this inspection. She found a fine, sheltered cave at one sleep time, clean and clear, by the look of it, large enough to shelter the whole team and herself, yet small enough at entry to block for shelter from the wind and cold and any unwelcome creatures.

When she called Nuna over to examine her find, though, the big white dog crouched low, hackles high and ears back. Furtively, she looked behind her to the left, then to the right, a deep growl building.

"It happens that the white bitch is keen," Sukitilan murmured as she patted Nuna's head. Both turned away and left that place, putting distance between the cave and their sleep stop.

As they jounced along on rocky terrain, Sukitilan wondered what Nuna had sensed. Only two creatures, she decided, would elicit such response. The white sea bear, perhaps with young, or else wolverine. She decided that they must have found a bear cave, because the pungency of wolverine would be detected even by her feeble human perception.

For the hundredth time on this trip she wished that Nuna could talk. Her nose and ears were exceptional, even for a dog. She was perceptive and wise, sensing and responding to the moods of those around her, human as well as creature. Sukitilan had no doubt but that the dog reasoned—she demonstrated this ability almost daily. So why not speak, Nuna? Why not share a wise dog's great knowledge with an unseasoned traveler on the trail?

Perhaps some day following the sleep, the big animal would come up to her and say, "It happens that an extra ration of food is necessary." Sukitilan smiled. Should that day come, she would not be overly surprised.

Chapter 10.
The Sunrise Sea

Inland tundra smoothed its deeper wrinkles to become rolling coastal plains. The travelers slept outside with a lean-to of uncut skins on a floor of robes. Pichikut had explained that an igloo was the best shelter when Sukitilan reached the sea.

Increasingly, for sleeps where the ice was right, especially if storm threatened, she built a tiny snowhouse just for practice, found it to be a snug mound impervious to gale where she could curl up with her brother and his foster family.

Ajak was plump and frolicking, too rough to leave alone with the baby. But as days passed, Nuna taught the pup to tussle in moderation—even as the human child developed strength and resiliency. It helped also that Ajak possessed her mother's tender heart.

After twenty-eight sleeps with cold deepening and now only the briefest and most pale mid-day light for a few moments on the south horizon, Sukitilan knew that she must stop to secure food. The nine-dog team specially picked from those owned by her family worked together peaceably enough. Iyarpok, the Laughing One, proudly ranged ahead and center in the fan-shaped hitch.

He sensed Nuna's rivalry and was unfriendly in cunning ways. He did not dare confront the huge female. He knew that she would shatter his bones if sufficiently provoked. So instead, he nipped at Ajak if the pup came close when her mother was somewhere else. Sukitilan worried that he might also consider the human child a target.

Or the sled dog might someday misjudge Nuna's location or her mood. He had so far been a steady leader, never brilliant or intuitive, but strong and biddable. He would be hard to replace before Nuna could wean the babies and be ready.

She warned Iyarpok off sternly whenever she saw him near either of the young ones. "Nuna is larger than Iyarpok, far wiser—half again as clever as this Inupiat who speaks," she informed him.

The grey-and-black dog cocked his head as if to understand.

"More important, she is a mother—fierce as a she-bear to any who might bother her offspring." Sukitilan thought about that. "Who might bother either of her young," she amended. Besides which, she thought silently, any dog that threatens the human child will die by Sukitilan's own spear.

Eh, how savage she sounded!

The girl knew the personality of each animal in the team. She used the strengths of some to compensate for weaknesses in others. Although they might not previously have run together, all knew her and understood her wishes. She rarely needed to use her voice and never the whip of split and braided walrus-skin that she had brought along to slice the air if some command required emphasis.

Sukitilan understood the wishes of the dogs, too. Chief among these involved an insatiable appetite. Provision available, they would devour all until they vomited, re-ingest that and look about for still more food. Nor did they fatten, for the team was hard-working and Sukitilan worked them hard.

So it was that as they sliced across the last ice of wind-scoured prairie to finally reach the coast, Sukitilan knew that she must stop and stay awhile to replenish food supplies. The first glimpse of the sea was illuminated by spirit lights churning above.

She looked at the flatness which stretched before her, now a swirl of pastel reflections. She saw also the black strip far out from shore, something Pichikut called a "lead"—a sparkle of black water which formed a boundary between grounded coastal ice and the traveling ice beyond—the huge, floating and forever rearranging islands of *siku*.

Food was here, on and under ice as well as in that somber lead, very likely all along the boulder-strewn shoreline. Sea birds and their nests were here, though in this dark season no eggs would be found in the near-vertical sea cliffs.

Perhaps the shy seal was nearby, a half-grown pup . . . all unfamiliar prey, even though Ananak had described and drilled her in the source and capture, then the use of each creature part. She must find a way to seek out whatever was here.

Shelter first, she told herself, and then—she could not keep her eyes from straying inland—the inevitable search for food. Far back upon familiar inland tundra—lost to her now and perhaps forever—was customary prey eager to give itself to any Inupiat sufficiently fortunate in the hunt.

No. She must hunt for sea and coastal prairie creatures; for soon, these would be all that were available.

Sukitilan sang as she used the snow knife to break through ice to sea water and make a rough circle. She told herself to be silent, but then forgot as she set herself to widening the hole. She was happy. She had made discoveries. Like all inland people, she was timid of the sea. Even though her village might travel often within a day or two's sled run of salt water, and even though she had actually come with her brothers to explore the coast, she never before had found an opportunity to drive dogs on ocean ice.

Once past the tidal crack near shore, it would be smoother even than freshwater ice in lakes and rivers, just as her mother said—and being without rocks, much smoother than land. Goose-down smooth.

If they could drive north on *tuwak*—the solidly grounded sea ice—and sweep over or around whatever pressure ridges they could not avoid, she need not mud or even ice her sled runners more than once during a full run between sleeps. Once again and this time about the ice—conditions would be as Ananak described.

She prepared a string of caribou sinew, threaded bait and line through the ice hole, caught herself singing again. Pichikut had reminded her, fish are transient visitors. Not like the cautious seal, an intelligent animal which will avoid its breathing hole for one or two full sleeps—perhaps forever—when it detects sound or moving shadow on ice above.

Fish, therefore, were easier to capture. Still, she must be quiet. She glanced over at the sled where the infant slept cozily in the nest with Nuna and Ajak. The team and of course dogs were scattered out, but unharnessed, hungry and hopeful. So was she.

A tug on the line she held told her that a fish was tasting and testing. A glance at the fur float combined with a new, steady pull informed her moments later that the bait was to its liking. She pulled hard without jerking. The creature below fought the now-imbedded sharp bone hook. Continuing to hold the sinew curled around her mittened fingers, she brought the fish up smoothly, hand over hand, until it slipped onto the ice and flopped a few times before going rigid with cold. Two of the dogs hurried forward, and her hand motioned them away. They stepped back reluctantly, sprawled onto ice, gazed steadily at the catch, a slim but substantial silvery fish nearly as long as the leg of the one who had caught it.

"Someone must have more of these before it becomes possible to eat," Sukitilan explained to her waiting team, and furry ears pricked forward. She restored her freshly-baited line to the sea, then looked down to address the single fish sprawled on the ice.

> Our thanks to Sea Queen Sedna for her offering,
> And all of us accept, for we have need!
> Grateful also are we for *tuktu*, the graceful caribou
> Who gave its sinew for the line,
> Its bit of bone for carving of a hook.
> Even *kapvik* do we thank, the fearsome wolverine
> Which answers for its dark and violent deeds
> To none but Paija—
> This *kapvik* gave his piece of pelt with air-filled hairs
> That float . . . to tell the tale to those above
> Of what is happening below.

Again, a slight pull made her check the fur bob and ready herself to set the hook. She was singing once more. . . . Perhaps fish enjoy poetry, the breath of Inuit? Are attracted by melody? Or per-haps—breathing a song or not—Sukitilan was someone who would always be successful in the hunt. So said her family, and so said she!

When seventeen fish lay like bones by the hole, she motioned to the dogs, gave one entire fish to each, and they retreated happily with their frozen prizes. They would gnaw and warm their dinner bite by bite, eyeing her reproachfully because it was fish instead of hare or caribou, but down every morsel before she harnessed them. She cleared the front end of the sled and dropped all but one of the remaining fish onto the base of caribou ribs.

Each icy corpse made a hollow thunk that reverberated off the nearby shoreline cliff. As she put her hunting bag on top, then adjusted Nuna's nest, she gave the white dog an extra fish, herself first cutting up and chewing some small portions for the pup Ajak. She wondered, Why do dog parents not feed their young with solid food, like wolves?

"If, near the sea, a person prefers to make her igloo on the land," Pichikut had said, "then it happens she must go far enough and high enough to escape rogue ice and tide."

The girl could not then imagine a time when she would wish to build her sleep time shelter on sea ice.

With her team well fed although not satisfied—not ever sat-isfied by fish—and with each dog separated and staked, Sukitilan returned to the sod-backed lean-to she had built on ground high above the tidal crack at shoreline. Would she ever trust sea ice to support them through a night? Certainly not ever on a night like this, with Ooangniktuk, the merciless north wind, wrathful once again.

Often, she awoke during sleep time with anxiety mount-ing as a storm wind shrieked. Tonight was no exception, and once awake, so she remained, fingers at her ears. Her mind rambled, picking a berry from this bush, then that one, never stripping a whole plant to collect a meal of anything.

She had always wondered idly whether her success in hunting while she lived at home might have been some kind of shaman trickery by Narluk. Or perhaps her brothers' elaborate bluff to give her confidence. But then, so she reasoned as she lay sleepless in the screeching night, would Pichikut not know? And if Ananak knew, she would not abide such nonsense. And if the daughter were not fortunate on the trail, then certainly her mother would not have expected so much of Sukit—no, not Sukitilan. . . .

She must take another name, and soon. She was so different now—and striving to be more so—from the terrified child-woman who fled family and village. Changed outside as well as in. She had chopped her long hair off to shoulder length because it got wind-tangled when her hood lay back, then became a dangerous source of perspiration on the trail when her hood was up. She possessed even less flesh than when she started, and what remained was firmly toned, muscular as a man. Never mind her ugliness, being tall and sinewy instead of round and comforting, for she had never aspired to possess great beauty.

She had eaten sparsely on the trail because there wasn't much to eat. Also, eating by herself was no fun—she would be glad when the baby could share a meal with her, could talk or at least listen with some understanding.

Many nights, after a day's run and after the dogs were staked and fed, she would roll into her robes and forget to eat at all—or be too tired to cut and chew. Her face was wind-burned, leathery to the touch in contrast with smooth numb patches where frost had bitten the tips of her nose and both cheekbones. She knew that these would appear colorless to an observer.

And inside this new person, this not-Sukitilan, was a stillness born of solitude. A new tranquility that came from being—along with her small brother and her dogs and sled—the only marks upon the snow so far as her eye could see in any direction. A hush that stemmed from knowledge of her growing strength and capability. The old panic visited her imaginings less often as time passed. She now knew that those late night fears were mostly without base. She could solve problems as they arose. If not perfectly, then at least acceptably—until a better solution came as she gained experience on the trail. For food here? She could catch fish, at least those.

And she could successfully hunt caribou by going inland if summer came before she reached the top of the world. Staying by salt water, she would manage somehow to find seal when seal were here, perhaps even walrus. When she found other people—and she would find them!—she could help take whale in spring. She was anxious for opportunity to prove herself to herself.

She and the baby would survive to find Pichikut's people. Oh yes, the Sukitilan who began this journey no longer existed, and tomorrow she must find a name for the woman newly born amid ice music on the trail.

She had no doubt, anymore, but that the coastal Inupiat in the high islands her mother had described would help protect the baby—would safeguard Pichikut's last child. In fact, they would take over as his family. So her mother had promised. "Someone is free of responsibility for the child after she finds her mother's village," said Pichikut, "for people there treasure little ones even as wolves cherish their young."

"Do they, then, not set a motherless infant out to perish?" she had persisted.

"They do," Pichikut admitted, "but only if continued life for the small one is without hope."

"Then how are these islanders so different?"

Eyes narrow in thought, her mother had picked her words carefully. "Like our people here, they would not see someone suffer—especially not a baby—with no prospect for good life."

"Suckling a dog . . . ?"

"—They have some strong prohibitions, as we do here—many of which were ignored long ago by a bedraggled and rebellious young girl—a *nuliajak* bent on survival. Using a dog to

70

feed an infant when no other provision is possible? Perhaps untried before, for this woman never heard of it—except the reverse, when Queen Sedna used her own Inuit milk to suckle her dog litters . . . so probably acceptable.

"In any case, the child can be weaned before his sister reaches the islands of Pichikut."

Sukitilan was assiduous. "Under such circumstance—Nuna's milk might be allowed here in our own village as well!?"

"No." The woman frowned, then shrugged. Differing from inland, her coastal Inupiat might be less hard-pushed for food in winter. They are perhaps more willing to gamble on feeding an extra mouth. If a child is cared for and prospering"—she lifted both shoulders and ducked her head as her voice trailed off. "Ahmi." None can say the future.

Sukitilan was convinced by her mother that Pichikut's village would be delighted to take any child of Pichikut. Right now, though, with confidence inflated by the remarkable fact of their survival to date, the young woman thought she might not need their help. Perhaps she could take care of—what name? The child too must have a name. She could not call him Pichikut, for no one carries a parent's name, even in such special circumstance. She liked the sound and thought of *ajak*, a wind-whipped sprinkling of snow. Liked it so much, in fact, that she had already used it to designate her favorite among Nuna's pups—never dreaming that she might need it for a brother. Once given, could she now take it back?

But two new names were necessary—one for this "new" young woman on the trail, and the other for Nuna's pup if Sukitilan appropriated "*Ajak*" for her small brother. Much to think about.

Chapter 11.
Visitor

Late the next day, bearing a dozen extra fish and a smiling face, Sukitilan with dogs and sled approached her lean-to under the roiling greens and blues and pinks of spirits tumbling at play in the northern sky. Someone was in her camp.

One person stood in light that had to be generated by his own lamp. He was not tall enough to be her father or Oojulit. Not thick enough to be Pajuk. Her dogs barked. Excitement and challenge rang in their outcry, not alarm. Sukitilan silenced and slowed them. Nuna stood up on the sled, braced against its movement. She was growling, hackles raised. When the sled stopped, though, her collar fur settled; and although she continued to stand, she made no further objection.

The girl walked up to rest an arm along the dog's back. She had ceased to tie the big husky. "A good mother will protect her small ones," she murmured with approval before she faded back to the weapons in her hunting bag. A stranger and his silent team stood looking at her and her team. The inspection went both ways.

Normally, a traveler among Inuit is a welcome sight, no cause for fear. Inupiats can and do arrive unannounced from any quarter in any season at any time, day or night, secure about receiving a hearty welcome. They might come alone or in family or hunting groups, might temporarily join a village or merge with hunters on the trail. Although they always arrive unexpectedly, since no means exist to communicate ahead, no one ever expresses surprise, for that would be discourteous.

Still, Sukitilan had been long on the trail without seeing so much as a sled track—nothing and no one since that morning long ago when she spotted her family following the marks of her earlier passage. Nor did she yearn for company, not consciously, focused as she was on surviving long enough to reach the high islands before summer thaw.

Still more angry about her family than apprehensive, she did not want to consider whether someone would be sent by Narluk, especially so soon. Shrewd and artful himself was her father likely to dispatch someone similarly cunning—a well-seasoned man—who would look like and pretend convincingly to be someone other than an emissary? But would Narluk possibly select someone this young?

The stranger had grave features but an unlined face. His eyes were steady and without any guile apparent. He too had the stillness of the trail about him. Yet . . .

She had no time to build anxiety. She viewed first with pleasure and then with trepidation the fur-clad human figure who stood beside her lean-to. On either side of him lay a shadowy lump. Seal, she identified by squinting. Saliva flooded her mouth. She smiled. Might oil for her lamp be forthcoming? Light and warmth—how she missed such luxuries!

"Someone would build an igloo for the woman, except that this shelter seems sturdy and the weather mild."

Eh, he had recognized her as a woman. . . . Back in her village filled with aging people, she as an unmarried female was still considered a child. She liked it that the stranger's voice was deep and rich, his sounds carefully produced. His inflection was like Pichikut's had been—eh, coastal Inupiaq. Wonderful tone, the young woman thought—then reminded herself that she had heard no human voice at all except her own in a very long time.

73

"*Kinaowit?*" she asked. What is the name to which someone answers? Ah, she knew her error even as the syllables were uttered. Not only was she rude to ask rather than wait for him to reveal the information; but if this stranger gave his name, then she must in courtesy give him hers. What name should she give? Not Sukitilan.

"Only genuine Inuit concern themselves with names," the young man laughed. "It is necessary to thank someone for proving that she is no spirit of the trail. The hunter standing here is called Tuk." And in a few moments, when she did not return the courtesy, "The woman's name, then? And that of her child?"

"The child?!" burst from her lips. Her brother was asleep in the robe nest on the sled. He had made no sound or movement. How did the stranger know about a baby? She looked to his sled and saw the tracks behind it leading from southwest. No instinct within her signaled fear.

Or did her ease come only from anticipation of the coming seal flesh and oil? She sighed. *Ai-ee*—at least, he thought the infant hers, so he did not know much.

She must not seem to hesitate, so she drew herself up and lifted her chin while she made two quick decisions. A name for her brother? Something close to but not the same as Ajak. Her own new name was easy—she supposed she had already decided what it would be.

Proudly, "This one speaking is called Kiti," she told him with great dignity. And she silently thought, *but not often, and not by many.* And a mother's child"—what was similar in sound to the name of his milk sister? "—is Arajik!"

There, done. Her little one had a name at last, and so did this new female. The sound of each title spoken aloud gave pleasure. Her little one? She shrugged and smiled. She had now confirmed Tuk's misinformation on origin of the baby.

"Kiti," the young man Tuk repeated, rolling each of the two syllables with equal stress, softly in the back of his mouth. He knew it would not do to speak a human name too loudly out-of-doors for fear of tempting spirits bent on mischief.

Then, "It happens that someone foolishly brought with him some small and possibly rotten seals that lay abandoned on the trail."

The old Sukitilan and now this new Kiti were impatient with the long-winded approach to presentation of a gift. No seal ever just lay deserted—not for long, anyway—not with ravenous predators including Inupiat craving the rich flavor. And the only way such a carcass would rot in winter would be for Inuit to cache and deliberately rot it to get that special, succulent flavor and texture. Her mouth weltered in contemplation of fat red meat to come. Not fish!

"Someone would be most grateful," he continued, "if the woman would take some of the meat—perhaps to feed her least valuable dogs?"

She smiled. "*Nakorami*," thank you. She watched as he expertly butchered the larger of the two. Fresh, certainly not rotten, and of fine size—*nathek*, the petite, sweet-meated creature with tallowy blubber to produce much oil for lamps. Regardless of the stranger's origin, heedless of his intent, she must accompany him on a seal hunt. She had gone with her brothers, but they were never successful, knew no more than she about capturing ocean prey.

On the trail returning from the sea, in fact, her family always had to trade in order to get seal and walrus meat and hide. Local hunters more knowledgeable about sea mammals were happy to get variety found with caribou or sea bear, were delighted with one of Pichikut's fine parkas trimmed around the face with *kapvik* fur, the weatherproof, hollow filaments from the pelt of wolverine.

Kiti must also try to learn what else this Tuk knew about her—and do so without asking any more questions.

The visitor shared the liver, and she ate the delicacy hungrily with deep appreciation. Never before had she been so honored. The two Inuit had their fill of seal while both dog teams gorged on the rich flesh. How could Kiti get Tuk to demonstrate his methods for hunting seal?

After light conversation without revelation, the stranger spoke seriously. "Skin and blubber in these creatures is too heavy for a lazy hunter to haul," he complained. Kiti knew his comment was not only an offer of more food and oil but also her cue to invite him to travel with her.

Here was a pleasing man. But was he an agent of *angakok*? One so cunning as to assuage her anxiety by deliberately indicating misinformation on the child?

Still . . . why speak of the baby at all, in that circumstance? Certainly Arajik would have revealed himself in short order. So if not through Narluk, how did Tuk know of her small brother's existence?

Or again, might this stranger be some youthful rogue male cast out by his own people for some unspeakable misdeed—and now preparing to prey on her? Pichikut always told her that someone could avoid deception by listening carefully to hear a certain echo in a voice. The imposter also tends to show great zeal in all matters, she had said. But mostly, the daughter was to listen to her own inner response. So said *Ananak*:Pay attention to the silent secret voice.

And in this instance, Kiti felt nothing amiss. She decided that Tuk was most likely to be exactly what he seemed—a young coastal Inupiat hunting alone for some yet unspoken reason. She quite suddenly knew herself to be so lonely that she wondered whether she was even in touch with her inner warning system.

Kiti had more faith at this moment in Nuna's secret voice, and the white dog seemed complacent. See how Nuna was making friendly overtures—unusual for her with anyone other than family!—by pressing her nose under Tuk's arm as he walked by.

But then Kiti's brain told her to be cautious. Nuna appreciated red meat and knew its source. So hungry for it, she had been, that she might well befriend evil Paija.

But Kiti (and yes, she liked the name so clean and simple!) had her knives and spear, knew how to use them, even the harpoon. . . . But oh, how she did long for congenial company. Instead of inviting him to share the trail, though, she rummaged at her sled for small bladders and intestinal sacs in which they could store seal meat. She would accept some packets of meat and oil for herself if he insisted strongly, as she hoped he would.

And she could reciprocate with—what? Fish was no great gift to any but a starving Inuit. Perhaps some *kapvik* fur, mending and apparel repair if needed?

Her mouth watered at the prospect of meat. Now she watched closely as Tuk cut the other seal to make an oil bag—a process that her mother had rarely found opportunity to undertake, one which Kiti had never taken the trouble to watch. Her own family along with many other inlanders traded caribou and processed hides with coastal Inuit to get the golden oil already formed in plump bladders.

Beginning at the creature's mouth, the man sliced delicately beneath the skin, sliding it back expertly as he cut so that he finally had a seamless and liquid-proof pouch into which they would together stuff cubed chunks of blubber. From the Big Feed, Kiti took especially sturdy sinew to tie off the opening. Within that pouch would develop a supply of the oil which would light Tuk's lamp, brighten his meals and warm him in a trail house. Well yes, if he pressed her strongly, she would also accept oil. . . . How long would it take, she wondered, to become liquid for the lamp?

And yes, she decided, here would be a good person with whom to share the trail. A coastal man. But could she travel with someone who might later be her undoing? Why not postpone any decision about inviting him—just wait and see? Stay right here at this fish camp for two or three more sleeps, stay alert to danger if it came, and give this stranger time to reveal himself.

Chapter 12.
A Plan

That night, the wind was calm for once, fog hovering thick, and Tuk rigged a ragged hide across the front of Kiti's lean-to. All humans plus Nuna and Ajak were cozy around the travel lamp which burned Tuk's oil—for he had by now seen that she herself had none. She had been without for many sleeps—but he did not need to know that. If he urged strongly that she accept oil, then yes indeed.

And she would reciprocate with wolverine pelt, she had decided, for she noticed that his *nuilak*, that fur which trims the face opening of a parka, was handsome enough but only fox, prone to icing up in storm and serious cold. If all went well, she would offer to sew in the new fur.

Tuk had by now observed that Arajik—how easily that name came!—took his milk from a sled dog. He had made no comment. His eyes had not so much as widened in surprise—for Kiti had watched carefully—the first time he saw the infant nurse Nuna .

Perhaps Tuk had seen them on the trail previously? That explanation was the only key to his initial knowledge of Arajik's existence, barring Narluk's information. Certainly, that prior sight was a solution to this mystery, a clarification that she wanted to accept.

Of course! He probably had known already that Nuna suckled the child.

Arajik. Her brother had a name. She thought happily about how, each time the snow was right, she would from this time on

79

adopt coastal ways and cut blocks to coil up a little house before each sleep. If she had seal oil for light and warmth—eh, what pleasure might be coming!

She looked across the lamp at her guest. Before entering the small shelter, he had removed his outer furs—his *silipak*—and beat off encrusted snow. Then he scraped and folded the apparel, placed it neatly into a bladder he had earlier carried inside. A tidy man. His eyes were half shut as he sat in his *illupak*, his underfurs, cross-legged on robes.

She saw a sturdy, well-built Inupiat, possibly twenty-some-thing winters, twenty-five at most—no older than Palunga would be now.

How could anyone like this, so generous and sociable and pleasant, be guilty of deceit? He had broad cheeks and a ruddy, clear complexion, soft smile creases around his mouth. Fully open, his sparkling dark eyes were centered in whites like new snow and surrounded by pale arcs of unreddened skin.

During even the brief and deeply shadowed light of this season on the trail, he must often wear *idgak*, his snow spectacles. These would be carved from bone or walrus ivory or even from precious driftwood scraps. They would have tiny, horizontal slits through which to peer and thus keep ground glare from blinding him. It being winter, she had not thought to pack such goggles for herself.

As a result, the rims of her own eyes were sore, and she knew that they must be crimson. She would have to craft something by springtime, when once again the sun showed its face each day for lengthening periods to reflect on snow that still lay on the ground.

They chatted back and forth, and she continued to observe the newcomer. On the upper edges of Tuk's cheeks were white patches which matched two fingers on his bare left hand. The Snow-walker had touched and then released him, for here were marks of frostbite. Similar pale marks probably showed in the numb places on her own cheeks.

As if suddenly aware of her scrutiny, he lifted his eyes to study her as well across the smoking lamp. What did he see, she wondered. Her dark hair glistened, that she knew, turning under at her shoulders. Perhaps a good point. But she would never be plump enough to be beautiful, even though her full, rosy cheeks—so Pichikut assured her often—gave promise of fine facial flesh to come.

At home, although not gaunt as now, she still had always been lanky, already nearly tall as her tall mother and towering over most village women. Not ever round and comforting as Inupiat women should be.

Kiti brought herself back to the present. A question must not be asked, but she needed an answer, anyway. "It may have happened that someone saw a person fishing on the ice today," she suggested.

He raised his eyebrows, Yes. "A hunter stalked seal on high rocks. He saw a woman take her team far onto ungrounded ice." His words held no rebuke. She knew even when she started out, this morning, that she might be taking a chance by going so close to the open lead. Just how much danger lay there, she was uncertain. Ice must be easier to slice through for fishing where it was not so thick. And most likely—so she reasoned then—fish would be more plentiful in open water. And had not the success of her fishing on this day supported her theory?

She had offered the fresh char to accompany seal for their evening meal. But Tuk insisted that she save the fish for emergencies on the trail. He must not like it, either. She would go out by the lead each day she stayed here before continuing north, do so with or without accompaniment. Beginning tomorrow, after the sleep . . . ah. . . . Unless . . .

She took a deep breath. "It may happen that seal is abundant near this camp." She had gone southeast to the coast for seal with her brothers two winters back. They had insisted that she hide herself and be silent. But even so—or possibly because she obeyed and stayed far from the seals, so *Ananak* scolded them later—they captured nothing.

Tuk sucked in breath, Yes. "On this day, at least. *Ahmi*. One cannot know the future."

"It could happen that two hunters can enjoy double the success of one." He did not need to know that her experience was so limited. Nor did he need to know that she wanted to learn from someone who came from the coast, someone familiar with sea creatures.

His eyes crinkled at the edges, but he did not laugh aloud. "Perhaps."

She remembered that Inupiat women do not normally refer to themselves as hunters—even if they hunt.

Later that night, although they shared the robes and sleeping place, Kiti made no signal of willingness to share more, no move to extend the courtesy common on the trail. Why not? She was no maiden, certainly, and knew she would enjoy a lusty romp in the furs. Here was a compelling man, balanced in form and mellow in manner.

Well, for one thing, he had made no overture—but even if he had, she would have turned away. She already liked him—and she did not wish to like him more until she knew with certainty that he did not somehow come from her father.

Still, she was curious, and she warmed herself and put herself to sleep by imagining what he might be like. She was aware of and sometimes a participant in activities upon the sleeping ledge at home, especially when one or another brother brought in some visiting woman to share the *iglerk*. But she herself had never sought out males from off the trail. Nor had she begged to expand her acquaintance of men by accompanying her family when they visited another village or joined with other groups in summer camp.

Still, she always agreed when someone asked her father to have her for the night, and he in turn asked her. And each time, her body had reveled in the play. But always, she kept her mind and manner separated. She wondered now whether she could keep this kind of distance if her partner were someone like Tuk. Villagers remarked—sometimes within her hearing—on her cool bearing.

How was she to learn a woman's secrets with such rare opportunity to receive advice and counsel from others on the sleeping ledge of her own home? How, without great experiment and practice?

Still, most of the villagers were much older, tolerant of someone whom they considered still a child. Eh, and the daughter of *angakok*, besides. *Pirtok*. So it was, and no help for it. The girl excelled in other ways. . . .

It was Pichikut that the daughter listened to. And Pichikut sent the same message in a dozen ways: Life can be long. No hurry.

Kiti woke up early. On impulse, she crept out to the sled and got into her mother's clothing. She proudly shrugged on the softly flowing *silipak* with *amoutik*, the trousers with adult woman's parka that had the extra hood, the *amaut*, for carrying a child. Everything was much too wide, but hardly too long at all. She pulled the pants high and then flapped the waist over and down before she drew the string tight as possible.

The parka fit like walrus hide would fit a seal. It did not—quite—drag the ground because she was after all nearly as tall as her mother had been although not so round. Arajik was resting and at peace when she plucked him up and cuddled him, pressing her nose into his fat cheek. She carried him with her to the sled, then lowered him gently into the deep hood that opened to her back. He nestled down immediately, perhaps pleased by unaccustomed skin contact. The girl now busied herself with preparation of her sled runners.

Tuk crawled out through the hide baffle of the lean-to just as Kiti finished a final ice coat. She was proud of her work, for the parallel strips glistened in bright starlight. When she walked over to the lean-to, though, Kiti realized that she had made a mistake by putting the baby into the *amaut*. All had been well while she bent to attend the runners, but standing up and having Arajik swinging in the tip of the carrier made him bounce against her buttocks with each step. He did not complain—in fact, his muffled chortles came to her. But the dignity she had planned to display was breached, and Tuk stood open-mouthed.

"It happens that the babe is not yet large enough for this hood," she explained. Any *soospuk* could see that the problem here lay not with the size of the baby but rather with the fit and sheer volume of the heavy fur clothing obviously not her own.

Tuk turned suddenly away to undo and fuss with fastenings at the front of the lean-to. His next words were muffled. Kiti listened as she twisted the *amaut* around and scooped Arajik from the hood. Then she plucked up clothing that fit from her sled and went back to the lean-to.

"Can it be that two hunters will soon go for seal?" her visitor asked finally. His voice was grave, but she could see in lampglow that his eyes danced with mischief.

Chapter 13.
Seal

Seal can be captured in two ways. A hunter may go out on ocean ice and search for an *aglu*, a breathing hole around which at certain seasons is built for newborn pups a circular ledge below the ice surface but above the water line. The breathing holes—and one animal probably has several—are used and kept open by the seal. They are invisible, or nearly so, to anyone who searches from above.

Even the huge white sea bear, whose great joy in life comes from capture of a seal and whose effective although time-consuming technique for hunting these creatures has been copied and adapted since the earliest Inuit, even this astute predator has difficulty finding these *aglu* on ice above the sea.

If good fortune rests on the hunter's shoulder—and perhaps luck comes from a hungry sled dog with a sharp nose—an *aglu* can be located. Then the hunter sets up a harpoon on bone crosspieces, takes out the killing spear and knife, puts a few layers of bear pelt between *kamik* and ice, balances a fur float in the hole . . . and waits.

Sometimes for only part of a day but more often for several sleep times and intervening dark days, the hopeful Inuit stands silent, motionless, hunched over the *aglu* to make the least shadow possible. He endures.

Or at least, Kiti remembered, she endured. Perhaps the seal would finally come. Or not. How many hunters had she heard about found frozen, stiff and spiritless over an *aglu* on sea ice?

The other method to catch seal is faster but less certain and involves the rocky shore. When the sun is bright, or even in winter when moonlight bathes the coast or lights display in the sky, seals in small number may pull up onto craggy boulders above the tide. There, they take an air bath to rid their fur of louse-like saltwater hitchhikers.

If a hunter is lucky enough to find the creatures out of water, and if this hunter is sufficiently skilled to get close, then several seals might give themselves in a single encounter.

So whether in water or on rocks, seals are never easy. Intelligent, wary, suspicious—but oh, so worth great effort!

Late on the second morning after Tuk's arrival, just as a pale strip of light showed shy and delicate, a mere glimmer on the southeast horizon, Kiti followed Tuk up an icy trail, creeping along, slithering like some legless creature, slowly. . . .

So far, the furry mammals well forward on a stone-strewn point seemed not to sense approaching danger.

In a roundabout way, Tuk had asked earlier whether a young mother had ever before hunted seals.

"Yes, on both rocks and ice." True, but that was all she had done: hunted. And even so, she had participated mostly as observer. This morning she must educate herself about searching out seal when she was alone on the trail. She could not reveal to Tuk that she had never even seen someone capture a seal, and she was relieved when he did not require specifics.

For not one seal ever gave itself. Not to her brothers, certainly not to her. Nor even to Narluk, so far as she had ever heard. Not even close. She had so far mentioned nothing of her family to Tuk, and she did not plan to. She still did not know how much he knew about her.

Kiti's neck ached from watching the *kamik* soles of this man who crawled along in front of her. Expecting glare on snow and ice in a clear sky after the stars faded—and even those very few moments of the hazy, early winter sun glow before it faded totally could damage eyes, he assured her—Tuk had given her a pair of his own *idjak*, slitted goggles carved elegantly from driftwood.

Her eyes ached anyway. They did not throb from the sun which even now faded into the southwest only a few degrees from where it had moments earlier stained the sky. But rather, they hurt from trying so hard to follow and copy every move made by the hunter in front of her.

Eh, would she now, as Pichikut had so often petitioned the trail spirits, truly be successful in the hunt?

When Tuk stopped going forward and rolled onto his side, she wondered at the action. And when he became frenzied with an arm bent at the elbow while keeping a mittened hand close to his side, she became even more curious.

She edged up to be even with him. They were now so close to the herd that wind might carry her voice to the seals, so she whispered her words directly into the hood at his ear. "Someone is well?"

He continued to wag his elbow, but more slowly, gradually turning so that he faced her. His quiet voice came to her. "It happens that a seal is vigilant."

She raised her eyebrows, Yes. She knew that.

"But also, it may be that seal eyes cannot distinguish details of shape at a distance."

Again, Kiti's eyebrows arched. New information, credible, but what did it have to do with Tuk's odd behavior?

As the man realized that the conversation was not concluded, he sighed. "Many the fine and fortunate hunter who lost his shot at seals upon the rocks."

He was watching her eyes, and she knew that some response was expected, some sign that she grasped his thought from the few words given. Nothing came to her.

"—Because," he continued finally, "the hunter forgot to scratch."

"—Scratch," she echoed woodenly.

"Scratch!!" Tuk's elbow became more energetic as it changed angle to fan a new spot.

Kiti lay staring blankly at the flailing arm.

"To rid oneself of itching pests."

The woman was mystified. She felt no need to scratch anywhere. The trail contained no troublesome insects during winter.

Even more patiently, Tuk continued. "It may be that a creature suspicious but blurry-eyed is reassured to see approaching figures scratch like any other basking seal."

Ah! Kiti scrunched back to her former position, grasped her trousers firmly, then thrashed her elbow with great energy back and forth. . . . She must become a seal, must try to envision juicy clams on the ocean floor. She must roll a little, sluggishly, as she had seen these ahead of them do, must be a seal awkward on land and away from its element. Must stretch and preen. And especially, now that the space between Inupiat and seals was lessening, she must remember to scratch?

She did her best to imagine an itch where her fluttering elbow might reach—which was no place—and chuckled softly until Tuk doubled back to peer at her.

"It happens that what seal lacks in eyesight is compensated for by acute hearing," he told her softly. "True seals do not giggle."

Kiti forced herself to become quiet, determined to become a good—no, a superb!—hunter of seals. But a broad grin split her face.

At last, the two reached high, rocky headland which contained a jutting table that tilted slightly downward to overlook a narrow lead of open water. Their progress now must be even slower;

for stones on which they crawled could easily shift and alert their quarry.

Kiti knew this part of seal chase on land from hunting with her brothers. She remembered the intense cold, too, that overtook someone creeping slowly along the ice.

Today was no exception, even though she tied the drawstring on her hood especially tight to prevent the entry of a freshening wind. Her view opening was only half the size of her palm. She had stuffed extra moss and qiviut—the wild warm wool of muskox—into her *kamik* before leaving camp this morning, but her toes were without feeling. She heard the sea lash onto rocks below, where the lead sizzled so close to shore.

She was too cold to shiver. She must not think about the chill, must not fear proximity to pounding waves. She must think only of seals—their shape, their killing spot, the taste of them as well—and she must continue to be a seal . . . eh, did seals ever feel the cold? Perhaps not, with their three Inuit fingers' depth of blubber under warm fur.

. . . And she must not listen to the wailing wind. She must not notice boiling clouds as Nigituk, the strong south wind behind her, blustered in its aerial sled lashed high with storm. Too bad that the only approach for the hunters was on the wind. The mammals they stalked would surely smell them soon and seek shelter in the sea. She must continue to inch forward, head up, squinting through her hood opening, to guide herself by the soles of Tuk's *kamik*.

Then she saw the young man stand up smoothly. Clutched in his right hand was his killing spear and in his left, a fire-hardened skinning knife. Kiti copied him to rise with one fluid motion. She carried similar weapons, hers made of bone instead of Tuk's less brittle driftwood. Because the two hunters were obscured by loose snow circling on itself and parallel to the ground before the howling wind, the seals did not take alarm—but Kiti knew that in one more moment . . .

Tuk shouted as he leaped among the creatures and drove his spear into the nearest beast, withdrew the weapon and thrust into another. Kiti scrambled across the rocks to drive her own shaft into one more seal as the beasts twisted and blundered clumsily to reach the cliff drop-off.

On the glaze of droppings that fouled the ledge, they rammed each other in panic as they flopped toward safety in the sea. Kiti thrust again but missed, realized that for the first time ever, she had not—and did not now—hesitate before attack. . . . She stabbed again, successfully—and saw Tuk do the same.

Five beasts. . . . Two by her own hand. Pichikut was right— Kiti could do what was necessary in the hunt, now that she herself knew the gnaw of hunger. Euphoric in triumph, she wiped her spear on snow, watching Tuk so that she could join his ceremony of thanks.

As she bent to clean the knife, she felt a stone slide beneath her foot. The knife flew from her mitt and struck rock dully as she fought for purchase. Then she was skidding on the slippery decline, feet-first after the seals. She scrabbled for a handhold, for leverage of any kind, felt herself continue to glide helplessly.

As her feet went over the edge, she consigned herself to Sedna and the sea, praised the spirits that Arajik was not here in her tunic—would Tuk care for him now?

But before she could speculate about the thought-question, her clawing mitt also slid across the slick edge and she dropped toward water and the babble of panicked seals splashing below. Falling free she wondered if seals might eat people as people eat seals. . . .

Chapter 14.
Delivery

Kiti felt rather than heard a rhythmic rumble that she gradually recognized as surf on rocks. Her ears were filled with the shriek and moan of the still-approaching storm above her. She no longer heard seals barking. Her hips and legs bobbled in water, but her waist and upper body were on flat rock. She had not yet been accepted by the sea?

She ached, those parts of her not numb; but she felt as if she were still all together—and so, so cold. Of course, her feet and legs had been without much feeling before she ever reached the herd. Going for seal was a cold business on rocks or ice. And now, in water as well?

Ai-ee! Five seals, up there. Tuk would have fine provision for Arajik and himself, for Ajak and Nuna and both teams. Worth the chill? Absolutely. Worth dying for? Umm. She wondered when and where her spirit would begin anew.

Wind-borne ice pellets struck the bit of face exposed by parka and cut into her passive reverie. Cautiously, she raised her head to look around. Rocks and pebbles were strewn upon the ledge on either side of where she lay. Boulders jutted at odd angles from the cliff above her—play-toys of some untidy giant child.

The relatively shallow but undercut cliff she looked up to inspect, the one over which she had fallen and now viewed from below, gave way—as she had noted earlier—to less daunting verticals on either side.

She raised a mitten to brush ice from her face, but the

movement slid her further into water. She then lay perfectly still, flat as she could. Waves poured around her, but the low ledge where she clung seemed to be protected, receiving only a mild surge. Pirtok. Who can question what happens by chance? Frivolous fate that she could not change.

Tuk would think her washed away. How could he investigate from the slippery ledge? Why would he? She would not know to search, were he here and she above. She would presume that he had disappeared forever beneath the dark surface as had other Inuit before, as would others in the future.

She would believe him taken up immediately by the Ocean Queen, would assume his spirit to be busily preparing at this very moment for return to his people as protector of some new person. If she were the hunter left above, Kiti would not risk sliding off the cliff recklessly to investigate what was after all a familiar tragedy . . . nor would Tuk.

She called out, realizing as she shouted that her voice could not be heard above the sounds of sea and squall . . . even if someone were listening. She shouted anyway, and louder. Shrieking gale overhead, slapping, sucking surf below . . . whoosh . . . splash . . . gurgle.

This would be the end of her life-day, then, the finish to the brief new Kiti who existed by this name for so few sleeps. Also the end of young Sukitilan, for whom this would have been her seventeenth winter. Sometime soon, the tall tide which Pichikut had described with such awe would come to collect her, offering her once again to Sea-queen Sedna.

Kiti closed her eyes, pulled in upon herself. She wished that Tuk and she could together have thanked the seals for giving themselves. She wished that Narluk had not been so stubborn about Arajik. That Arajik had possessed a name from the start. She wished her mother had not died. She wished that Pichikut had not left her coastal Inupiat so long ago. . . .

Tuk had not spoken of his origins, but he must be of these same north and coastal people. His speech. His ease on sea ice. The *idjak* he had given her, formed from precious drifting wood still tucked into an inner pocket of her parka, now poking at her ribs. What a waste, to sink with them, when so little sunlight pierced the sea.

Carefully, so that balance was not disturbed, she dug out the spectacles, held them. Perhaps if she released them they would float onto some bright beach one day. Then it might happen that someone who had need would find and use—*ahmi*! Who can tell the future?

But *idjak* such as these were too valuable to drown. She put them back, resolved to set them afloat as she herself slid beneath the dark water.

Wood. She wondered where it came from. Only coastal people could find much of it. Tuk's spear of wood with blackened tip. No sled runners of bone, as with her inland people, but again wondrous wood, substantial, that drifting or shore bound material rarely seen in any size on tundra waterways. She wondered for the hundredth time what manner of creature left such a malleable skeleton.

Tuk would of course take Arajik to his coastal Inupiat. Perhaps by chance even to Pichikut's people? How strong was her mother's spirit in the babe? And although the people of the ice islands could never know that Arajik"s mother was one of their own, the child would be safe with them. So *Ananak* had promised.

She remembered with relief that she was wearing the skillfully constructed clothing fashioned by her mother. How tight the stitches of her boots and trousers. . . . She was embarrassed to recall her own slapdash work, required to be undone and done again not once but three times, sometimes four, *Ananak* dissatisfied even then.

Tiny stitches with sinew stuffing every opening can make the difference between breath and death for Inuit, Pichikut would tell her. Now Kiti understood those words. She vowed that when she lived again she would sew only the tiniest stitches that did not ever pierce pelt fully. And like what she wore now, would not leak water. She realized her feet and legs were dry!

Lived again? But might it be that the time for finishing this life had not yet arrived?

Arajik! Here she lay on stone and water . . . passively awaiting death. But she had an obligation—a baby, her small brother . . . and had she even tried to save herself? Arajik needed her. . . .

Eh, to move at all might slide her fully to the sea. But would that not be preferable to having tide drink her slowly? "*Soospuk!*" she muttered aloud. What a nitwit.

She must not change her grip of both mitts pressed along the ledge. But could she gradually draw those chilled legs and feet up to the rock? She still had feeling in her hips. Bit by bit, she brought her knees up, slowly curled her *kamik* around and onto the ledge, then loosened the tunic drawstring and tucked her legs inside, beneath her, to get warmth and feeling. Doing all this smoothly took strength, control, great effort, much time—and then at last was done.

She raised her body up to get belly above knees, then crouched low, completely free of the sea, still pressing as much of herself as possible against the ledge. With a cautious mitt, she rubbed along the side of first one calf and then the other, finally massaging feet and ankles hard but not so vigorously that she lost balance. Ice fragments driven by wind flew in the tiny opening of her hood to sting her eyes. She clenched them shut.

At last, she decided that her feet and legs might hold her up. She peeled away the frost that sealed her eyes, then tightened her parka opening even further, and finally stood bent against the wind.

She squinted up to inspect the rock wall before her, then looked in both directions where jutting boulders tilted out and downward to the sea. North, to her right, the ledge itself seemed to widen but was pounded in half a kayak's distance by the full force of wave action from a building tide. She could attain it, but she would never manage to resist those wild waves, not even by inching along on her stomach.

How fortunate was the seal hunter, she thought now, not to have fallen in that place instead of this.

South, then, into heavy wind. Bracing against the cliff, she felt her way inch by inch, squinting eyes meanwhile searching upward for a place where the hill descended to her ledge. Those seals got up to the rocky point by land, she reasoned. True, a seal can leap up with force to bring himself above water level—say high as a single Inuit, at most. But no seal can leap to the height of two or three people, no, not the distance to the top of the cliff before her—eh, presuming that she was now directly beneath the point from which she had fallen.

The seal herd could easily have bounded onto this low ledge on which she crawled, though, even juveniles, and then chosen an indirect route to reach the stars and spirit lights—much as she should do right now.

Yes south, then, along this narrowing shelf. She bumped her head on a sharp outcrop, explored its upper surface, tried to dislodge the formation with a sudden yank. Solid. Why not clamber up, then trust to luck that she could find another gripping place and yet another . . . and finally gain the top? Certainly not what seals had done, but she was no seal.

"Ai-ee-ee!" she shouted once, then saved her breath. . . . If Tuk were nearby and if he heard her, he would believe her shout to be the wail of some sad wandering spirit. *Pirtok.*

She took off her mittens, thrust each into a soggy parka pocket. For this climb, she needed sensitive bare fingers.

Energy coursed through her as she climbed, strength and balance beyond any she had ever known. She could clamber to the moon if the stars would make a ramp. Power centered in her hands and arms. Her fingers should be numb by now, but they were not. Kiti would survive this accident, return to Arajik, continue with this same life for a while longer.

In a crashing gale that continued to fling stinging particles before it, she slowly climbed, discovered toeholds, handholds as she went—fortuitously—each lucky find perhaps her last . . . moving carefully, taking time, waiting for lulls in wind to allow vision. Up. Over. Up again, zig-zagging.

At last, her nose level with a lower grade of the same rocky hillock where the seals had been, she pulled herself face down and gasping onto the icy ground amid swirling snow already beginning new drift around boulders.

Safe from Queen Sedna and the sea. Here she was—feet and legs and now hands also numb with cold. She replaced her mitts, clapped her palms together, slapped them against her hips, then tucked them under her tunic and finally down inside her trousers to the warmth between her thighs. Her furs were of course wet where they had floated on the sea—*kamik* and *silipak*, boots and trousers, stiffening as the salt water froze.

Still, the sea had not actually seeped through the inner fur-skin, the *illupak*, to her skin. Hard to tell, because they were saturated from perspiration born of fear and great exertion in the climb.

A shudder jolted her. She must find shelter up here. The old drifts were hard-grained granules impossible for burrowing and now topped by nomadic crystals rearranging constantly before a wrathful wind.

She must get warm and stay that way until her clothing dried. She had no food, no sheltering house or robes, no dogs and sled . . . no weapons? She stood up, braced herself on a boulder to keep from yielding to the gale. The threatened storm had arrived in earnest, a tempest rushing by on an unbroken howl of air from the southeast.

Up here on the exposed point, the stinging particles peeled her face. Once again, she tightened the cord to close her *nuilak*, the face opening of her parka, this time to a peephole the size of a lemming's eye. Her own eyes were useless, anyway, in the writhing air.

She felt her way as a blind creature, stooping to assess the ground, grasping to pull herself along on boulders, up the last bit of incline from the south to the killing place. The tilted bedrock where seals had been was now frozen dry, for she could feel abrasion on the soles of her *kamik*.

The surface was studded with ice particles, far less treacherous than before; but she moved gingerly nonetheless. It would not do to fall back to the sea through some widened crack.

Then she stopped, astonished. In the lee of giant stones, it was possible to see pale mounds lined up together like a family on its *iglerk*. All five seals. Her killing spear and skinning knife were side by side, outlined with snow on a rock nearby. Tuk had not taken any meat—well then, how could he, *soospuk* Kiti?—without at least a team? He had only pulled the carcasses high to ease loading after the storm. . . . He would certainly return.

How long, she wondered, had she lain on the sea ledge before her spirits collected themselves and brightened? Perhaps not so much time, she decided; for even with the building storm, some quarter-glow glimmer of mid-day remained. It had seemed the duration of a full sleep, maybe two, that she had lain inert—first surprised to be alive, next discovering herself unhurt but helpless, then feeling sorry for herself and waiting to die—and finally knowing that she must make an effort.

She peered about to find shelter. Besides driving snow, she saw nothing beyond the white lumps of seal, her own weapons and the surrounding boulders. She stumbled over to drop shivering onto the nearest carcass. Big beasts, this one perhaps a third of a kayak's length.

Warmth would be inside, she thought dully, for creatures of the ice and sea are well insulated—except, she thought, for puny humankind. She looked around once more, but now could recognize nothing, as the frost-hardened snow granules swarmed and swirled to create an opaque low fog.

Shelter might exist. Nearby could be a cave among these very boulders; but even the captured seals were barely distinguishable. She felt around to find them.

Drifts were building. Even if the snow were right to make a snowhouse—which it was not—she would freeze before she finished building. Anyway, she had foolishly left her broad snow knife back on the sled. Then as her body quaked with chill while the storm blasted her, an idea came.

Why not make a cave?

She must have shelter, or she might as well have stayed on the rocks below. Her whole body shuddered with rolling quakes of chill as she crept over to retrieve her weapons, then crawled back across the seals to find one surrounded by other carcasses and therefore protected from the gale.

She made a long incision in the belly, carefully removed viscera, rapidly separated out the bladder-like materials which could later be used for containers and floats. Then she flung the still-steaming remainder over the cliff edge. Let sea predators feast, she thought, for it was best not to invite land carnivores, however unlikely they were to come in time of storm.

She would crawl inside a seal to warm herself. If any predator sought out the seals during her coming sleep—and if any were so greedy as to select the largest creature in this group—it would be surprised, would it not?

She placed her killing spear and sharp knife inside the opening, then slid through the cut to lie beside them in the moist, bloody cave she had created. Relief. Out of the wind at last. Snug and protected, she listened to the moan and shriek outside, the driven pellets thud-a-thudding onto the pelt above her; and she felt wind gusts tug against the carcass.

She was in a warm place. Her body heat would keep it so. After sleep, she would have to scrape her furs carefully to get them soft and pliable again. *Pirtok!*

Chapter 15.
Flesh Or Phantom?

She must think through what was likely to have happened here. What would Tuk do when he thought Kiti lost to the sea? What would she do, were she Tuk?

Go back for the one sled they had brought, this morning—her sled bearing Arajik, Nuna, Ajak, along with the hunting bags. Tuk would drive the team up here. Why had he not cut into even one of the seals—ah! Less likelihood of losing all. No ravenous, always-foraging white sea bear would be drawn by the scent—no sly white fox, no wolf, no insatiable wolverine. She hoped she would have been so clever, were the situation reversed.

Tuk had drawn the seals together, for he was a tidy man. She liked that. It would have been he who found her weapons, too, for she remembered that she had thrown them back as she slid. His plan would be to collect everything when he returned.

Was it too much to believe his rapid return to the sled was to care for Arajik? She had felt restive from the very start of the seal hunt about leaving the baby for so long. But Arajik was at least as safe with Nuna as with her. Eh, that a young male stranger abandoned fresh meat and took trouble for a mere babe was perhaps too much to credit.

Tuk had gone back to shelter from the storm. He had gone back to see to the closest dogs—hers, as it happened, since tracking far into the face of the storm would be impossible. He would feed them, be sure that they were safely sheltered from the weather, no doubt worry about his own *kringmerk* back at camp.

Then he would harness the team when the blizzard was spent, and he would bring the sled up here to transport seals. He could do the butchering anywhere and at his leisure. He could pack and fill with blubber those empty bladder bags from camp that they had with such anticipation collected this morning before they set out.

"Ai-ee-ee!" The cry wrung from her lungs automatically, the sound startling her in her primordial shelter. Would her sled team pull for Tuk? Each dog had such different temperament, such unique personality. They needed to be run with a certain order in the harnessing—no question, Iyarpok would rip the throat of any dog that tried to take his spot.

Lacking Kiti's hand command, Nuna too must be restrained. In fact, the girl had lately wondered whether Nuna could ever peaceably become lead again if Iyarpok remained on the team.

And why did she worry about something over which she had no control? Tuk could harness the team or not. The dogs would obey his commands—or not. And if not, he would have to return on foot to the lean-to for his own sled and dogs. A long walk. . . . Both teams would be hungry, but they would survive. And coming soon—what a fine feast of seal to compensate!

She hoped a bit of shadowed light would show at midday after the storm . . . hoped Arajik was well . . . hoped Tuk was not someone sent by Narluk . . . hoped she would find Pichikut's people . . . and that her new little family would survive. . . .

Sound awakened her, and not the howl of wind. She was disoriented. Momentarily panicked, she struck out wildly as she found herself restricted on all sides. Then the opening slit in the seal skin let her bare hand feel the cold of outside air, let her see dim moonlight—and memory returned. The storm was past. What was the sound?

Spear in hand, she emerged with caution, quiet as possible, let her eyes accustom themselves, again heard movement nearby. Not bear or wolverine, she beseeched the spirits. A wolf? He and she might share a meal.

Then she saw Tuk. His back was to her, and he was at the sled by the cradle *upluk* with Arajik. The baby was shouting with his usual morning exuberance. He would by now badly need a change of birdskin on his bottom. Plus, water must be mouth-warmed to dilute the rich canine milk. Would Tuk have observed this practice? Would he think to do it himself? He would not know her reason. They had exchanged no words on the subject.

Kiti stood up stiffly, stretched her cramped muscles, then picked her way across icy rocks. "It happens, someone needs to find clean clothes," she told the man.

Tuk wheeled to stare at her, incredulous.

"Ah, the visitor was skillful to harness Kiti's team and bring it here," she said. "Someone is pleased." She pushed past him and went to Arajik. But she did not want to touch the baby, covered as she was by now-frozen seal gore. Instead, she spoke softly. He quieted his shouts, eyed her gravely, smiled, then began once more to exercise his lungs in glee. A noisy one, this final child of Pichikut!

Ignoring Tuk, for she knew he wrestled with disbelief, Kiti tried to reassure him by walking and talking normally, by attending regular tasks. She dug into the filled bladder packs lining the sled until she found her mother's *amoutik*, the big parka which had so embarrassed her that first morning after Tuk arrived.

Only three sleeps ago? She was once again a different person, her body having now been declined by Sedna. Should she select yet another name?

No. Kiti suited her. Far back in the mouth, strong—a carrying sound. She shrugged out of her matted parka and trousers, her *silipak*, then looked down at her fairly unscathed undergarments, her *illupak*, to assess their condition. Her own extra set of *silipak*, she realized even as she inspected in dim shadow the fully dry and reasonably unsoiled hareskin and ptarmigan she wore, were still at the lean-to in their base camp. She had brought Pichikut's clothing on the sled yesterday only because she wished to take no chance of losing the garments to a dog that came unstaked or to a hide-hungry wolverine.

Shivering and unclothed in the wind without her *silipak*, she shook out and then shrugged into the oversized furs of her mother. She glanced surreptitiously at Tuk as she drew up the waist and lapped it over, tightened the strings and knotted them. The young man was lifting empty bladders from their store, now starting up the rocky hill toward the five seals that awaited butchering. He had not yet spoken to her.

The girl laid her sullied outer furs to freeze more fully atop the sled load, stood to catch the eye of every sled dog scattered in the snow. As each gave evidence of recognition—wagged a tail, pricked ears forward to note her attention—she looked pointed-ly at the clothing, shook her head and then frowned at that dog. Delectable as the pelts might smell—bloody leather with fur!—each animal now knew that the apparel was not to be chewed.

Nuna, she need not bother to tell. Kiti sucked breath into her lungs and raised her chin to show satisfaction. The message was clear.

Not far away and on the craggy top of the hill, Tuk stood watching. "Does it happen that this person someone sees is real or some cunning spirit?" he demanded finally. That he questioned her directly indicated the depth of his disquiet.

Kiti laughed as she came up, reached out to apply pressure on his sleeve. Human touch, surely impossible for a specter.

"Mortal Kiti stands before Tuk. She can show her bruises from the fall."

The young man gazed at her steadily, his jaw working. "Then the person must forgive this ignorant hunter," he said softly. "A boy thought her spirits flown absolutely when she slid from rocks and disappeared. He even heard the splash."

Perhaps, but more likely he heard seals. Only her feet and legs had gone into the water. Praise be to Pichikut for her fine, waterproofing stitches to keep the feet and body dry! Kiti raised her eyebrows, held them up. Yes, emphatically. "As would anyone hear and then believe," she said alound.

"An ignorant person looked and listened near the edge, closely as he dared—but saw only frothing waves. He heard the bark of seals for the first few moments. Then no more sound but wave wash."

Again she raised her eyebrows, Yes. "Nor would Kiti linger longer, were she above and Tuk below," she tried to reassure him, "especially with a storm arriving and a long walk waiting. And a babe neglected through the day?" She watched Tuk's eyes to see whether Arajik had been a factor, but she read no change of expression.

Her words seemed to relieve him, however, and they both together set to work at loading.

The butchering of one seal accomplished back at the lean-to, all dogs fed festively. Fire danced on a freshly twisted wick in the sheltered travel lamp. Kiti beat and scraped her furs, put them on, folded her mother's garments back into their bag. It was time to share experience across a meal of sweet seal.

"A hunter thanked the creatures for giving themselves." She asked without asking.

Tuk sucked in a ragged breath, Yes. "Right after the capture, before returning to the sled."

Kiti recognized that the man was not yet fully at ease with her, uncertain still as to whether she were flesh or phantom. *Pirtok.* Time would convince him—seeing her do what all people do naturally—the many unconscious and automatic links to humankind.

She cut raw seal meat and blubber away from her lips with a quick flick of her *ulu*, the sharp semi-circular utility knife. Tuk did the same. Let him talk a bit, and let Kiti respond before she tried once more to get answers from him without direct questioning.

But Tuk was pensive and given to few words. After he finished his meal, he got up and walked over to observe Arajik suckling Nuna. Ajak the pup was now weaned by Nuna's insistence; but she liked to cuddle with her mother and foster brother.

After a time and without comment, Tuk returned to the lamp and sat on robes. He seemed self-absorbed.

Kiti knew he still pondered the miracle of her survival. But she had no way to help him other than to be her own human self. She found her thoughts beginning to scatter, now that the marvel of her continued existence was receding, at least for her. She knew herself to be the same mortal, certainly no visiting spirit. She knew she still drew breath and lived in the human dimension—but what else operated in this moment?

Yes. She guessed the answer was quite simple: Pichikut's daughter, so far at least, was—indeed!—most fortunate in the hunt.

Storm clouds had cleared completely, and the moon was bright. Both teams of dogs were sated with seal meat, now silent and asleep in their ice caves. Arajik nestled in the front of Kiti's parka while the girl worked at sewing her own *amaut* attachment, the small child's hood-pouch that would fit within her own parka to contain Arajik.

Here was a good time for discussion. She had already decided during the meal, when Tuk was not forthcoming, that she had little to lose by asking what she needed to learn in order to keep from bursting like an over-full bladder.

"With Kiti gone, it is supposed that the man was astonished to find himself with a baby in addition to even more dogs."

"He was not fully certain what to do," Tuk answered slowly.

"About the baby," she prompted him.

"*Ee-ee.*" Yes.

Someone was uncertain about the child? What could be uncertain about the dilemma in which Tuk had found himself? He was obligated to care for Arajik, was he not? But she forced herself to be silent as she waited for more.

Then his lips moved and his voice was low. "It happens that a hunter should have helped someone in mortal danger—but then did not."

That was worrying him? His lack of action on her behalf was centering his focus? Guilt? Kiti tossed her head impatiently. "As said before, Tuk did exactly as any other reasonable person would do. As Kiti herself would do. All realize that no chance of survival exists, none at all, for those who slide into the sea. No Inuit can swim."

"But a man should have checked to be certain."

Both knew that even if a person could somehow buoy the head above the ripples so that breath were possible, cold water will paralyze a human system within minutes. Soon, the body ceases to do what it has always done for itself—stops drawing breath. The heart ceases to beat. Tuk knew this as well as she—better than she, for he was of the coastal people.

"Still, a companion should have made certain—"

Kiti interrupted. "—And shortly after that, the Inuk in water lets loose all protective spirits and sinks."

"Yet someone did survive, inexplicably, and should have had Tuk's help."

Chapter 16.
Dispatch

Well, the man was finally talking, but not about important matters. She laughed. "It happens that someone troubles himself needlessly. . . . Kiti has always possessed capable helping spirits . . . and she is always success—eh, fortunate in the hunt."

He sucked in breath to agree. Then, "The girl—the woman—displayed great resourcefulness, to make her igloo of a seal." His tone belied his words. He sounded sad, lost.

He wanted her to need him, was that it? An aspect of the male that Pichikut had told her about, always chuckling at the irony. That Kiti survived without Tuk's help was a spear in his gut?

Every female knows that it is the woman who processes and chews the hides for boats and blankets and clothing—which she then makes to fit each individual and keeps in good repair. Pichikut's words: And she it is who bears and rears the children, who keeps the household going and ministers to the body and the soul of every member. It is her responsibility—as a daughter has noticed and complained about quite bitterly—to obtain and store oil for light and warmth, a woman's disgrace should the supply run out when blubber or even tallow is yet available.

"Yet, it is the woman who eats last or not at all in time of famine," the young Sukitilan would observe.

What the man does in exchange for woman's succor is hunt. If he is skilled and fortunate, creatures give themselves readily, and all men—most women as well—feel that the activities of life are properly balanced. If the man lacks skill or if he is unlucky, he will die and his family will die before him.

"All know this to be true." Sukitilan had to agree then, and certainly Kiti knows it to be so.

"But when a woman hunts with skill—through necessity or through predisposition, as in the case of Pichikut and now her daughter—and when she is favored by the spirits of the chase, then men believe life's balance is disturbed."

Kiti remembered asking, "But is it not always better within a family to have the greatest number of hunters possible?"

Pichikut laughed. "Of course, so long as all of them are men. So young Sukitilan must never seem to be too skillful on the trail." Her mother had stressed the word "seem."

But the daughter had frowned.

"Eh—fishing is fine. Berry-collecting in season, also. But never must she seem to excel in hunting that requires valor and strength, skill with weapons. At least, never among the barren lands Inupiat."

"This ignorant young woman fails to understand."

"A daughter must consider. Has someone seen a man chew hide to soften it?"

"Never."

"Of course not, no more than birth a baby—but also, has someone ever seen a man carry on his back an infant child who continually drools and spits and voids?"

The girl laughed aloud at the image of dignified Narluk so burdened even within the privacy of his own igloo. "*Ananak* says that this is so among those of the inner barren ground. Does she mean that coastal people view the matter differently?"

"When this woman was a child whose aging father was unskilled and helpless on the trail, she had to hunt or starve. She soon learned to go alone and carefully hide her ripening prowess."

"The family used what their daughter brought?"

"Absolutely. The mother knew that her only child had fortune in the chase, as did the other women in the village. But the father believed, as did every other male, that Pichikut took the sled she had made out onto the ice until a trail spirit she had subdued loaded the sled by her command."

Slowly, "It happens that it was necessary for them to believe so?"

"*Ee-ee*," Pichikut responded softly, "and it is therefore also necessary that no woman of this household appear to have particular prowess in the hunt."

Kiti focused on the tormented young man who sat across the lamp from her. Then she grinned. "Would someone prefer that Kiti perished when she received no aid from the other hunter?" she asked.

Tuk frowned at her impertinence and did not answer at first. Then he smiled briefly, shrugged. "*Owka*," No.

Perhaps this visitor was not of coastal Inupiat at all. With Pichikut, no topic was ever too grim for laughter. Kiti changed the subject. "Someone puzzles over what the man says was meant to be done with Arajik."

Tuk was silent for a long time. Kiti checked the new wick without losing her fire, twisted several more fine sinews for later use.

"Take him to his own village," Tuk said finally, "if the village could be found."

A vast shiver shook Kiti, and then she turned to stone. A voice that sounded as if it belonged to someone else questioned discourteously, "And how would someone know that village?"

He looked up, startled by the tightness of her tone. Once more, he did not reply immediately, only went back to watching the lamp flicker. At last, "A traveler first saw Kiti and her babe lying on the snow-laden prairie late in the sleeptime," he confessed, "then followed her to a village—to assure safe passage, he might say, but mostly for his own purpose."

Kiti's chin went up. Her breath came short. "Tuk has tracked someone all this way on the trail!"

He shook his head. "*Owka,* No. Only come across her later, once again by accident. . . and recognized her then."

Kiti's thoughts spun. "It must be that it was Tuk whom Kiti saw on the crest of a hill that night of her departure—as she lay on ice with the newborn babe and Nuna!"

"Newborn?!" He was astonished.

"Ee-ee, that same day."

Tuk raised his eyebrows, Yes. "Hoo-oo." Most women did not take the trail immediately after giving birth, especially not alone.

"And someone has perhaps stalked Kiti ever since!"

He had already indicated no, but the girl was thinking fast and not attending his words so much as searching for the truth beyond them.

If Tuk saw them only on that night while she waited in the dark for Arajik to suckle Nuna, then he truly did not know much. Their activities on the tundra would have been in deep shadow, for that night had shown no moon and few stars. Nor was he likely to know that the baby had earlier been set out to die.

Yet he knew about her village moving, and that would be more than he could learn by following her to the sleeping town, staying long enough to see her leave—and then returning immediately to the trail.

She tried to control a surge of anxiety. And if he did knew more about her village, then he might know Narluk and her circumstance. He might have been sent . . . white anger suddenly burned through her. No matter what he saw or did not see. . . . He admitted knowing of the village. . . . And because he followed her that night, he knew that she departed alone—silently, in darkness.

And yet—and yet, he had such small respect for her that he would return the child, after her death, to the very village he had seen her leave in secret? She leapt up, glaring.

"The newcomer must ice the runners, pack the sled, harness the team and leave this place!"

"Tonight?" He was stunned. Here was a joke, surely.

Her fury somehow related to his plan for the child, and she had not thought it through. She only knew that Tuk represented possible danger. He had already seen too much, if Narluk had sent him. He must go!

Tuk stood up slowly, consternation on his face. "This visitor planned to return Nuna as well, so that the child would not starve."

"Go now." Kiti's voice was cold. "Take the seals. This hunter has no need of them."

"But—?!"

He was without words. Good. Let him figure out her reasons in the desolation of his lonely days. He would take the child back even knowing she must have strong reason for escaping in the dark of night. She was only a woman—some diversion never to take seriously? Hoo-oo!

Then, once at the village—no easy task finding it, she reflected, for by now it had certainly relocated but he seemed to know that, too. And once again a man among men, would he not agree with Narluk that small, healthy, hearty Arajik . . . must die?

She clutched her killing spear and drew herself up to look fierce as possible.

He watched her without words, his handsome face expressionless.

KITI

She turned to the sled and withdrew the harpoon as well, held it high, though pointed to the ground. "And should Kiti see Tuk ever again—" she shook both weapons, and the harpoon toggle rattled—"she may not allow him to live!"

He squared his jaw, and firelight flickered in his eye, perhaps anger there as well. "Just this, before departure. A person meant no harm. Not then or now. He saw a beautiful young mother safely to her village, then watched her leave alone with sled and babe."

Kiti spoke suspiciously, "Someone still wishes Kiti to believe, the meeting here with Tuk was only accident!"

"One recognized the woman on the ice, that's all—off and on for several days—"

"—Then someone should have made himself known sooner!"

Tuk hesitated. Then, "The man had good reason . . . please do not ask."

"—Go now!" Her voice came out a shriek, and staked dogs around them lifted their shadowy heads to observe. Nuna growled from the sled.

This man, Kiti believed, could destroy her life by destroying Arajik—he was her child, now, and so she regarded him. Tuk could let her father know where they were? And then he and her brothers could pursue. She should kill the man here—now!—leave his body on the ice for predators and birds. Or drop it into the lead.

One small cool voice inside advised caution. Tuk spoke with the tune of coastal people. It might be that he did not come from Narluk, would not report back to him.

A part of Kiti stood aside to observe the rest of her. How easily her thought turned to killing. Unreasoned violence . . .certainly not *peeusinga*, not the Inupiat way. Was this great rage within her beyond the custom? Or was such ferocity found in every species by a mother whose young was threatened?

She brandished the harpoon and lowered her voice to make it even more savage. "Go!"

"A traveler hopes Kiti's husband will soon return and protect his fine family."

Did she hear wistfulness in his tone?

He looked at her evenly for a long moment, but she did not respond other than to lift the harpoon higher. Could she do it? Oh yes. And that she knew herself capable of dispatching an Inuit life spirit frightened her.

Tears came later, as she huddled between the robes. They washed from her eyes like mild tide. Why? After all, Tuk had taken with him only a little of the seal meat.

Chapter 17.
Thief

Trail time north became a haze of ice fog and storm. Each day, each sleep as winter darkened and deepened became routines of non-routine—whiteout so severe that she must halt or take the risk of driving her team into a trench inland or on ice into the open sea.

Stopped, she would claw out a cave in whatever drift she found by touch. That failing, she would dig a pit in ice and even dent the frozen ground—for endless wind scoured higher levels bare of malleable material. Sometimes the surface under her *kamik* was only rock-hard permafrost beneath perhaps a skid of ice.

She would settle the dogs, often simply staking them in a draw on wind-scoured barren prairie with tails wrapped around their noses. Then she would snug the baby into her tunic and crowd among sleep robes with Nuna and Ajak, the pup now bigger than Arajik but dependably gentle with the boy.

Sometimes, Kiti would drag the loaded sled across a pit she had hacked into some declivity. Days on end brought whirling snow—rarely new flakes falling, more often white crystals already present rearranging themselves before the wind.

In fact snow seemed to plummet upward from the ground. Visibility at such times included less than the full team fanned in front. In a whiteout, she could not see her mitt at the end of her arm.

Cold, cold, cold. On the trail, she tied a soft ptarmigan skin across her nose and mouth, then pulled the hood opening tiny as the eye of a fish—and still dared breathe only through her nostrils for fear of freezing her lungs. In camp at night, or in whatever passed for camp, she could press her face into, and breathe through, the wolverine *nuilak*, that fine fur trim on her hood.

She laughed when she remembered how, on finding this wondrous pelt in her mother's cache, she had thought she could "always trade it for food." Where? With whom? She felt guilty for not having shared more of this fine fur with Tuk.

She wanted to travel on the smooth grounded ice along the coast. But in fact, she rarely ventured there because its groans and cracks were so alarming. If the people who actually lived on sea ice for eight full moons of the blackest winter did not anticipate th espring breakup correctly, they could get stranded, lost forever when stable *tuwak* became nomadic *siku*—when the mooring thawed so that formerly grounded ice began to float. Then it traveled south and east to who knew where? And always melting, getting smaller all the way.

It was on one of these newly wandering bergs that her middle brothers Karikit and Mamak disappeared. Palunga it was who vanished alone on barren inland tundra as he headed for the sea. Thus, only Palunga was at all likely someday to reappear. And as new winter deepened, the chance for that diminished. A man alone without dogs and sled in wintertime?

If Tuk were truly of coastal Inupiat, he would know about ocean ice. . . . Why had she not asked him? The spirits knew, she had asked him nearly everything else that came into her head during the time they were together. In fact, she had sounded like a child of four winters, she thought now, for too many of her questions were not cloaked in the attire of a statement.

By each sleep time, Kiti was exhausted from unloading the sled to ice the runners, then re-loading—three, four, five times in one day's run, always depending on the number of jagged rocks

115

that jutted up through too sparse snow cover. Depending also on whether she could stay on this frozen cover so that her runners did not strike barren ground. The sled might be gliding smoothly in the now continual dark of night and day, skim up onto a rise—then grate sharply on earth scoured bare by gales.

Disaster for mud pack and ice on runners. And if the runners themselves were to be saved, they required immediate attention.

Kiti placed her seal and fish store in bladders, then bound everything in bags. She had heard of people using their food supply as a sled without runners, hitching it up to be dragged by the team. She always wondered how people harnessed their teams after the travel party consumed the "sled."

One night, the four of them including the two dogs were huddled among robes in a shallow pit she had slashed down into ice. She covered the top of the hollow with a ragged hide made secure by the heavily loaded sled bridging the top. Then she slid into the cavity and rearranged the covering.

She awoke late in the sleep time to hear the fear song of her dogs . . . rhythmic, sustained moaning with a trembling edge of panic. Something or someone fearful to them was nearby. She rolled clear of robes, put on mitts, then grasped her spear and knife. No head space in the hole allowed her to sit up, and she lay there alert, every sense tuned, listening, sniffing—what was that stink?

When the wind abated for a moment, she could hear movement at the sled above. Reaching up, she pressed with a bare hand the ragged robe on which the runners rested, felt vibration counter the gusts of wind. Not bear, not wolf—for either of these would first dig in to attack the staked and helpless dogs. Then what?

Nuna was growling deep in her throat. Now the white dog extricated herself from the robe, and by standing gradually she pushed upward with her croup and shoulders against the rough hide ceiling. That failing to move the sled, she rolled onto her back, trying to dig her way through the restraining pelt. But her claws caught in patches of repair, bringing part of the old hide down on all of them. The dog pawed through ragged folds to rise once more, this time to heave directly against the bottom of the sled.

She began a song of treble yelps, high, hysterical, punctuated by snarls. Once again, she was on her back, paws working this time at the crossbars. Only the weight of the laden sled kept her from pushing it away. Even so, the runners began to slip and Kiti feared that the load would shift and bring the sled with its cargo down upon them. Kiti whispered at her to stop, then reached up herself to steady the runners. She wanted protection. Nuna would be trapped, as well as she—good. . . . This dog had to survive.

Gradually, over and beside the sounds of the dogs, the girl heard other noise—low, uneven grunts of effort, muttered growls—eh, glottal hissing . . . *kapvik*? Yes, that odor could be wolverine. . . . She had smelled it only twice before, both times from a distance.

Kiti kept one hand firmly on a runner cross rib, grasped her spear with the other, ready to thrust if the creature should try to come at them. "Nuna, drop!" she commanded, and the dog subsided in the shallow hole, still rumbling, clearly displeased with the order, but obedient.

Kiti could now hear splitting and ripping overhead, gulping, gnashing, the pops of tearing cord. The creature should not eat their food—must not chew the lashings, devour the bags and bladders, consume the precious oil—

"—*Owka!*" No! The girl slid up beside the sled as she had entered the pit, came surging from the sleep cavity, spear swinging before her, the knife somehow clutched in her other mitt. "Ai-ee-ee!"

The creature that crouched on the sled load was a mass of dark fur that blew out so steadily that its outline was a blur, even in bright moonlight and the slow shimmer of spirit lights. At one end of the triangular blotch of rippling pelt was an acute angle impossibly low for the size of the animal. Small eyes caught sky shine to glitter above bared fangs white in a mouth agape, growling far back in the throat and hissing at the same time.

"Khssh-shh! . . . kssh-shh. . . . kssh-shh-shh-shh . . ."

The shadow with indistinct edges crouched to turn continually and face her as she circled the small cave beneath the sled—it now lurching forward, reeling back, then shooting out low and fast as if to strike before it faded back. Kiti leaped along one side of the sled, around the end, then along the other, herself darting up, withdrawing—moving rapidly, never presenting a target.

Her body was taut, alert to looming danger, tuned to each motion of the raging creature. The spear was ever pointed at the beast, braced hard against Kiti's shoulder, pointing forward and a little down to impale *kapvik* if it actually lunged up at her.

"Kssh-shh-shh!"

She realized gradually that this hissing servant of the devil spirit Paija was slow. It kept turning, yes, was menacing indeed. But dark *kapvik* was awkward as it rustled around packets on the loaded sled to meet her attack. She knew from hunters' tales that no wolverine was sluggish when those fearsome teeth and claws fastened into flesh. But as she leapt and circled, shouting, the creature had a hard time staying face to face.

Kiti also realized, as her eyes adjusted to the nearly nonexistent light, that the animal had already chewed away the lashings that secured the load. It had pulled food bags from their bundles, torn them open—created the sort of mindless, evil havoc for which *kapvik* was known. The only true criminal of her land . . . the only living creature which seemed to destroy purely for pleasure.

"*Ai-ee-ah-ah-Ai!*" she shrilled as she moved ever more rapidly to taunt the struggling animal twisting on its short front legs, trying to stay high on the shifting packets still remaining on the sled.

The body was not as long as a sled dog but bulkier and with much shorter legs. Why would it not run away? She was taller, her head well above that gaping mouth even when the wolverine stood here on the sled packs. True, she might not be as strong as this terrifying beast—but she was armed and she was at least as angry. The thing should scurry off. Kiti had no need for its fur; and no creature she knew or ever heard about would eat any meat that *kapvik* sprayed. Would any eat the wolverine itself? She doubted it.

Just go in peace, she thought. *Take whatever can be carried, and go. It may happen that this woman will throw more, and she will be generous.*

Brandishing the spear, she wished that she had some idea of where to thrust if *kapvik* did attack. It having billowing fur and she lacking knowledge, the throat was probably best. But crouched as the creature was, even the pointed muzzle arrowing to the sled, no throat or chest was exposed. Could a killing stab be made behind and somewhat above the left foreleg? But the creature's legs could not be distinguished clearly from the body mass. Too much hair. Too much movement. Too much wind. Too much excitement.

"Ksshh-shh!"

How long the grim dance lasted, Kiti did not know—she leaping, bobbing, shouting; and *kapvik* pirouetting in cadence to the hissing growl, the dog team at last silent as they listened.

But then the creature lurched suddenly and a horrid stench met Kiti's nostrils. What had before been unpleasant now became eye-watering fetor. She watched with disbelief as *kapvik* ejected a foul liquid from beneath its raised tail. She saw or imagined the steam spreading across opened food and what few packets remained sound.

"OW-KA-AA!". . . NO-OO! she shrieked. On inspiration, she placed the spear tip inside the creature's mouth as it hissed and pressed hard without stabbing. The wolverine gagged, backed up, slid off the far side of the sled, then turned to scuttle off to south and west onto the prairie.

Kiti could have pierced its throat, but she wanted no further reek of wolverine at her camp. She could in fact run to overtake the animal, possibly separate it from its odorous spirits. But she lacked heart for slaughter without need . . . for killing only in retaliation for the giant weasel's doing what wolverine does naturally.

Instead, Kiti retched beside the sled. Arajik in her tunic shouted in dismay as the musk reached his nostrils. Arajik? She had carried him throughout the encounter. Had the wolverine come at her, it was Arajik in the front of her parka who would have taken the impact of those fangs and hooking claws. . . .

Great heat flooded through Kiti, and she felt suddenly as if she could ride the moon. To use the surge of energy, she ran past the dogs moaning in their snow caves, ran toward sea ice, away from the stench, away from the fleeing wolverine—and away from the grave problem that now awaited her.

Strangely, her one coherent thought was that she must hurry to complete the *amaut*, that special hood to let her brother be carried more safely on her back.

She returned to camp at last, near-frozen with hip-high fog following in a swirl from off the lead. Pale pink spirit lights with a dancing crimson hem towered over them and swirled gently. They were oblivious to the wild drama recently played out beneath their glow. And of course were unaware of the calamity which had befallen Kiti's camp.

Nuna with Ajak sat waiting well away from the fetid sled, a reproachful glint in her pale eye, a questioning cock to her head.

"Did odor reach the robes?" Kiti asked aloud. If the terrible liquid had dropped upon their sleeping furs, they would have to accustom themselves to the smell, as no more coverings were likely to come soon.

Because her nose rebelled as they approached the sled, Kiti turned her head to breathe with her mouth through the fur—oh yes, this sweet-smelling wolverine fur—that trimmed her hood. The staked dogs were stretched at the farthest limit of the thongs which held them, facing away, complaining in low moans, not even turning at her approach.

She smiled. "First thing, we'll move a team upwind," she promised them. But doing so delayed only briefly the enlightenment she feared and the necessary job she hated. She must take stock of damage.

The sleep robes, for a miracle, were not contaminated. The food was. Two wrapped packets on the lower layer of the sled might be usable, for the creature had only ripped the hide coverings without yet actually having torn the bladders when its ravage was interrupted.

Food she could replace in time—but gone was the security of having good packs of seal meat remaining from the hunt with Tuk. Gone also was the reserve of bags and bladders for storing extra provision against the inevitable time of need. All of the lashings were ripped and chewed, no longer usable. Repair would get her nothing more than a mass of stinking shreds and knots. Walrus hide. Split and carefully twisted tight and strong—how could she replace walrus hide?

The precious containers, all but those two bladders that had been at the base of the sled, were beyond help. The pouches of blubber and seal oil, thankfully, had been in her hunting bag at one end of the sleeping trench. As had two more drinking bladders. She could still ice runners. They could still have light and warmth within their shelter every night . . . to accompany their growling stomachs.

Until she replaced the bladders—could actually capture big game on her own?—there would be no way to preserve anything she might seize beyond daily use. Without containers, the dogs would take any meat, even fish. Predators would come.

Pirtok, she thought, *there is no helping what has happened.*

Chapter 18.
The Hunger Beast

For five sleeps, she stayed on that same prairie by the sea. There, she hunted without success. Even Nuna could find on ice no *aglu*, no breathing hole for a seal. And though it snowed without wild winds to sweep away ground cover, she found no creature tracks to follow, not even hare. Not lemming.

On the first new day, the dogs refused the meat which had been opened but not actually defiled by the wolverine. On the second day, and with no other food, they ate of it reluctantly. On the third day, they gobbled what remained and looked for more.

There was no more. On the fourth and fifth days, they went hungry. As did Kiti. Only Nuna got food. The woman was now desperate.

She knew that all of them needed good tallow or blubber—animal fat—to withstand the cold. But she was not even catching fish, and the sea ice appeared devoid of life. It was as if an angry Sedna had taken all sea creatures to her palace at the bottom of the sea.

Should she butcher a sled dog? She needed the nine she had. Without transport, all would perish. Only Ajak could be considered surplus, and that pup was too small to satisfy more than Kiti's appetite. Not that she would have appetite, where Ajak was concerned.

They must leave this place, then, continue north while they had energy. How many hunters died along the trail from lack of food, she wondered. And where was Kiti's great good fortune on the trail?

So they moved on sea ice within sight of land . . . or else on land in sight of sea ice. They went slowly to conserve energy and to stay alert for sign of game. Dark days dragged by—sometimes with storm, other times with starlight and a moon, often fog, never a glimmer of sun. A little snow might come during sleep. Or more likely, existing snow would rearrange. Gale wind drove it low above the ice on land and sea.

Up a pressure ridge they went, then down. Always searching for tracks. Would she tackle a white bear? Yes. A walrus on the rocks beside the sea? Yes, yes. . . . Seals? Come, seals. . . . "Ai-ee-ee! Food!"

In a desperate gamble with disaster as the stake, she finally ran the sled far out on smooth sea ice. She no longer had energy to repair runner icing every time they struck rocks on land. The coast had shown itself barren of game—and all too often for her sled, barren of snow as well. Perhaps, now that the dogs were truly hungry, one might sniff out an aglu near the lead. . . .

Her trail party would stop for rest and she would fish through ice . . . but again nothing, nothing except dark and cold and always the hunger beast gnawing at her belly. Faint and dizzy when she moved. Close the eyes and tend the inner spirits lest they bolt, she ordered herself. Sleep, sleep, slow the body processes.

Did Palunga hunger so, she wondered often in the night, as he walked silent and alone upon the tundra? Did her favorite brother feel the torment of a gut so empty that his spirits tried to flee their inhospitable host?

And then one morning, strangely, when she rolled from her robes, no craving for food remained. A lightness in her head let Kiti see whatever creature she sought. Only it wasn't there. She would lift her killing spear and hurry forward. The bear or ermine or even caribou on sea ice would continue to stand as she had seen it. But no substance met her weak attack. These were only pictures floating on the surface of troubled eyes.

Danger. . . . The lead, the open water was too close on their right as they dragged north. Black water. Ice could be thin. She must turn away from this empty river of salt. Yes. Search elsewhere. Sleep. Run with the team when possible, lighten their load, help to push the sled. Even Nuna's food was near an end. . . .

Palunga? You whose sled and dog a sister drives . . . you who know the agony of starvation—eh, what must Kiti do now?

And then before her on the ice was first one mound and then a whole village of snowhouses. Silent. No glow welcomed strangers. Another fantasy, she thought—and like the others, it would not be tangible.

They drew closer. The mounds were still there, although her dogs did not react. But why would they? They would not imagine what she would. Besides, they too were torpid with hunger and fatigue. Kiti closed her eyes and shook her head to clear her mind. But still, when she opened them, a hunting camp lay scattered on the ice. The girl moved up to touch an igloo wall, be certain it was real.

She felt substance, so coughed weakly outside the tunnel. No response. But who could hear above the shrieking wind and cracking ice?

She coughed louder at another porch. Still no answer. Sleds leaned on their sides against the arching walls. People could not get far in winter time without them. Perhaps the villagers hunted nearby. On foot, in winter time?

She tried to make her fogged brain reason. The sleds were here—where were the dogs? And especially the Inupiat, where were they? She came alert.

"*Ai-ee!*" she tried to shout, but the call came out a whisper.

Still her team showed no excitement. Kiti crawled into a snowhouse. But the dark was too intense, and she came back. She staked her dogs, emptied the sled of its light burden, upended it on impulse to later make her own lean-to sheltered from the wind. She got fire going in the lee of a sunken porch at one snowhouse, then pushed the travel lamp ahead of her as she crawled down the tunnel once again. Nuna nosed along behind her, and Kiti was grateful for the company.

Inside, she saw three still figures upon the sleeping ledge. She touched the woman and knew no spirit warmed her. Nor the man. Nor the half-grown boy. Turning, Kiti looked around. Two seals on end were near the tunnel opening. A Big Feed nested in the wall near a dark, untended lamp. Nuna whined, and Kiti reached back to reassure her.

She left her lamp burning there, but dragged a seal out. Her need was great and immediate. She cut it up for Nuna and the team with a little for herself. The dogs with their slim bellies would over-eat, expel the food and gobble it again.

But Inupiat knew to nibble just a little right at first, then more until the shrunken stomach could acquaint itself with food once more.

Kiti checked the remainder of the encampment. Six among the eight cold igloos contained the husks of fourteen Inuit with spirits gone. The remaining two snowhouses, both deserted, looked as if their occupants had planned their leaving, for no provision or weapons remained and no sleds but only kayaks were nearby. In the village was no *umiak*, the big round whale boat which Kiti thought would normally be brought out to a seal or whale or walrus camp on ice.

Kiti returned to the original snowhouse. Nothing was here to fear, for the dispossessed spirits would by now have wandered off and upward to the sky party above, awaiting opportunity to return. She retrieved the other seal from that first igloo, then could not resist opening the Big Feed—in this place, it was a black basket artfully woven of darkly gleaming whale baleen. Inside were treasures quite different from those Pichikut had hoarded.

Kiti removed a handsome white bear pelt. The coarsely worked amulets of walrus ivory, she left on the *iglerk* with the people. These were some *angakok's* domain, not hers. A neatly sewn little pouch of ptarmigan hide contained strange green stones. She examined them in lamplight, and each seemed to possess a glowing spirit within. Finally, she pushed the puzzling packet into a pocket of her parka to be studied later.

She looked around for lashings, found two long braids of split walrus hide, coiled them around the Big Feed, then dragged the whole bag outside. Certainly she would use the container. She would plan her sled space after checking other igloos in detail. At present, she was carrying on Palunga's sled only robes, the sleep nest, her hunting bag and what had been Pichikut's Big Feed.

Energy from food and burgeoning excitement coursed through her, and she interrupted her exploration only to feed the dogs again and nibble more herself. Then she stood tall and strong and faced the crimson lights dancing above and north. She grinned at them, then opened her mouth wide.

"Ai-ee-ee-ai-ee!"

Life returned on that day to her and to the team. They stayed at the dead village for three days and nights. Between meals—and meals were many!—Kiti sorted, considered carefully, and then took all she needed from the six igloos where inhabitants were spiritless. She did not touch the contents of the two abandoned snow houses. She packed her sled with food in bladders which, remembering *kapvik*, she had this time placed in thick hide bags double-tied secure, and as scentless as such a bag can be.

She collected stored seal blubber from pouches in the various snowhouses. This she cubed as she had done with Tuk, then stuffed it into many small, well-scraped bladders to await its transformation into golden oil for the lamp. She packed one sturdy pouch made of caribou hide full of nothing but rope and lashing, tough split walrus and the delicate, more elastic strips of seal hide. She selected two more soft robes in addition to the splendid white bear fur.

What has happened here? she wondered. The people did not starve, for food was plentiful. Their bodies were well padded, faces peaceful. Here was a mystery, she realized, for which she was unlikely ever to learn the answer.

As vitality and clear thought returned, the girl considered all that would be lost in this place when spring tides came. At season's change, deluges would break up thinning ice in this dead camp. What did not sink as the melting islands upended would surely float away. So before continuing north, she spent her last dark day in using a village sled to transport everything she could onto a land ridge high above the ice. She took weapons, lamps, stone food bowls—and every bit of food that she and the dogs were unable to consume and could not fit onto her sled.

She built a stone cache for the edibles—and then still remembering *kapvik* as well as the predations of unwatched sled dogs, all of whom take pleasure in chewing up animal hide, she added all the extra robes to the top of the well-protected cache. These would also muffle the scent.

She wished there were some way to let travelers know that they could have whatever they needed without the usual obligation to replenish everything at first opportunity.

She could have her choice of sleds, several with runners of carved driftwood. But her own was lighter, and it was Palunga's.

Besides, she was uncertain about methods for icing wood, even though she had observed Tuk prepare his driftwood runners.

In the end, she piled sleds and kayaks and weapons on and beside the cache. But then at the moment of leaving, she retrieved a sturdy little kayak that she tied across the top of her own sled. *Ahmi,* who can predict the future?

"*Nakorami,*" Thank you! she told the spirits hovering near the cache, then repeated her thanks as she with the sled and frisking team hissed north in darkness on sea ice past the silent village. She was more at ease, now, less leery of traveling near open water. For one thing, deep winter was upon them, so that ice should be very thick indeed. Also, she knew that the village was built by coastal Inupiat who knew much about the sea. If the ice could hold them and their snowhouses, so Kiti reasoned, then certainly it could support one woman with dogs and a laden sled.

Chapter 19.
Tuk's Tale

At her camp and before sleep, under the flow and churn of pale spirit lights on a windless night, Kiti sat talking to Arajik, to Nuna, to the team. She wished that someone could speak back to her. Arajik responded with a chortle. Then he laughed aloud, jumped up and down in her lap as she braced his arms. He wore a miniature tunic and feet-in trousers that she had finished making for him only one sleep ago. She had used hides gathered from the dead village, delicately cured caribou and hare pelt for trim. What a pleasure to make clothing for this baby. What a comfort he was. . . .

Even so, at times—and this was one of them—she would give all her food and half her robes to hear her native language from lips other than her own. She wanted to discuss things. She wanted especially to hear another person's guess about the village that had saved them. She wanted to plan with someone to hunt for Sedna's large sea mammals. She had heard walrus barking and bellowing on floes for two sleeps, now.

Yet she knew it would be foolhardy to take the new *kayak* into the lead for walrus. The huge males were peevish when disturbed. Or so she had always heard, and so Tuk said. But if another person were with her—perhaps someone with a big stable *umiak* to accompany her *kayak*. . . .

The team stirred, and Nuna gave a low grumble, looked toward the northwest prairie, then subsided. After a time, Kiti saw a slash of sled and dots of dogs lit by the swirling pink and green of gentle spirit lights. One person with a large team came forward. She hefted the harpoon from her sled, grasped a sharp skinning knife in her left hand, watched them come.

Why did her dogs not give alarm? She tightened with dread. Their silence would mean that they knew who now approached. Her father? Oojulit?

At first, she did not recognize Tuk. The confident stride had vanished. This person's footsteps faltered as he slowly staked his dogs, then lurched toward her lean-to. Not until he crept into the lampglow and released the hood string on his parka did she realize that she knew him—and even then could not be certain.

They stared at each other. What she saw made her lower her weapons. Dark pockets shadowed sunken eyes. The pads on his cheeks had vanished, the bones of his face now thinly fleshed. He stood weaving in the light, dull eyes fastened on hers. She took a folded robe out from still unloaded sled gear, spread it thickly on the ice before the lamp, motioned him down.

He dropped wearily. She stood watching him. His eyes closed, unmittened hands working into the warm fur, bringing the lush folds around him.

"Someone saw lamp glow on the ice," he muttered at last.

That was all. He didn't care that she might kill him. Or perhaps he knew she wouldn't? No, he could not know that. She did not know that, not until she saw his condition. Once more, she walked over to the load still stacked on her sled. She unwrapped seal meat, sliced off a large chunk and handed it to him.

Then she went back, dug deeply until she uncovered choice *muktuk*, crisp whale skin with blubber attached, a special crackling treat she had found in a Big Feed at the dead village. She rustled for a slim stone bowl she had also found there, heaped more food upon it and set the dish before him.

When Tuk saw the mountain of good raw meat, his mouth fell open and his eyes widened. His hand came from the furs to slide into his tunic pocket and retrieve his sharp little *ulu* used for eating.

He shook his head in wonder, glancing up before he grasped the whale. "Where? How?!"

But he waited for no answer, only fit a corner of the frozen delicacy into his mouth, hacked it off at his lips. She noticed that both of his hands trembled—not a good thing for someone wielding an *ulu*.

Kiti turned away, picked up her skinning knife, grasped another split seal and dragged it out to feed Tuk's dogs. If he was hungry, so must they be.

It would have been companionable for her to lay out lots of food, then sit and eat with her visitor. Not many moments ago, she would have given much to find someone to share the evening. Now, though, she quivered with strange, conflicting feelings which put an uncomfortable echo into her belly. Also, she churned with questions that could not be asked.

So she busied herself around the camp, expanded the lean-to, then played with Arajik. At last, she lowered the lamp wick, spread an extra robe for Tuk , then rolled up wearily in her own sleep furs, one hand kneading her cold ear lobe.

Nearly asleep and strangely relaxed, she realized that the few words Tuk had spoken . . . even in such unsteady voice . . . eh, a wonderful sound notwithstanding. . . . She would get him fed and warmed, back to himself once more. Then—should she let him stay? Would he want to? Should she ask him to join her camp?

But he had come here, had he not? And come straight in, despite her prior threats. Did he know more about this new Kiti than did Sukitilan?

Once more, her imagination leaped to and lingered on the worst possible scenario she could conjure. He might still be a threat. He knew where she came from—Even had he not been formerly, he might now be in communication with Narluk after this time of travel.

But a persistent, wily voice inside brought another view. All right, if she had to believe that Tuk truly was in some way connected with her family, then why should she not have him right here so that she could keep an eye on him? Yes, she liked that thought. Besides, he could have taken Arajik earlier, quite easily as she reviewed their time together, might even have hurt the child—or Kiti—if he had been told to do so by his shaman . . . but he had not. Perhaps his task, if he had one, was only to find her and report back?

So where had he been throughout these recent sleeps?—and this she needed to know. How could he possibly have visited her village recently, and then arrive back here in this condition? True, it would be far away from here. But her people would not have let him go without plenty of food. He would have hunted with a group, had he joined any village or trail group at all, then shared what was captured regardless of who had thrown the killing spears.

And he personally successful on the hunt or not, any but a starving group would have provisioned him before he left. *Peeusinga*, the People's Way.

But no. He came hungry, worn out, perhaps ill—and something else, besides. She could feel a sadness in him. He may have risked his life to find her camp. Or any camp at all?

Right now, he seemed not to care whether his spirits stayed or fluttered off forever. He seemed to be heavy with *Perlerornaq*—the weight of life, the futility of drawing breath. Tuk would not be first among Inupiat to succumb to this shadow on the spirit, this strange rapture that beset a person who followed a lonely trail in solitude. The everlasting darkness of deep winter. Such isolation on the trek that senses blur . . . and free will diminishes, even that innate determination to survive. How often she had heard of this mortal malady from tales dramatized beside the lamp.

She wondered, had she herself come close to this condition before she stumbled on the dead village? No. Her perceptions had been mischievous and misleading, especially her vision and hearing. But she had not once thought life too troublesome to be continued

Of course, she had Arajik. No doubt, he made a great difference in the strength of her purpose. Too, she must remember that her guest had been upon the trail longer than she. Nor may it have been his choice to leave family behind.

She needed to know about Tuk. Why did he say nothing? Time, talk, good food and warmth—right now!—would surely chase the shadow from Tuk's spirit. Perhaps this time she could wait patiently for him to talk.

But this new woman Kiti, unfortunately, seemed to be no more patient than the old child Sukitilan. She really must learn to exercise more discipline . . . and soon.

They remained in camp while Tuk ate and slept. His dogs, as it turned out, were hungry but not starving, slim but not emaciated. And a very little food, both seal and fish, still remained on Tuk's sled. He wanted her to use it with her own. She smiled privately. She had so much, thanks to the silent village, and he so little.

The young man's pride returned. He was recovering.

"One found no helping spirit anywhere," he related over a meal three sleeps later. "Nor is this hunter strong enough to go on and on without the sight of other Inuit."

Kiti remembered the strange visions she herself had—the imaginary creatures and active, fur-clad hunters on ice—during the time of great hunger after the wolverine destroyed their provisions and before they came upon the village of the dead. But that invention was from lack of food, she told herself now.

She remembered also how she had yearned for another human voice on the very evening Tuk appeared recently. But that was preference and desire, not need, certainly not necessity, she decided.

Could it be that Kiti was becoming independent? If so, Pichikut would be pleased. True, they would have starved had the village not appeared. But so would any hunter unable to find food. That no game had come to give itself had little to do with her growing self-reliance. . . .

Resilient as all Inupiat, Tuk rapidly gained energy, strength and vigor. His hearty spirit returned. He now spoke more readily than before, as if he and Kiti were established friends. Or perhaps it was only that Kiti listened better, for she reveled in the sound of Inupiaq spoken in another's voice.

He told her, "It happens that even wind and sky are enemies when too long in one's own company."

Kiti smiled, raised her brows in agreement. She was determined to let him do the talking so that she could learn everything possible. She could not, however, keep her mind from formulating questions silently. Where had he been? What was his destination as he wandered unfamiliar terrain in the blackness of mid-winter? Did he know her father?

". . . When the gale drones words that Inuk understands, then madness is nearby," Tuk told her thoughtfully before the fifth sleep time since his return. He was now up and energetic, had gone hunting alone inland that very morning, not successfully. Nor was Kiti fortunate on the ice she chose to search. Still, much food remained available to them at her camp.

At the end of the next full day, Tuk described his futile efforts to find game after he left her so many sleeps ago. "Near the end," he told her, "even though some food remained, this Inuk could not eat or sleep or think in a straight line. He could not plan or hunt. Often, he had to remember even to draw breath."

She smiled at him encouragingly, sympathizing without speech. This was not the time to mention his *perlerorneq*, that terrible weight of life which can overtake a solitary hunter on the dark winter trail.

She had by now decided that no, she herself definitely had not had such a problem. Or if so, she had handily laid it to a different cause. Her difficulties came from trying to hunt on ice and land when both were bare of life. His dilemma? The same, or only loneliness? A matter of perception, she decided—how two separate people interpret an identical situation differently . . . and both, she decided with an audible snort, may be incorrect. The true picture might be something else entirely.

One evening, Tuk finally unraveled a part of the tangled straps of his origin. "When a young man's family died suddenly— both parents and a young sister, as well. . . . Did someone tell this tale before?"

Kiti dropped her eyelids, No. By the intensity of his voice, Kiti knew that her visitor would soon reveal a reason for his sadness. "A woman never invited explanation," she told him, suddenly ashamed. Certainly she had been saturated right from the beginning with curiosity about his beginnings, reasons for his current solitude.

She still was. She slept poorly when he was in her camp because she kept going over and over the possibilities—mostly dire—in her sleep-time imagination. She had maneuvered from him instruction on hunting seal, on better ways to load a sled— even some information about Inupiat routines when living by and on the sea. How could she not have managed to get from him some answers to the truly vital questions?

Well, she knew why. She had not wanted him to have such information about herself, so she avoided altogether the subjects of origin and current isolation.

"It happens that the family was far inland as winter began," Tuk told her, "because they had gone south as summer ended to follow the beasts called *tuktu*"—caribou. "But then they returned too slowly, well past time of tundra snow. Still, transportation could be rapid for that very reason, now able to use sled and team. Here was an adventure. A father found a sun-dried caribou carcass to make a sled, hitched up the team and started off to join friends at their own familiar village by the sea.

"But still far out on barren ground, it happened that a family came upon two coastal Inupiat. Both strangers, and they seemed frightened."

Kiti waited while Tuk stared into the fire for a long time before continuing.

"At first the two gave no explanation for their traveling west when others of the coastal folk had gone to meet the sunrise half a moon before. Most by then would be already in igloo within fresh-ly-built villages on sea ice."

Kiti's mind flashed a memory of the two deserted snow-houses in the village of death. "On the ice," she stated, an obvious query tucked into the words.

Tuk raised his brows to show assent, but his voice continued hollow, echoing: "One day, Tuk's beloved family was vigorous. Then a little coughing on the sleep ledge in the night. By the next day, their spirits had fled."

He raised his mitts on either side, palm up and empty, looked at each. "One day, four happily together. The next, one sadly alone."

His eyes were tormented when he looked at her, his jaw working. She wanted to comfort him—clasp him to her as she would Arajik. Who would not in such circumstance fall prey to *perlerorneq*? Of course he was melancholy!

"So it happens, Tuk did not choose to be alone on the prai-rie," she murmured.

"Who would!?" he gasped. "Did Kiti?"

She hesitated, realizing for the first time how well her moth-er had equipped her for this trip. Not only skills, but also how her mind worked—the pride in doing for herself, the determination to rely on her own reserves so far as possible.

"Yes," she told him softly, "Kiti selected solitude from among those morsels offered in her bowl."

He frowned, staring over at her, but did not comment further. And she did not ask.

Chapter 20.
Sighting

The musk oxen were on nearby prairie. *Oomingmak*, "the creature with skin covered by shaggy beard." Tuk said he had seen some, or thought he had, before he found Kiti on the ice. These were the only living creatures, he told her, that he had seen in many days. And they were not considered possible targets for capture, certainly not by a solitary hunter.

Big hoofed beasts, shorter but built more roundly than caribou? Ai-ee-ee! Kiti's mouth watered. How could anyone resist . . . so much food with a single thrust of the spear. . . . Of course they two must search before Tuk went away!

"Coastal people do not pursue them," he warned her.

"Nor do those of Kiti's old village. But why not? Does it happen that the flesh is foul, like wolverine?"

"Owka, No. For if this were so, then someone would have said it."

". . . Then perhaps they wait for two young hunters who have sufficient desire."

Tuk's hand on her sleeve to caution her, Kiti now gazed with awe over the top of a rise at the small group of *oomingmak* below them to the south. Not tall like caribou, adults looked blocky, long and strong. Their cascading coats were luminous under the filmy pink and green swirls still lighting the sky at a time that would be dawn if it were summer.

A fur skirt commenced beneath the creature's chin with streaming overfur that seemed to be as long as Kiti's arm. This great fur joined the rest, all flowing out in the wind, nearly hiding those relatively delicate legs. All the adults, male and female alike, had downswept horns that curved back up to swing out sharply at eye level. What looked to be the largest males had a thick plate across the brow.

Kiti had of course heard of muskox in lamplight tales. Dangerous creatures, fierce and swift, to be feared and left alone. So said the storytellers. But none professed ever to have actually seen one up close, only herds in the distance and then but rarely.

Often, Kiti and all villagers had plucked from tundra grass and rocks the clotted clumps of wool discarded lavishly during the summer molt. The long dark overhairs could be twisted to make a strong thread. Or handfuls could be stuffed into *kamik* for fine effect to insulate against cold.

The shorter underfur could be hand-wound as elegant trim for parkas and trousers. Contrary to its coarse appearance, the material when washed was softer to the touch than the most delicate belly fur of a young rabbit. But preparing and working it into a design was more demanding, to Kiti's mind and to her mother's also, than mere beauty was worth.

These animals Tuk and she saw grazed placidly, five adults and three juveniles, at lichen sites beneath the ice and snow that they had stomped bare. Kiti moved up toward the crest of the bluff to get closer. But she found Tuk once more grasping the sleeve of her parka.

Softly, "*Owka.*" No.

She glanced at his anxious face, then retreated to where the hill crest hid them from the creatures. "They are violent?"

"*Ee-ee,* when they feel threatened." He sounded unsure. "Like all beings including Inuit, large fear becomes great anger. And musk oxen are said to be suspicious by their nature."

"But good to eat?"

"Opinions differ."

Kiti chuckled. "Someone wonders whether any who had these opinions ever actually tasted the flesh."

The corners of Tuk's lips turned up. "None I heard ever spoke of doing so."

Both hunters were quiet when Kiti grinned over at Tuk. "Can it be that the two mighty seal hunters will capture *oomingmak* on this day?"

Without answering, Tuk squinted and eased upward to peer once more over the top of the hillock. Then he slid back, picked up his spear.

Kiti clasped her own bone weapon as well as the big harpoon she had lugged from the sled. A large creature is worthy of such a weapon, so she reasoned.

Just before they crested the hill, Tuk reached over in curiosity to heft the harpoon. A quizzical look swept across his face. Although small for a harpoon, it was still quite heavy. But he did not laugh.

"It may happen," he said softly, "that someone could move more easily with only the spear." He pointed his nose at the sharp implement she held in her other hand, raised his head rapidly.

Kiti's jaw tightened, especially because she had to admit to herself the truth of his words. "It may also happen," she retorted, "that the spirit of one's grandfather who made this harpoon will aid the granddaughter in its use."

Tuk shrugged. Who could argue?

But why did she say such a thing? Ananak had always maintained that her father—the ice island grandfather whom Pichikut's children never saw—was a terrible hunter. A good weapon-maker, yes, but a hard luck *Inuk* on the trail. It was for this reason that young Pichikut had to take responsibility for feeding her family.

"Should a shaggy skin attack," Kiti continued, "this woman will throw the harpoon and retreat swiftly."

He motioned her back to whisper again. "Tuk has not hunted for nor eaten of *oomingmak*, this is true," he said. "But from a safe distance he has observed angered bulls outrun wolves easily and use those sharp horns to send the spirits flying forever!"

Kiti's eyes widened. "Then it happens that puny Inuit cannot outdistance it, should one attack."

"So it's important that no reason for anger be given."

As if this provided all the instruction Kiti needed, Tuk returned to the crest and then inched down toward the beasts. Kiti watched him creep forward. In fact, she had trouble seeing that he moved at all. Leaving the harpoon, she followed his lead, fancying herself a boulder set in the hillside here and then there at this lower place and now here in this new spot.

At this pace, Kiti decided, the juvenile musk oxen would be fully grown before the two swift hunters ever reached the herd.

Half way down the little hill, the two were perhaps eight sled lengths from the nearest grazing animals. Tuk's hand again was on her sleeve in warning as they crouched there, the strong south gale in their faces so that they remained downwind, peering at their quarry.

"Now what?" Kiti finally whispered into his ear.

Even that slight sound, however, was picked up by the sharp but invisible woolly ears below. The biggest animal wheeled to face them, and the hunters crouched motionless, twin shadows against the snow.

Let the bearded ones see nothing but furry boulders. Kiti concentrated fiercely on the idea, just as she had focused on becoming a seal when she hunted on the rocks. See? Here are two stones covered with animal pelt, she amended her first thought, set firmly in the earth. She lowered her eyelids so that the whites would be even less apt to reflect what little light existed. She tried not to blink or even to breathe, for fear some ripple of parka fur unnatural to the wind might betray her.

She wanted to see what Tuk was doing but dared not look. She knew the creatures could not scent them, for they had staked the dogs well back and taken pains to keep all downwind.

141

Yet, the herd knew something was different. They sensed some small change in their surroundings. With no signal Kiti could distinguish, adults in the group moved in together haunch by furry haunch, youngsters tucked between and behind, all facing the hillside where the two Inupiat hunkered stiff as rock cairns.

The big heads tossed. The ends of the line backed around to form a half-circle, arcs swinging back on either side of what Kiti took to be the boss bull. Juveniles peered out curiously from among their full-sized kin.

Now came a timeless period. The Inupiat crouched motionless, furs blowing. Five bearded adults also stood on planted hooves, noses testing wind, eyes rolling, skirt furs flowing in brisk breeze.

The spirit lights gradually faded and disappeared while the hunters waited. Now a bank of black clouds which had hidden moon and stars passed by, and the sky afforded to the stationary scene a cold blue light. Perhaps a glint from one of the smooth weapons gave them away. Or even the sparkle of an eye. Whatever it was, the bull suddenly fastened his gaze on them. He snorted, pawed with a front hoof, rubbed his muzzle on his foreleg.

Neither Tuk nor Kiti moved. The girl felt her stomach lurch to the base of her throat as the whole herd advanced a sled's length forward, still in that curious formation. Then no more movement for a time, until one of the smaller beasts suddenly broke free of adults and darted toward the hunters. A full-grown muskox surged out to nose the youngster none too gently back behind the rank. That movement, and the small one's squall of protest, broke the spell only for a moment.

Then all was as before. Standing. Staring. Breathless crouching. Fur rippling. Kiti slowly closed her aching eyes completely. As she did so, every other sense sharpened. Here is a good thing to know, she thought, and applicable in other circumstance.

She became restless. Her muscles ached from holding still. Ice underfoot breached the moss lining her *kamik*, her boots, and cold gradually numbed her feet and legs to the knee. Knowing what she now knew, she wanted to go back in time to the moment when they first saw *oomingmak*. Then, having seen, they could return to their teams and take the trail to hunt elsewhere. And before the sleep tonight, they would then have that unusual experience of seeing *oomingmak* to muse and mull over at the lamp.

She was the one who had pushed for seeking out muskox, she now recalled; and their dilemma, therefore, was her blunder. Neither of them had any idea whether these beasts were even good to eat. Neither knew how to catch them. Of two things she was now certain. Only a *soospuk* would try to capture musk oxen in a herd. And she also knew that in this situation, the hunters were far more at risk than any of the creatures on the flat below.

Another good thing to have learned, she thought, wondering whether she would live long enough to apply this new wisdom to the trail. Truly, could a small herd of musk oxen dispatch a whole pack of wolves?

The two different species, human and beast, studied each other for what seemed to Kiti at least three sleeps. She felt herself become a lump of ice before the big leader turned and walked away with grand nonchalance. The herd broke rank immediately and returned to feeding without another look at the interlopers. Tuk and Kiti were forgotten.

Chock-chip, a sharp hoof dug through snow. *Smoo-oosh,* a blunt muzzle bent to snuffle and scrape noisily, then move on. Much sound, little food, Kiti thought as she watched the creatures graze slowly south to greater and greater distance before the intrepid pursuers dared to move away.

Chapter 21.
Oomingmak

Kiti was startled when her parka slid back as Tuk put his mouth to her ear once again. His question reached her more as thought than sound. "Does it happen that someone sees the lone beast on the next rise?"

She looked to the west, across the narrow valley and up another shallow hill. Yes, a solitary creature stood in silhouette against the deep black-purple of the starlit sky. She raised her eyebrows to let him know that Yes, she saw something, anyway. And that bit of movement, just lifting her brows, was a vast relief. She took a deep breath, turned to put her own lips to Tuk's ear.

"Can we reach him?" She knew that somewhere near most herds of caribou—the only other grazer that she knew—one or several exiles can be found. Usually, these would be old males, probably no longer vital enough to challenge other bulls and win cows, yet unwilling to leave their kind entirely. Or, the solitary animal could be a scout. Who knew?

Tuk raised his eyebrows, Yes. "Perhaps when the herd has moved further away."

"But won't the single one attack?"

"It happens, *oomingmak* is not foolish. Here to face him are two, he but one."

Kiti thought about the words but said nothing. The male she had seen up close was more than equal to the two puny Inupiat who observed him. Even from such distance in poor light, those twisting horns looked very sharp. She pictured in her mind the demise of a ferocious pack of wolves . . . their carcasses careering high, one by one arcing to fall inert.

Still the hunters waited as the herd moved off. Kiti felt herself an extension of the frozen ground and not much warmer, either. Tuk kept shuddering, an arm moving up spasmodically, a foot changing position. Was he cold also, or only restless, Kiti wondered.

Suddenly, he spoke with a full voice. "One more thing is known about a herd of these shaggy beasts, this when they no longer feel immediately threatened," he said. Then he braced his legs and took a deep breath. "Ai-EE-EE! Ah-ah-AI-EE!! He jumped up and down, waving his arms.

Startled, Kiti watched him for a moment, then sent her own howls upwind. The shouts still echoing, they watched when the herd well south in a deepening valley wheeled as a single creature and thundered away.

Kiti glanced up. The shadow on the hill crest to the west remained exactly as it was. The wind was shifting, now toward northwest. It would have blown their shouts south and east toward the moving herd, opposite from the solitary muskox. The two hunters walked down to cross the frozen prairie.

"If a woman still wishes to take this animal . . . ?"

"Yes." The two teams of dogs were going rapidly through her food supply. Tuk's provision was gone entirely, and they had not yet captured any fresh game. They could backtrack south to find the cache near the village of death, but it was several sleeps back and Kiti would consider doing this only if she were truly desperate.

Besides, she needed skill and knowledge in the capture of every creature. This attempt to take *oomingmak* would be part of her education on becoming more self-sufficient. She had already learned—just today!—not to approach a herd of *oomingmak* unless accompanied by an entire village of well-armed hunters. Even then, she would know to be most cautious.

A *whole pack* of clever wolves?!

"The creature may easily become provoked," Tuk warned. "A solitary herding beast is not a bachelor by choice—so is rarely pleased with his fate." They had reached the other side of the shallow valley, had circled around to be downwind, and were now ready to climb the hill on which the lone bull still stood head down and foraging. Sounds of his stamping through ice and scraping for lichen came to them on the wind.

Tuk searched without explanation among rocks and boulders which had rolled down what must in summer be a streambed, perhaps becoming a waterfall in heavy rain. Two giant stones leaned against each other at the foot of the dry course. The tops met, but a spear-high fold gaped narrowly from the ground to form a high triangle. Into this opening, Tuk pressed himself. Kiti heard him laughing, and he still chuckled as he emerged.

"One hunter will draw the beast, then fly into these rocks for safety," he told her. "The second will be hidden above and will step out to plunge the killing spear as the creature charges the first hunter."

Just like that. Kiti looked at Tuk with new respect. A plan. She thought a moment, then snorted. "And which hunter will do what?"

"This decision belongs to Kiti," he told her.

"Who drives the spear more strongly?" she asked as if she did not know.

"And who can run more nimbly?" he asked with a crinkling grin.

"Phfft! Kiti's decision!" she laughed. Then soberly, she handed him her harpoon. "Might this be better?"

He studied it once more, turning it thoughtfully in his mitts. "The grandfather will continue to aid in the weapon's use when another hand holds it?"

"Perhaps as much as if the one were kin," Kiti heard herself say. She put a bare hand up inside her parka to rub her ear.

It is unlikely that the spirit of Kiti's grandfather could help regardless of whose hand held his handsome harpoon. And here she was, sinking in the muck of her original lie and unable to retrieve herself.

"Eh, and perhaps not," Tuk mused. He leaned the harpoon against one of the boulders, far back by the hill so that she would not stumble over it as she dived for the opening.

"The spear man is likely to have but one opportunity. He must use a familiar weapon."

Kiti put her own spear carefully on end inside the safety gap. She started up the incline. Tuk followed. She selected as she went what was likely to be the surest path to take down the snow-covered ice on rocks which made up the streambed. Her descent would be at full speed, and likely not knowing whether the creature followed. She must memorize the most stable route.

From time to time as they climbed, Tuk would grunt and point out some jagged stone or possible dark sink hole that she might not have noticed but needed to avoid.

As they neared the crest, they crouched low. They were silent in their stalk, cautious—once again nearly motionless, so slow was their crosswind approach. The solitary bull seemed unaware as he snuffled in the still-green graze he uncovered.

At last, the hunters were at the top of the hill, two sled lengths away from where the creature stood with his shaggy backside to them. Rocks and a few boulders still lined even the upper waterway. Behind one of these latter Tuk now positioned himself, pulling Kiti toward him, once more placing his mouth at her ear.

"A hunter should not get too close before she lets the creature see her," he warned. "Someone needs wings for a flying start."

Kiti raised her eyebrows, Yes. Based on what she saw when the whole herd whirled away, a runner on flat ground would have no chance at all. A thrill of excitement accompanied her fear. She shivered, grinned. Now she moved away from Tuk to let him hide himself.

She straightened up suddenly. "Hoo-oo!" she called tentatively from downwind, feeling like a child play-acting, unsure of her voice. The creature did not move.

"HOO-OO!" she tried again. Nothing. He was intent on feeding. The blast out of the north caught her words and carried them away.

She stepped closer. Then she drew a deep breath, flapped her arms and jumped. **"AH-AI-ee-EE!"** she shouted.

The animal leaped straight up, came down turning toward her, bellowing, feet churning ice. As Kiti dashed down the stream bed, she wondered whether he was annoyed enough to follow.

He was. He did.

She did not know when she passed the place where Tuk hid. Rocks skittered beneath her boots. She fell and rolled, got lightly to her feet, continued. She heard a crash behind and above, but dared not turn to see what happened. Perhaps *oomingmak* had fallen as she had. Perhaps Tuk had taken him. Perhaps Tuk himself was down. Rocks rattled behind her, passed her on their steep descent. Was it she or the animal that had disturbed them? She raced to the boulders, slid smoothly inside, hunched far back to make herself unreachable by horns if not invisible.

Except for stones that rattled down the stream bed—first many, then few, finally none—she heard no more. No sound rode the wind—no bellow of angry beast, no shout of triumphant hunter. She waited for what seemed a long time before she peeked out and around, then emerged. Nothing. Staying by the gap, she shouted. No answer. She waited. Impatience overtook her. She could not remain here through a sleep. Whatever was to happen had by now occurred. Tuk might be wounded. Might be spiritless. The beast was either mortally injured, dead—or had long since run away. It certainly had not followed Kiti all the way down, for she had watched from safety and would have seen him pass.

She picked up her spear and knife, left the harpoon for later. She needed to investigate. She also needed to get back to Arajik and the team, regardless of what was happening in this place.

Cautious, quietly as possible, she clambered up the stream bed. Every sense was alert to possible danger in the near-black of early afternoon. But no sound came. The smell of blood reached her nostrils. At the crest, she saw a large dark shape lying on the snow. *Oomingmak*, the bearded one, was down.

"Tuk?" Her own voice startled her.

No answer came, nor did the creature stir. She moved closer. Blood that pooled from underneath the beast showed black upon the shadow of snow, spreading still, frozen at the edges, crystals sparkling in starlight. She removed a mitten, touched the muzzle. Cold, with a frothy, frozen pale mucus at the nostrils.

She replaced her mitt, walked around the animal to observe. A broken spear shaft extended from under the creature. She kept walking. Something irregular caught her eye as she got to the belly side. Spear poised and ready, she bent down to peer more closely.

A *kamik*, Tuk's fur boot. . . . She reached out to pick it up, found it attached to a foot, heard a muffled sound from beneath the animal.

"Spirits, help me now!" she beseeched as she backed up to the carcass and dug both of her own boots into the snow, pushing against the dead weight with all her strength. She barely nudged the big creature.

Now she put her spear deep as possible under the belly, careful not to puncture Tuk or the creature, then pulled up on the end until she knew the weapon strained and was ready to snap.

"Wait!!" She raced to the other side, pulled out the remains of Tuk's spear and took it around. Then placing the handles of both weapons together and bending low, she pushed them far under and lifted once again.

This time, the big body shifted. She pushed back for fresh purchase, lifted steadily.

Tuk's boot and leg wiggled. While she levered part of the weight, he crept out from under, spitting wool and sneezing. At last he stood free, plucking away whole handfuls of qiviut fur from face and ears and tunic. The pale light overhead showed him to be unharmed. The black smears of blood appeared to come from wounds inflicted on the beast.

The two thanked *oomingmak* for allowing himself to be taken. Neither Inuit was certain of the conventions in this instance, but their prayer of thanksgiving to the creature spirit was sincere.

Afterward, Kiti fixed Tuk with hard eyes and a set mouth. "Why is it, the hunter did not move out immediately from beneath the creature? Did not at least manage to call for help?"

Tuk raised his mitten, palm up to her. She placed his broken spear shaft into it, and he examined it ruefully.

"At first, the muskox still possessed fierce spirits, who knew how strong? The spearman dared not move."

"And after? A woman hiding below thought all was lost."

Tuk sucked in breath—yes, she had a point. "Later, as it happened, and for the first time since the sleep, the mighty hunter . . ." and his voice trailed into silence.

"For the first time . . ." Kiti repeated, then waited.

"This mighty hunter found himself . . . for the first time . . . well, to be comfortably warm!" He looked across at Kiti with mbarrassment, raised his eyebrows, then his shoulders helplessly, kept staring at her.

Only silence.

The girl was encased in snow where she had fallen on her trip down the hill. She must resemble a delicate white she-wolf, head up, alert—and very shaggy.

His eyes still steady, Tuk's lips twitched, and he held back the rising chuckle with a strangling sound. . . .

Kiti looked at him. She knew that her anger issued from anxiety—fear for his well-being—not real annoyance. Wads of wool remained on his hood. Shreds that he had missed in his hurried scrape-off stuck out everywhere.

She snorted. The young man stood before her like a spring-molted white sea-bear, clasping in his mitts the useless shank of a broken spear.

She grinned.

He continued to stare with grave dark eyes until he choked on his laughter. After that, he raised his woolly chin to the sky and bellowed.

Suddenly, both were rolling in the snow, smothered and helpless with mirth and relief and triumph and joy following a successful hunt.

Chapter 22.
Release

The meat was edible if not exactly delicious. Thus, the first solid food for Arajik turned out to be muskox. *Oomingmak*. Kiti thought this a good sign—exotic fare for an uncommon child.

She cut the flesh into fine pieces, stirred in still-warm tallow from the thick layer of fat under the creature's skin. She had to heat the baby's meal near the lamp, for Arajik of course knew only warm sustenance. Then Kiti mushed it with a rock she had picked up at the stream bed, a smooth stone rounded on both ends, a cobble that fit her hand perfectly.

Interesting alluvium had slid down the stream bed behind her rushed retreat. Or had been uncovered by her fall and slide. When the two brought in the sled to pack out the carcass, spirit lights were rippling. In the pastel flicker, both hunters took time to look through the gravel of rocks and pebbles.

Beside the natural pestle and a small soapstone having one concave face—exactly right to hold her brother's food—Kiti picked out the clearest from among a great many of the translucent green minerals such as she had seen only once before. Back at camp, she added them to those in the pouch she had found at the dead village.

Tuk discovered a largish lump of pale, slick mineral which he turned over and over in his hands, feeling its smoothness and observing its shape from every angle. He was certain, he told Kiti, that the bearded one, the spirit of the very *oomingmak* of their chase, was hidden within. The creature only wanted Tuk's chipping knife and hand-stone mallet to release it.

Tap-tip-tap. Tuk was intent on this liberation of a shaggy beast before the sleep when Arajik dipped his fat-cheeked face into the new bowl of freshly warmed meat. The baby brought his head up, snuffling and snorting, but with wonder and delight making his eyes sparkle. Meat and tallow were thick on nose and chin when he looked at Kiti and laughed aloud, spraying a share of his meal. Then he dived back to the bowl as if someone might take it away.

Tap-tap, went Tuk's chipping knife. Tap-tip. "One questions," he said mildly, and pointing with his chin at the child, "whether that one can ever now be satisfied with only fish and seal."

Kiti giggled when the grimy face came up again for air. "Arajik must not get attached to muskox. This hunter has small desire to capture another."

"Hoo-oo!" Tuk said in mock distress at the thought.

Then, slowly, "Someone wonders whether it may happen that two hunters can see the baby grow in these next moons, or only the child's mother."

He was asking whether they might stay together for a time. Kiti was pleased at the thought, then confused by her pleasure. She dipped a warm, wet ptarmigan cloth from a bladder suspended over the lamp on a caribou rib and scrubbed at Arajik's protesting hands and face.

"Eh, this on the outside cannot be saved to later go within!" She kept scrubbing and murmuring to hide her strange sensations.

Perhaps Tuk would not notice that she had ignored his question. In most ways, it would be good to have him with her. Easier—for he was knowledgeable and strong, could and would share work along the trail. Safer as well—for two could help each other in a time of trouble. She no longer feared him. Together, they had faced danger without fleeing, and together they had laughed often. . . . They were in harmony.

Too, he had given seal oil generously at their first meeting when she had been without heat and light for half a moon. He had also been liberal at that time—despite her noisy hostility—about leaving so much seal from his own capture . . . . That *kapvik* had promptly ruined it was not Tuk's fault.

Kiti reflected now that she too had shown good faith, despite her misgivings and threats of violence, by ministering to him seven sleeps ago when he came off the trail confused and half starved. Even if the worst were true—even if he were Narluk's spy or emissary—there was a kindness to this young man . . . and something else she could not yet name.

Something good and mysterious and tantalizing. Something still forming richly in her perception. Perhaps she would invite him to share her body on this night. . . . What a very pleasant prospect!

But wait. He was an enigma still, even though he had explained his circumstance. She sighed. And had done so without requiring that she reveal her own situation. Despite his tale of tragedy—and yes, she did believe him—some questions continued to plague her. For example, why—after his family died and winter came—did he not go back directly to join his coastal village? Or at least find some people?

He was not a person to thrive in solitude—perhaps he did not know this when he started? And also, since by his own admission he knew her village, how could he not know Narluk? Was it possible to be there and not meet her father? And even more confusing, was it possible to be there, meet him—then not know, at least from other villagers, that Narluk's daughter had vanished with *angakok's* newborn son? How much was known by those people there—how much Narluk had said—she had no way to tell.

She wondered where Tuk went after she sent him from her camp following their capture of seals. Not her concern, she realized—not unless. . . . What if some treacherous sinew really did tie this man to Narluk? Was it not more prudent to continue as they were, hunt together by day and sleep separately at night? Then what? It would be easier, that way, to send him off alone after both had provisioned themselves.

But Tuk was not someone pleased for long in his own company. And why did her logic go in circles each time that he visited, with always the same questions about the same unknowns? And too few answers.

Eh . . . and why does Kiti continue to say nothing about her own circumstance? She had good reasons to be unaccompanied. . . . But he did not know that, and yet he never pushed. Supposing Tuk as well had solid grounds. . .

Chip . . . tip-tip, tap. . . . "It may happen, someone's husband would not wish for Tuk to join her on the trail," the man continued as he worked.

Ah, this gentle probing on his part invited but never did demand that she explain her domestic status. Of course he must suspect by now that no husband would be coming. Kiti felt heat rise in her once again, fury like all anger born of fear. Be done with him, she told herself. *Don't take chances when Arajik is at stake.* Still, if she knew the answers for questions about Tuk, then she might freely explain her own situation, might even permit—no, welcome!—his joining her while their coastal routes converged.

And yes, if perfectly at ease, she would open her sleep robes to him.

A quickening overtook her when she got to this phase in her revolving fancy and recognized that this was no new thought conjured up today. In fact—but then and automatically, her right hand reached for her ear. The white bear peacefully asleep within the ice is not to be disturbed. Who had said that? Not Pichikut. But never before had the young woman anticipated the player above the process.

Hoo-oo! No words to Tuk about this matter. She would not wish to make herself more vulnerable than she already was. Any Inuit alone for unlimited time outdoors in winter dallied with disaster. Pichikut hadn't said that, either. But Kiti's brain told her that a woman like herself was at risk . . . young, inexperienced . . . with an infant . . . her family probably still searching and possibly still with violent intent. And these were not matters to be thought on at one time, let alone to be spoken to a stranger.

Well then. Let Tuk be for you not so much an outsider. Perhaps this man chipping on a stone only awaited opportunity to reveal himself. What question had he only just now asked? Ah!

"Any husband would want companionship for his wife on a long and lonely trail," she said. "Just as any wife who could not go herself because of late pregnancy or illness would want her man to take a woman with him for aid and comfort on the trail. Such selfishness would be unimaginable in either situation."

No response.

She would provide Tuk with another opening to reveal more: "Still, a man's village must be worried even now about his welfare."

"Owka," No, he said mildly as he tapped the muskox stone and turned it in his hands. "The village will believe that we are a family together and have made a choice."

Eyes half closed, Tuk seemed to perceive the mineral with all his senses rather than observe it with eyes only. Then, "Someone knows the beast is there. But how is it placed within this rock?"

Kiti chewed her upper lip for patience. "Perhaps the people of Tuk's village will send someone to search for missing members long overdue," Kiti persisted.

"No, they will believe that it is by choice that a whole family has not returned. Families after summer can go anywhere. . . ." His voice trailed off but the chipping did not slacken.

Kiti raised her eyebrows, Yes. She knew that villagers were free to attach and unattach.

"They may believe that someone chose to join another village?" Her own people usually stayed with the same group unless there was serious dissension. Or unless it became necessary to find a group with other sons and daughters of marriageable age.

Would her own family have changed villages when Narluk decided that his daughter really ought to take a husband?

Tuk made no response. His mind was not on her words or on his village. . . . It was on his carving, his releasing of the troublesome muskox. "Hoo-oo. . . . Where's the head for this creature?" Tuk inquired of the soapstone.

"Otherwise," Kiti concluded, "some villagers would have searched for and found Tuk by now."

"This is true—ai-ee! There the horns! the brow! the muzzle!" Triumphant, Tuk moved closer to the lamp, bent forward to his work.

Kiti watched as he chipped and tapped rapidly, patiently. Small bits of brittle stone flew up. Half hypnotized, Kiti saw the head of *oomingmak* emerge from the rock and as time passed gain realistic proportions. This young man possessed an artist's skill.

Finally involved, Kiti focused on Tuk's project. Several of the men in her village carved in stone or more often bone—usually to enhance the appearance of some useful tool, a spear or knife or certainly an amulet. Women did not. But then, such activity took place in spare moments. Women processed and mended hide at such times.

"Someone wonders how it is that someone can invent creatures from stone."

Tuk frowned over his work. "*Owka*, not invent. The creature lies within and fully formed. The worker only chips away all that in this instance is not muskox."

Kiti thought about that for silent moments as birdflesh pricked up on her arms. Would this long winter trail be the craftsman that chipped from Sukitilan all that was not Kiti?

She wanted to free the thought into the air for Tuk's consideration, but then compressed her lips. For what reason should she say such a thing? Neither of them had lived long enough, neither had observed the ways of life sufficiently, even to make a guess.

Before plucking up Arajik and rolling into sleep robes, she tried one final time to give Tuk a chance to disclose himself and the nature of his extended travel. "Even so, someone supposes that Tuk's village is concerned about his absence."

Tip-tap, went the mallet. Pop-chunk, went discarded pieces. Tuk smiled as he worked, confident now, fully at ease. Kiti tied a soft birdskin filled with summer moss around Arajik's bottom, smoothed the sleep robes as she crawled in and tucked the child into the layers with her. She had in fact nearly forgotten her last words when the young man finally spoke.

"As one supposes Kiti's village concerns itself with her."

She did not respond from the depths of her robe, only reached up to finger the slick lobe of her right ear.

There followed eight days of successful hunting. Neither had enjoyed great fortune on the trail in the moon apart after their first meeting. Did they now bring luck to each other? Far more likely, Kiti thought, that sea and coastal creatures have a rhythm of appearance, like sun and moon and a woman's blood. Cycles with a pulse unknown to Inuit or at least unknown to her.

Throughout the time of their success together with the spear and fishing line, both tried to get the other to reveal personal circumstances. Kiti smiled grimly as she thought back. She knew her reason for being so close mouthed. But Tuk—who was he really?

Again, the thoughts were circular, as usual involving home and family, but ending nowhere. Mostly conjecture about Tuk. Like her thoughts about Narluk and her brothers—their whereabouts and their intentions.

Perhaps her father knew somehow that she was on the coast? Given that Narluk still searched. Given that he wanted to send out someone familiar with the prairies by the sea. But why would he use someone so young? She kept getting back to that. Because his daughter too was young? That worked well for Kiti's reasoning—but Narluk was not likely to trust such youth, and especially not a callow stranger. She knew him well.

Besides, none of this surmise fit easily into her heart. Not the idea that her father still searched. Not the concept that he would embarrass himself by telling others what had happened.

The great *angakok* unable to control his own daughter? What rode least easily in her head was the idea that he would send any emissary rather than come himself . . . or at the least send her brothers. The Narluk she knew—father and wise shaman—would tend to keep a family matter within the family.

And was Tuk capable of trickery? She did not believe that the open-faced, kind and playful young man she knew could deceive for long. Although she became ever more certain of Tuk's integrity, day by day, her mind continued to advise caution.

And soberly, in a last talk on the final night they spent quartered together, they agreed that they should take their own trails. Or was it that Tuk respected a decision Kiti made? He was, after all, the guest in her camp. . . .

At least, he did not argue. The next day, each prepared sled runners and loaded up, harnessed teams and started north. Tuk went far out toward the black lead, Kiti along *tuwak*, that solidly grounded ice near shore. In winter's daytime darkness, the young man soon disappeared.

Before leaving the camp, Kiti picked up the muskox stone carving from where Tuk had discarded it in the snow on the very night he finished it. It fit neatly into the palm of her mitt. She was not sure why she wanted to keep it. After all, the carving was complete and therefore without value. It was a bit of Tuk, though— attractive and pleasant and skilled—a reminder. She wondered as she admired the craftsmanship whether the artist himself were not constructed in the same manner—graceful, intricate parts that revealed themselves slowly to a patient artisan.

Oh? And did the young Kiti who traveled endlessly on ice consider herself sufficiently skilled? Patient—now or ever? She folded the piece tightly into some *oomingmak* wool and dropped it into her hunting bag. *Ahmi.* Who can know the future?

Chapter 23.
Company

Dark, dark. Kiti tried to imagine summer sunshine, attempted to find at mid-day some hint of light on the south horizon. Sometimes she clenched her eyes shut during a rest time when she rode the sled, telling herself that all she need do now was open them to be dazzled by a brilliant day.

These inventions amused her as she moved north, but of course they must not become real. If spring were a reality, the ice would thaw. *Tuwak* would be unsafe. Her speed would dwindle when she took her team onto rocky terrain that lined the shore. She would spend much time mudding and icing runners, then would finally halt entirely because too little ground cover for the sled remained.

More time spent building a cache for sled and all provision that she could not carry on her back—that would be most of it. Food for Arajik, for her dogs and for Nuna and herself would depend on what she captured daily.

Only a *soospuk* wished for summer sun. . . . Besides, she could not with Arajik and the dogs reach ice islands when open water separated them. . . if these islands existed at all. So when she finally reached Pichikut's original home at the top of the world, should sunshine arrive now, she would be able to see the shrinking ice fields, perhaps, but not reach them until next winter because the bridge of thick ice would be treacherous or gone.

And should she decide to abandon her dogs—something neither she nor any Inuit was likely to do under any circumstance— and should she paddle the small kayak to those dots of tide-washed land—she would find no people.

Ananak had warned her. Within half a moon's time following appearance of the full sun arcing the south horizon, ice island Inupiat will be gone to summer themselves on the mainland.

She must find Pichikut's people—or some far-north village of people who could direct her—before spring break-up. How fortunate she was, to have come so far in only two moons. How lucky to have at least one more moon cycle of good ice in which to reach her destination. Ah, but she was truly weary of darkness.

She took from the sea enough for needs day by day and when possible a little more—something to save in hide and bladder bags against times of storm or places with scarce game. On her sled was a fine stack of packets, mostly seal and fish, also what was left from her share of the muskox. Although some food still remained from the dead village, much of what she had now came from those days when she and Tuk had been so successful together on the hunt.

The whale *muktuk* from the silent village was gone, unfortunately; but she and Tuk and especially small Arajik had enjoyed each morsel. Meantime, her half of recent food captured with Tuk meant she was well provisioned at this time. *Ahmi*, who could ever say the future?

The girl loped along beside the sled in the darkness of day, Nuna pacing her on the other side. Arajik poked his hooded head from her *amaut*, jabbered ceaselessly and punctuated the stream of sound with whoops of glee and howls of merriment. How he loved the bouncing trail. . . . He reached up now to pull at Kiti's own hood, managed to get toeholds in the pouch enough to let him pull around to her face and grin. Then he braced himself back at the top of the pouch and shouted at the dogs.

This Arajik would be a great traveler. A strong dog-handler, besides. So very much alive. . . . Eh, if Narluk could see the boy, would he—no. Kiti must not allow her thoughts to take that twisting track.

These nine dogs pulling Palunga's sled were trail-hardened. So was Kiti. *Kringmerk* were solid and dependable. Kiti hoped that she was, too. Iyarpok would never get the team's respect as Nuna did. But the dogs feared him—so the result in pulling day by day was nearly the same. And Nuna so far was content to keep the *ananak* role. Most of the team also put up with young Ajak capering beside them, took in stride the pup's teasing, her playful yips and nips.

Iyarpok, though, still tolerated none of this. Ajak learned rapidly and painfully to give him space.

Kiti studied the rangy lead dog. He was normally good-tempered, patient—named as he was by Palunga for an innate sense of humor. Iyarpok, the Laughing One . . . but not these days. He still must remember that Nuna had been the lead before maternal duties claimed her. And he apparently had no intention of giving the position back to her—as he quietly continued to let her know. He would crowd away any dog that approached her to show friendship. A team when it was feeding normally allowed a nursing female to keep a bear's share uncontested. Iyarpok, though, would corner for himself the choice and largest portions of meat thrown to the dogs—not knowing that Kiti fed Nuna privately, better and far beyond what went to the pack. No fish for Nuna while rich mammal flesh and blubber were available!

Iyarpok would not attack Nuna outright nor let himself become the object of her wrath, for he was no match. Carnivores appeared to know each other's limit without full test, Kiti reflected. The cheekiest crow would never taunt an owl. Nor would the most rapacious wolverine directly challenge a healthy adult sea bear. A pity that people did not have this special sense fully developed.

Nuna ignored Iyarpok. With Ajak weaned and fairly independent, the bitch was devoted to Kiti's little brother, permitting only the girl and Ajak to get close . . . and Tuk, when he was present. Now here was something to consider, a thought far more useful than trying to conjure up sunlight in her memory. Why does Nuna allow Tuk to touch Arajik?

Kiti should have factored in Nuna's acceptance of the young man at her time for decision-making—but she had not. No matter, for she was not likely to see Tuk's face again.

And just as well, she told herself then and now. In fact, she told herself often. Odd moments, frequently just before sleep, Kiti would run her finger along her ear lobe notch and wonder what Tuk was doing, where he was right now, what had become of him . . . then tell herself once more how good it was that he was gone.

Strangers visible in starlight traveled up from the southwest in late morning. From an *aglu* far out on grounded ice, Kiti saw them in silhouette as they drove the crest on a prairie hillock parallel to the sea, passed her by and disappeared. Two Inuit, one long sled with a high, flat load, more dogs than she could count at such distance . . . a great herd of kringmerk, she decided. Twenty? More? How could someone feed so many? Worse even than Tuk's mob.

Then the travelers must have swept around, for she saw them later coming toward her from northwest across the ice. She with Arajik and Nuna were still at the seal hole when the men drove up boldly between her and her team.

They stopped. Their dogs growled and her team howled. Kiti silenced her own group. The shorter of the two men shouted at his *kringmerk*, finally used his whip with speed and skill, but struck directly on the flesh of his dogs with no prior snap and snick in the air. Nor did the newcomers make any move to change the awkward placing of their team.

The girl stepped away from and folded up her bear rug, collected her crosspieces, pulled apart her harpoon, put everything into the hunting bag. She was annoyed. She had waited many hours at this *aglu* already, and now no seal would be captured today. The strangers lacked consideration.

Nuna grumbled far back in her throat, a sustained bubble of

sound, as the two men came toward Kiti. Then Nuna went forward and stood between them and the girl, the dog's feet planted solidly, hackles high, muscles rippling and at the ready. Her mouth was agape, nostrils wrinkled, fangs showing.

Both men stopped. The shorter one raised his spear, looked at Kiti and lowered it, smiled.

Smiled? The girl was close enough and sufficiently intent to see the glittering cold eyes that made a liar of his mouth. She walked forward cautiously to stand beside Nuna, her mitt resting on the dog's head. She did not smile. She, too, could be discourteous.

"Hush!" she murmured to *kringmerk*. "Some travelers wish to rest?" Kiti asked in a neutral voice.

The growl ceased, but the stance continued to send a hostile message: come forward at grave risk.

The taller man stepped up. "Great weariness caught us on the trail." He looked around.

"A woman's poor camp is on ice not far from here," she told him. She returned to the *aglu* to grasp her hunting bag, then circumnavigated the strange team to reach her own dogs and sled, all the time hanging onto Nuna by the strap looped around her neck. The men made no move until Kiti with the team was underway, but the girl was uncomfortable to have them behind her.

She forced herself not to look back, for to do so might reveal the apprehension she felt but must conceal. Or might indicate to them a congeniality which she did not wish to convey.

But Kiti's instincts this time were clear and exceedingly strong. They told her to fly. Leave the snowhouse and its content, all that extra food she had been saving . . . take the team, the sled with its precious nest and hunting bag, then go as far and fast as possible.

Kiti has been too much alone, her brain objected. She was unaccustomed to strangers. And besides, Kiti cannot outrun them, should they decide to follow. True, her dogs were fresh. But theirs were many, and with two people besides—one to push the chase while the other rested. And if they did not follow, there was no reason to run. . . .

Chapter 24.
Intrusion

Kiti pulled to the far side of her igloo before halting the team. Her animals still in harness, she went back with the driving whip to be sure the other dogs gave her team space. No one needed a dogfight on the ice. It was well she interposed herself, for the big team did not slow until she first put out her arms to give the signal, then finally brandished the whip. Even then, the lead and both wheel dogs peered back for their driver's instruction.

Kiti did not move, and the dogs halted. At the sled, the two men spoke rapidly, voices rising as if in argument, but Kiti could not distinguish words except to know with certainty that they spoke with the cadence of her familiar inland people.

She staked and fed her own team without offering hospitality to the great throng of new canines, then rolled away the outer ice block and entered her small snowhouse. She sighed. Certain conventions of the trail had to be observed. The strangers must be permitted to share her shelter if they wished.

To make space, she stacked deep into the harness porch the packets of seal she had left inside her igloo. The men need not know the extent of her provision. She felt niggardly to harbor such a thought. What is happening here?

The lamp glowed cheerfully, and Arajik was playing on the robes with his foster family of canines as the men crawled in, each coming down the tiny tunnel and through the baffle. The girl put a hand on Nuna's head to keep her still. But the dog stood with nose wrinkled, upper muzzle raised to show her teeth as she stared unblinking at the strangers, first one, then the other, back and forth. Nuna disliked them equally. Her hackles bristled.

"The woman has a child!" Both men seemed genuinely surprised.

Why the surprise? Many women have children. If these two were sent by Narluk, they would know about the baby, Kiti reflected. Unless, on her father's assumption that the infant had perished, they were not told of his existence. And unless they were not actually sent by Narluk.

She forced a smile, telling herself that she should feel relief at their lack of information. And telling herself also that she must not imagine every male on every trail to have been dispatched by *angakok*.

"The boy is Arajik, and his mother is Kiti," she informed them.

The men exchanged glances, but the girl could not read their expressions. The taller one had to stoop inside the snowhouse. He promptly sat down on the ice floor, using a still-folded robe he plucked off the *iglerk*. Anyone could see that the sleep shelf was too small for three. Besides, the pushy one now on the robe might expect her to share more than the *iglerk* later in the sleep time.

"This traveler answers to Tonratu." His words were cordial enough, but his manner was patronizing. He seemed to be exercising forbearance with a difficult child. Well, and he might not be far off. Kiti was no longer a child; but ever since this pair usurped her space there by the *aglu* on the ice, she had felt a strange determination building. She recognized no fear, right now, only cold certainty that she must hold her own with them to keep her family safe.

The shorter, somewhat older man who had earlier drawn his spear on Nuna now stood just inside the baffle, kept his eye on the dog, speaking not at all. Kiti was relieved that he did not offer up another ghastly smile.

"One's silent companion is Odlerk," the first man continued. He twisted to look at that other. "Someone should go to the sled for seal—" he turned back to Kiti—"and perhaps *muktuk*?"

The prospect of such unexpectedly fine fare—the latter always her favorite and also always in short supply among inland Inupiat—thrust a smile onto her face despite the resolve to be formal and grave.

"For the child!" she blurted. Arajik seemed to have the insatiable appetite of his foster mother and her kind. When Tuk had introduced him to *muktuk*, the whale meat with its attached blubber, the baby had savored it even more than the flesh of *oomingmak*.

Nearly a moon ago, that would be. She wished Tuk were here at this moment; and this time no prissy inner voice interrupted her thought to say how good it was that he had gone. Kiti placed food into Arajik's little stone dish kept warm on bone rails above the lamp.

The blocky stranger named Odlerk returned in a few moments with a split of frozen seal along with a bulging leather pouch. From this he withdrew the promised whale blubber, the *muktuk*.

"Nakorami," thank you, she told him as she cut off a small chunk, then pulverized it with the pestle in the warm dish. "The babe will enjoy it."

"Take some for Kiti as well." Odlerk spoke for the first time with a voice half-growl, a thick grating sound unpleasant to her ear.

"Take all of it for this household!" Tonratu corrected.

Kiti intercepted dark looks between the partners.

The evening was short and quiet. Iron rules of hospitality required her to offer shelter certainly and food if she had it. Not just surplus. Any food at all was to be shared with visitors. Kiti had plenty at this time, and she offered much. In normal circumstance, she would be proud to have such bounty. But with these two, she was reluctant even as she chided herself for greed. Ultimately, her need would be far greater than theirs, with only herself to find more and with much trail time still ahead.

More, she wanted to possess nothing and do nothing that would make them remember her. To the extent possible, nothing must set her apart from any other Inupiat they might meet on the trail. Kiti refilled the lamp as she thought these things, twisted the wick to bring up the light. She was glad that her face was hidden when the absurdity of her wish struck her, for she nearly choked on sudden laughter rising from nowhere.

Of course she was unremarkable. What could be more ordinary than to come upon a young, solitary woman having a small baby suckled by a dog, the tiny party on ice near no village whatsoever . . . with full team in mid-winter dark? Kiti planned to make herself invisible? She coughed several times, cleared her throat to chase back her private amusement at the irony.

As it turned out, the guests chose to eat exclusively from their own supplies—an ungracious gesture on their part—rude—which nevertheless suited Kiti well. It was not essential in the name of hospitality that she feed their dogs, but certainly this would be the friendly thing to do.

She did not. It was necessary that these visitors not feel too welcome, she reflected even as she deplored her own mean spirit. She wanted them to move on.

Kiti managed that evening to keep Arajik from nursing Nuna while the men were in the snowhouse. She dreaded sleep time. The dog must stay in at night for the baby, and Nuna was warming to the strangers even less than Kiti. Besides, the igloo was far too tiny for five.

Tonratu got up at last and solved the problem, oil from the meal glistening on his skimpy chin hairs in lamplight as he stood hunched over beneath the low curve that roofed Kiti's shelter.

"The night will be fair," he told her, "for the sky is clear. The unloaded sled of the visitors is vulnerable to wild creatures."

"Yes," Kiti agreed, not quite daring to hope where his prediction would lead.

"The two visitors have built with hides a lean-to for sleep outside." He got down to crawl past the baffle, and the girl dared to relax a little. Then he added softly, "It happens that a larger snowhouse will soon be built."

Kiti gulped. Good news, that they would stay outside. But a larger snowhouse? For them, perhaps. Not for her. Hoo-oo-oo, they planned to stay so long? She picked up the robe Tonratu had sat upon and spread it with others on her own shallow sleep ledge. She covered both Arajik and Nuna when she did so, and the baby shouted with laughter.

"And does it happen that a woman's husband will return from hunting by the sleep time?"

Kiti jumped, unaware that Tonratu had not yet left the shelter. How dare he ask such a blunt question, as if she were a child?

She gazed at him steadily to let him know she disapproved. "Perhaps not."

"Ai-ee-ee!" the man said softly, but Kiti caught laughter in his eyes. "It may be that a visitor will ask a question when the man comes back." His lip rose on one side to form a smirk.

Kiti flicked up her eyebrows, not long enough to indicate agreement but sufficient to let him know she understood his words. She gave no other response. He was telling her that he wished to ask the husband if he might sleep with the wife. And why the unpleasant smile?

The strangers must leave very soon, she decided—so they need not trouble to build a new snowhouse. Or she must move on quickly. So long as they were not sent by Narluk to find her, then they would not think it odd that she anticipated a husband's return. Nor would it be strange that he did not appear. Hunters on the trail were delayed more often than not.

Eh, that Tonratu thought her to be accompanied by a husband gave a glimmer of reassurance . . . unless that ancillary smile came from satisfaction with his own deceit. The other one, Odlerk, was large and brutal.

But Tonratu appeared clever and therefore to be feared particularly? His words were sharp on both ends. He might at first sight be less unpleasant than Odlerk, but something in his voice put her off balance—a mockery, as if he harbored some dark private joke. As if he played a game of fox and lemming—enjoyed each cut and leap, anticipated some future final pounce.

"This lemming," she later told Arajik softly, "will dig in too deep to unearth."

Tonratu had disappeared through the baffle to join Odlerk outside, to tend their dogs—to sleep elsewhere.

Pirtok. Whoever they were, wherever they came from, the men were here and she did not enjoy their company. She realized as she rolled the ice lump door into place that the men would have had to sleep doubled up if they tried to lie down within her trail igloo. She smiled. She must remember to build such tiny dwellings always.

Chapter 25.
Violation

The next day and the next, Kiti left early with sled and team. Alone, she went far out toward the lead to seek seal. Both times, she wound up only fishing through ice. Nuna showed no interest in searching out *aglu*. She was nervous, kept her pup nearby and continually checked Arajik on the sled. She would stand motionless for a long time peering west, then south and finally north, her ears pricked forward, to see that no one approached. She paced restlessly between every such inquiry.

Later, the woman fed her team far from camp, then returned long past the sleep time. Her message to the visitors was clear: be gone. But still, the interlopers were there—bedded in a snow cave outside and silent when she returned.

It was late during the third sleep time, long after she had collapsed into her furs, that Kiti awoke suddenly. A blast of cold was coming down the tunnel of her snowhouse past the baffle. Someone has moved the block.

Among the blankets, she reached first for Arajik and then flailed out with both hands to find Nuna or Ajak. None but herself were in the folds of her bedding. More, the lamp had gone out. She came alert fully.

Holding her breath, she listened for sound, aware that the stream of cold air was no longer noticeable. Now someone has replaced the block. She heard scuffing steps on the ice floor.

"Nuna!" she called softly. Why would the big dog take the babies from their furs? And where would she take them? No dog could roll away the big ice block at the end of the tunnel.

Then the furs above her lifted and a human hand pressed her down.

"*Suwit?*" What does someone want?

"The comfort of a woman for the night." Tonratu's voice.

Kiti tried to sit up, but the man's palm held her back. "This is not acceptable. No one has asked a woman's husband, and the husband of course has not asked his wife whether—"

Tonratu laughed. "The visitors know well—" and his voice ceased as Kiti stiffened beneath his hand. Then he began again. "The visitors believe that no husband will appear at this ice camp."

"A hunter is delayed."

What is happening here? And what is well known by the unwelcome visitors? And where was her small family? She must find out. "Arajik. . . . The dogs?"

"The unnatural child is with its dog-sister and the nursing bitch."

Again, Kiti tried to rise, and again his hand pressed her down. She reached out to remove it and he slapped her fingers away, then placed his fist against her stomach with great pressure. She could tell from touch in near-total black that the man wore only underfurs—his *illupak*—and these were askew, half open. As he bent close above her, she could smell his flesh—warm and moist and sour.

Never mind the discourtesy of asking a direct question. "The child and two dogs—where?" His hand restraining her, his rough swat on her fingers—these were violation far beyond discourtesy, surpassing all she knew or had ever heard about.

"The white dog would not easily be taken from the igloo," she said. And never by you, she thought but did not say. Not willingly.

Tonratu hoisted himself fully onto the ice shelf and kneeled above her, then yanked her soft *illupak* trousers down so roughly that she heard the sewing sinew break. Then she felt herself torn from the robes and thrown to the ice floor. She twisted and crawled toward the baffle. If she could reach the weapons in her hunting bag—

The man scrabbled after her in the darkness, grasped her leg, jerked her back. His strength overpowered her, and she did not understand what was happening. If Nuna were here—but she was not.

Kiti was dizzy, jumbled thoughts hissing past rapidly like a poorly-packed sled pulled by forty dogs on slick sea ice. Too fast to capture one idea and examine it closely, too jumbled to make sense of anything. She raised her right hand to her ear lobe, pinched it painfully. Better.

But nothing she had ever heard about, let alone experienced, prepared her for this, and nothing Pichikut had told her— resentment rose in her.

Not so much of the man behaving so strangely—of course his actions were despicable—but rancor regarding her mother. Why did Ananak not tell of this? Why not prepare her daughter for this horror? Perhaps because her mother did not know that such could occur. . . .

When her brothers brought some woman to the *iglerk*—and such a person would have to be from the trail, some other village— for no young or even half-young women beside herself lived in their own community—both were happy at the prospect of uniting. And when Narluk and Pichikut copulated, usually with each other, they did so with affection and mutual respect.

And when Kiti—eh, Sukitilan!—came together with a man, it was a time for experiment and laughter, for hearing and heeding instruction, for general joy.

No *inuk* ever need take any woman by coercion. For anyone on the trail—woman as well as man—common hospitality at any village will produce for someone so inclined a choice of willing partners for the *iglerk* at sleeptime.

What of some creature like Tonratu? Yes, she decided. For village wives would be curious even if repelled by his manner. Variety and new experiences are generally welcomed as enrichments to the chapter of one's life.

Then she realized with a shudder that the Paija spirit of the monster above her had interest not in copulation but in violence and power. She inhaled slowly and deeply as possible, fighting panic.

Kiti tried to steady her breathing, tried to listen beyond the drum of heartbeat in her ears. This cannot be happening—yet she knew it was no dream.

"Enough!" she told Tonratu firmly, once again attempting to sit up. This time, though, he grasped both her shoulders and slammed them onto the floor ice. She waited for the pain to subside, for the shock to recede, for rational thought to be possible.

What can someone do in this situation? She felt the man's *ussuk*—his penis—probe her *uttuk*, the sensitive woman's portal, the vulva. No. . . . The Inupiat woman has a right to choose. . . . And she did not choose Tonratu.

"Kiti is unwilling to *kaoyuk* with this man!" she quaked.

But he ignored her, placed a hand at the opening to facilitate entry.

The woman tried to roll, but the fist only increased its pressure. She could think of nothing except to get away. She reached one hand down to find the tender place between Tonratu's legs, fumbled to grasp his genitals and twist.

"*OwKAH!*" No! he growled, and capturing both her hands with one of his, forced them up beside her head.

"*Pinnak!*" Don't! she told him.

His whole body held her down, but the fist and its pressure were gone.

She could try to take a full breath now. Perhaps he had not understood her before. "A woman chooses not to copulate," she gasped.

She heard the unpleasant laugh once more, and then felt a strap encircle her left wrist, stretch across her neck and loop the other wrist. The man pulled the binding tight, and again she fought for breath.

"A strangle thong around the neck will coax cooperation from dog or inuit," he panted. She twisted to loosen the strap, but it held and she felt her body stiffen with horror.

Would he kill her now? Had he already killed Nuna? Arajik could not survive without the nourishment she still provided. Ajak? Had he killed all three?

When the man ripped apart her lower *illupak*, she wrapped her legs around him and clenched hard with full and considerable power.

He grunted, and then his right fist pounded at her ribs. As her breath left her, she felt and heard something within her crack. At the same time, tension on the strap increased, and she gagged. She relaxed her straddling grip.

She tried to draw breath as the line across her throat loosened slightly, but then stopped short as new agony shot through her when she inhaled. Her ribs. . . . He had battered the cage of bones with his fury.

She could not breathe? And if she could not find breath, how could she live to care for Arajik? She tried to calm herself. As she pushed frenzy away by strong will, the space it left open filled with hot anger. Rage flowed through her mind and her body like seething spirit lights. The man was inside her. How dare he!

Here was violation of her body and of her spirit. An end to what she was before—that Kiti she had been testing and exploring— and doing so with delight, she realized. Liking much of what she discovered. And now—how could someone do this thing?

Starvation was a natural finish on the trail. Or becoming the meal for a white sea bear. Even floating far and finally on a broken bit of independent ice. These and other such calamities, she could and did expect and would accept. But not this. . . .

The snarling man who strained and grunted at her here could not be real. He must be an emissary—not of her father Narluk but of Paija, that queen of evil deeds. A malevolent trail spirit is here, she assured herself, not Inuit and surely not Inupiat. She wondered at the distended *ussuk*. A spirit was equipped thus? She felt the tearing of her own *uttuk* as the creature pounded on her body.

For this one, she was prey. And Arajik's life—if Arajik still lived—depended on her survival in whatever form she now must take. How dare Tonratu do this to her? Pichikut, help me find breath.

Again she tried to expand her lungs, and the pain on her left side made her gasp and need even more air. Sharp sleet swam across her closed eyelids. She felt rivulets of perspiration roll from her head and into her ears, drip from her jaw. And she felt herself withdrawing. . . .

No. . . . Stay alert. Try to make the anger monster go away, for that one also requires air. Do not mind the pain. Breath is more important. She forced her mind to full awareness and once more inhaled, this time slowly, and felt her lungs expand. A miracle of comfort came with what she had always before thought her due. Blessed air. She breathed again, wincing with the anguish of the movement.

How did this devil get Nuna out without Kiti's hearing what must have been a battle? Her imagination flashed a rapid chronology of images before her eyes. She pictured Tonratu rolling inward the ice block up at the end of the tunnel, then cunningly scratching on it enough for the dog to hear but not enough to disturb the human occupants of the igloo.

As she left the sleeping shelf to go investigate, Kiti envisioned Nuna—imagined Tonratu ready with a strip of walrus hide—perhaps the very thong against Kiti's own flesh throughout this ordeal—to rapidly encircle and jerk tight at Nuna's neck. She could see her dog being dragged out through the opening, all four legs stiffened against the pressure of the pull, breathless, unable to protect herself or vocalize alarm. Where had he staked her, still choking, while he re-entered the igloo for Arajik and Arak? And where was Kiti's sled with the nest right now—how far from here, how safe?

With fury still foremost and strengthening her, she focused on the creature hovering above and pumping at her savagely. The demon had mastered her, but he would never be her master. Perhaps the new Kiti was not ended. It might be that this horror when it passed would somehow leave her fully except in memory. And stronger. She breathed again, cautiously, shallowly, triumphed in the seep of air.

She gathered the anguish of her broken side into a small, tidy packet, consciously wrapped it tight and placed it mentally into a bladder to be examined later. Once more she inhaled. Better. Now breathe again. How soon before she could rise and dress and walk out to assure herself that all was well with Arajik and the dogs?

At last, Tonratu seized and grunted like a gut-pierced caribou. She felt him shrivel immediately, even as he withdrew. Eh, this is no true man!

He pulled away the strap and left. Kiti heard the rustle of his clothing, listened as he crawled past the baffle and up the tunnel, moved the block without replacing it, for chill swept into the igloo and did not cease. The woman lay shuddering on the ice floor. The anger remained, but it did not heat her. Thoughts fled from what had just happened and centered instead on what she must do.

Dress for the cold. *Illupak* and *silipak*. Inner wear—she had that of her adolescence with which to replace her own until it could be mended. The old *illupak* would be uncomfortable—too tight, short at the crotch, high above her ankles. But it would temporarily do its job—wick moisture from her skin and hold close the heat her body generated.

And its discomfort would remind her to mend the one that fit. She was fortunate to have that outgrown spare of undergarments with her—for she had been unwilling to leave it with her family as a reminder. Most people had but one, and the *illupak* was essential. Without it, someone would freeze on the trail. It struck her now that Tonratu would believe she had but the one underfur—yet he put her at grave risk by deliberately tearing it.

She must go find Arajik and Nuna with her pup. If she was successful and they could travel, she would leave this place. So she must get her hunting bag and dog hitching from the storage bubble. Have weapons ready if Tonratu or Odlerk should try to stop her. Carry the harness. Take her team with their sleeptime leads well away from camp—along with her sled if it was there. If her family could not be found or found dead? She would return to this camp—to kill her visitors or die herself in the attempt.

Chapter 26.
Odlerk

Shaking with cold and outrage, she tried to rise but was caught short by the sharp pain of injured ribs. She rolled onto her right side, then slowly brought herself up to a sitting position. Taking shallow but frequent breaths, she placed both hands on the sleeping shelf to draw her trembling body over and ease herself from the floor onto the top of the robes. Brr-rr! She reached out to draw up a loose cover.

Only a few moments for warming. Someone needs to review once more the actions to come. First, find her family . . . including her team.

While she waited for her body to stop shaking, she went over her plan. Hunting bag and harness. Weapons and now-torn underfurs, then *silipak*—full as possible dress against the cold. Return to pack and leave camp or, if her family were hurt or missing, to take vengeance.

All must be done silently as possible, she reminded herself as she left the furs. This would be a cold day without the close-fitting underfurs of her *illupak* that Tonratu had torn. At least, she would not have to deal with the now-painful effort of rolling away the heavy block at the doorway.

Outside, she padded around to collect her dogs on the leads which anchored them at night. Her sled was gone. Destroyed? More likely, hidden. The snug little pallet was on it, the babies' *upluk*, their nest. Surely, surely the little ones were warm! She knew that Nuna would have had to be tied. Did Tonratu use another choking strap?

It would require that to insure silence. Perhaps the unwelcome "visitors" did not yet realize that Arajak suckled Nuna.

Slowly, each breath a separate agony, Kiti led the team and carried the harness away from camp. She watched the dogs for any signal of what direction to take. The outdoors was moonlit, seemed bright after the blackness of the igloo. The hummocks showed detail as she passed, and the black of open sea glistened not far away.

She called softly for Nuna, but there was no answer.

Close to the black lead, Kiti found her sled, Arajik and Ajik asleep safely in the *upluk*, the nest. Nuna stood head down and silent at the end of a choke leash that the woman released with a single flick of her *ulu*, the food knife always in her pocket.

Kiti stayed out for the remainder of the sleep time to reassure a distressed Nuna and to calm her own troubled spirits. Movement and drawing breath were both painful. But she realized as she assessed her situation that she was still—amazingly—the same Kiti she had been before. More experienced, now—and some inner wisdom reassured her that such expansion was bound to have value in the future.

Gullies of perception had been deepened. The sleeptime had contributed greater terror than she had previously known. Not so much for her own well-being—one life has small importance—but for Arajik and for Pichikut's Plan.

Too, Kiti was now for the first time beset by physical pain connected with simple acts like moving and drawing breath. Surely this discomfort would pass? She would learn in the days ahead.

And finally, overriding all other sensation, was a white-hot calculating anger that swelled once more to rage. Energy rocked her. She wanted to race to the western horizon. To lasso the moon with the long cracking sinew she used to guide the team. To leap up into and collect the spirit lights and force them to do her bidding

. . . do all of that if only she could walk and draw breath without torment.

She returned to her ice camp in mid-afternoon on that day, determined to pack up food and go. But as she came closer, she saw that her small snowhouse was demolished. She gasped in dismay, mouth open. Ruined blocks lay strewn haphazard across the frozen sea. Glistening in the flickering reflection of spirit lights was a new igloo having a porch, a long tunnel and a large extra storage dome that formed a blister on the side. In debris tossed over the ice were Arajik's concave little stone food dish and Tuk's muskox stone-carving. These she picked up and dropped into the hunting bag still on her sled. The strangers with their many dogs were nowhere in sight. And once again, Kiti felt violated.

Nuna refused to enter the new house. She stood beside it and stared at the structure, fangs bared without making a sound. Kiti rolled away the door block, painfully crawled down through the tunnel. Inside were her robes and lamp and packeted food, including what she had stowed in the harness porch.

Her tools were there, and both Big Feeds—her property that no one had the right to touch without express permission. Fresh anger made her so warm that she threw back her hood. Everything not presently on her sled—or discarded among the ruins of her igloo—was now mixed with belongings of the men . . . food, lamp oil bladders, blankets, extra clothing. What were they thinking?

She hauled her robes outdoors and stacked them beside the sled. Still fuming, she pulled out the lamp and food pouches, then the extra *amaut* belonging to Pichikut. How dare they? Why would anyone destroy the home of another? True, they had built one far grander—but for the two strangers to sort her belongings—actually decide between them that this item had value, that one not. . . . Hoo-oo-oo! . . . Never mind, she was leaving this place.

The girl went back to drag out food, careful to take only what she was certain had been hers. She left the whale *muktuk* behind, even though it had been given to her and even though Arajik and she both loved it. The manner of these men was not *peeusinga*, not the Inuit Way. Even though they spoke Inupiaq perfectly with the inlander accents most familiar to Kiti. This folly today was no more acceptable than their interrupting her above a seal hole when they arrived. Than their placing of the huge team between her and her own dogs and sled. Here was insolence, a show of flaunted power—blatant contempt. Nor was it peeusinga to have at the edge of camp their frequent private chats and arguments and sometimes laughter, often looking in her direction.

And the horror of last night was not even to be considered. The reason for her present pain in walking and drawing breath was beyond her power to address on this terrible day.

This afternoon—now!—was the perfect time for her to go with no further loss. But before she could bring out the last of her bladders and food packets, her dogs growled and began to bark. She plucked her spear from the hunting bag, then turned to gaze south across the ice, the direction which seemed to be their source of alarm. The big sled finally visible in moonlight came in, but with only one driver—Odlerk.

He slowed his team, halted, walked toward her, kept coming closer, too close. She realized that she had not studied him before. No taller than she, Odlerk was thick of torso but short-legged with inordinately long arms. He had a low forehead, she saw as he shrugged off his hood. A few black hairs of finger length drooped from a dark mole located on his lower cheek to the left side of his mouth. His eyes were small, close together, glinting darkly in the flicker of starlight high overhead.

Kiti could turn her dogs and run, as her heart told her to do, for *kringmerk* were harnessed and ready. Arajik was in the *amaut*. But she had not yet loaded and tied on what belonged to her. What she would need on the trail. Almost everything was stacked beside the sled. She'd soon be short of food if she left now. She and Arajik could not survive without the robes still piled on ice.

Now she smiled, shook her head. Run? Kiti could barely walk, on this day.

Odlerk was examining her preparations, and she saw his eyes narrow. Given the desire, he could overtake her easily with his huge team. Or the men together could find her later, if they wished, tracking at their leisure and relentlessly. And if they did not wish to chase her down, so her brain informed her, then she had no reason to bolt.

She was still aching and disoriented from the events of this past sleeptime, and tired besides. And she was of course further incensed over the destruction of her snowhouse. Over the vaunted lack of respect for her and her belongings. And besides that, she was furious with herself for feeling fear.

Lips drawn tight, she marched up to make the gap between her and Odlerk even narrower—an impudent act, especially given the difference in their ages and the fact that she was female. Nuna insisted on staying ahead of her, and Kiti restrained her by looping a section of the whip loosely around the dog's neck.

"Does it happen that someone marvels at such a comfortable new home?" Odlerk taunted in his grating voice.
"Hoo-oo!" she disapproved.
The man brushed against her as he might a boulder along a narrow trail. He walked on past to reach her sled and team. He gazed for a few moments at the dogs, then walked around and inspected very slowly and deliberately every article on and beside her sled. Although he did not touch anything, he kept slapping his driving whip against the fur on his right thigh—sluck, thwap, sluck-sluck, thwap!

Nuna's deep bubble of disapproval began anew, and Kiti moved up to cover the dog's muzzle with her mitt. The sound ceased, but the canine muscles remained tense, hackles quaking half-high. Nuna and Kiti together moved up toward their sled and the man beside it.

He turned. "And where will Sukitilan go now?" Odlerk sneered. "Back to her father to beg forgiveness?"

Kiti stared at the man. The ramification of his words left her shuddering. All that early suspicion so unfairly misplaced on Tuk? And then followed by mostly ignored instinctive apprehension with arrival of these two men? To be a *soospuk* can be fatal.

She smoothly removed the strap from Nuna's neck and rested her mitt on the broad shoulder. Waiting for Odlerk to make the next move, she recalled how she first saw the men come from the southwest. Then, not knowing or perhaps not caring that she had seen them earlier, they pulled in as if to arrive from the coastal prairie northwest. Even though she had noticed all this at the time, she had consciously marked only that they were inlanders, barren ground Inupiat who spoke with familiar intonations. Yet, she realized now, their doubling back to reach her camp had niggled at her from the start.

"The people said the unnatural babe would be dead long ago," Odlerk continued.

"And Narluk—?"

"—The great Angakok is unknown to this person." Odlerk shrugged. "As is also the dark spirit named Tonratu met wandering on the trail."

Kiti was silent. The two are not friends, then, only travelers who met by chance. That would explain the constant differences of opinion. And if this irritable man uttered truth, then Narluk has not sent him. She chose her next words carefully.

"And now it happens that two men can find favor—"

"—One man only. . . . *Ingminek!* This one and no other!" His eyes disappeared when he scowled. "Someone does not reveal private plans to evil that walks on two legs."

So he has not spoken of this matter to his companion? "But Tonratu—"

"—Now walks alone, and may his feet—!" Odlerk's voice broke. He spat on the ice and did not continue.

Kiti looked beyond him, but saw no shadow approaching. "A shaman did not send a traveler to find his daughter," she said, "and yet the traveler knows her childhood name." This today was by far the most speech the two had exchanged.

Nuna remained tense under the woman's mitt. But, Kiti reflected, this dialogue was almost cordial although everything in her warned her to be wary. Also, the effort to pull air for talk and the pain of making that effort were taking a toll on her energy and patience.

Odlerk continued. "It happens that all Inupiat know of the willful woman's defection. Narluk will be pleased to have his female child returned to him."

Chapter 27.
Encounter

What a *soospuk* is this woman to have relaxed. . . . Kiti drew herself up and inhaled deeply despite the pain. "Someone can see that a woman stands here. Narluk has no female child. Nor is the adult once called Sukitilan someone to be returned like a borrowed sled."

The man's face darkened, eyes obliterated by lowering brows. He stepped forward, and Nuna rumbled. His face lowered to the dog, and his right hand produced a broad knife of sharpened bone.

"The seal should never taunt a walrus." Again he glanced at Nuna.

Kiti stepped up to stand between him and the big dog. "It happens that someone needs to find his friend and leave this place," she told the man in low but emphatic tones.

Odlerk stepped even closer, the corners of his mouth turning up in that cold smile she had disliked from the beginning. Kiti put the mitt resting on Nuna to her side, the fingers clenching into a fist. Her right mitt grasped more tightly around her spear, but she did not raise it.

Time stopped; all motion halted. Even the spirit lights towering above seemed to cease swirling and appeared to glow steadily while the woman collected her thoughts.

Odlerk spoke at last. "And Narluk will no doubt rejoice to have the spiritless babe disposed of as—"

"—The boy Arajik has strong spirits," Kiti told him softly, "and he is now son to the woman Kiti."

As if he followed the dialogue, the sturdy child pushed himself up in his hood bag so that he could regard this man with the rough voice.

"Give him over," Odlerk rasped. "We'll see how easily such powerful spirits can be dispatched."

Kiti and Nuna stood motionless, now side by side, Arajik still perched at the top of the carrier on his sister's back. One practiced shrug tumbled him deep into the *amaut*, and he objected loudly. Still, Kiti reflected, it would take time for him to climb again to the top.

It was at this moment, with Arajik howling and Odlerk watching them expectantly, Kiti and Nuna standing silent together as they waited for Odlerk's next move, that the puppy Ajak decided to attack the threatening man. She gave no warning sound, only flung herself at him, grasping and chewing fiercely with her sharp teeth at the knee of his fur trousers.

Odlerk grabbed her up with both hands, his face filling with rage, his eyes bulging. Kiti heard the man's clothing tear, and she gasped. The tiny teeth were still fastened in a portion of trouser hide when Odlerk raised the puppy above his head and dashed her straight down onto the ice, then kicked the small body two kayak lengths through the air. Ajak made no sound. She did not move from the spot where she landed.

Nuna saw what happened, but for a wonder did not stir while energy poured into every muscle of Kiti's aching frame. The girl felt her *kamik* seem to rise off ice, her body float on air—able to spring forward or race away, unrestrained by any normal law of weight. Her mind considered and discarded first this action and then that.

She must not be precipitous. Must wait to see what happened next. Be ready to respond. She knew that she was no match for Odlerk physically. Her fingers tightened on her spear, but still she did not raise it.

The man frowned, glanced past her with an anxious, jerky movement, his eyes straying back beyond his team in the direction from which he had come. Is he making sure Tonratu is not here to see? Kiti wondered. Or checking to see whether help is coming?

Then Odlerk shifted his spear into his left mitt and took from the pocket of his *silipak* a killing knife. He held it before him, flat and ready.

"Give over the child!" he growled, lifting the weapon.

But before the words had fully left his mouth, Nuna was on him—all fur and fang and fury. Her great forepads hit his shoulders and he toppled backwards. Her gleaming incisors closed around his trachea before he hit the ice, and the man's startled bellow became a gurgle.

Kiti tightened the grasp on her own spear and hurled herself into the battle. Odlerk was down, thrashing, his right mitt still holding the knife, stabbing in wild arcs at the dog above him. Kiti looked for a body target not dangerous to Nuna, then plunged her spear sideways, under the man's left arm and through his ribs, deep into the place where his evil spirit dwelled. That done, and diving across the dog, she caught Odlerk's right arm and pinned it to the ice, finally kicked the knife far from his fingers.

Struggling for breath, fighting the pain, Kiti watched the man's movements weaken, then cease altogether.

Fighting increased pain brought on by not only the excitement but also the physical effort, Kiti crept around the still form to pull out her spear. She watched blood follow it from the wound to darken the ice and freeze. Blood bubbled also from the neck, around Nuna's teeth, dribbled from the mouth. But then the woman frowned as she realized that Nuna herself lay motionless across the chest of the downed man. Dark splotches were blackening her pale fur.

Kiti knelt to encircle the dog's middle and tug gently.

"This matter is concluded," she told the big dog, but the creature did not respond.

"Come!" The white dog twitched and quivered as Kiti loosened the teeth from Odlerk's neck and pulled Nuna away from what was clearly nothing but the husk of a brutal Inuk. Kiti leaned over to inspect the man. His throat was torn open, and the now-bloody mole hairs rested across it were crystallizing as she watched.

Resulting from Nuna's attack, the spirits of this man might have been soaring even before Kiti thrust her spear. She hoped not. She wanted to—no, she *needed* to be part of his finish.

Nuna collapsed beside her, sank to the ice when Kiti released her grip to run back to the sled for a robe. This, she worked under the dog, then brought up the edges for warmth. She pulled small bladders from her hunting bag, got out certain summer moss and from a neat birdskin packet some web material to press into the dog's wounds. These would stop the blood and soothe the pain.

"If only . . ." she spoke gently, but the dog did not respond, shallow breath rasping high in her throat.

When Kiti finished doing all she knew to do, she found her own body quaking. She was grateful that Arajik had subsided, was aware that the infant was at the top of the *amaut* again, taking in all that was happening, and for once without sound.

Kiti went over to Ajak, the small blizzard, and lifted that valiant little body now limp and spiritless, cooling rapidly. She carried the pup back to the team, laid her gently on the ice, then herself sank down onto the sled and wept for the first time she could remember. The speckled snowstorm had resembled her dam not only in having a tender heart. She also had her mother's fierce loyalty, the instinct to protect at any cost—but sadly without Nuna's restraint born of experience. Kiti removed her mitts. She rested her left hand on Ajak while she gasped for breath around the anguish of her ribs and straining lungs.

After a short time, the girl realized that she must mourn the pup later—possibly mourn Nuna as well—but not until they were safely on the trail. For that matter, she had never taken time to grieve about her own mother, about Pichikoot—but that loss was not the same, for Pichikut had not gone far. Or at least not for long. Right now, though, Kiti must plot for the survival of her remaining family. She grasped her ear lobe with a bare right hand and rubbed slowly.

Think, she told herself. Go step by step without mistake. . . .

Where had the two men gone after building the new igloo? Why did Odlerk come back alone with the full team? Where was Tonratu at this moment? Why, for that matter, would those two dare to be away when she returned from fishing? Would they not know that she would take what was hers and run? Or perhaps they thought her so simple as to welcome their destruction of her inferior igloo and replacement with such a grand structure? Thought her so bland as to be undisturbed by their heavy-handedness with her belongings? Or . . . they were secure in knowledge that they could catch her whenever they wished—again like a fox with a lemming.

Kiti got up, loaded the sled, then circled the team around so that the *upluk* was close to Nuna. She placed another blanket over the now-unconscious dog. It would be far better for Nuna's recuperation—assuming that mending was possible—if they could stay right here. But she dared not remain unless . . . kill Tonratu if and when he appeared?

That she had helped the dog slay Odlerk gave her no conscious distress, at least not yet. But the idea of causing more human bloodshed deliberately—even with the memory and abiding pain connected with this man's obscene assault during the sleeptime—such behavior was beyond her.

Odlerk had indicated that neither man knew her father Narluk. If she could believe him—and the creature seemed too doltish to be cunning—Odlerk by himself had planned to take her back to ingratiate himself with the *angakok*. With increased certainty, Kiti believed that if Narluk required destruction for Arajik, and possibly serious retribution for the father's wayward daughter, he would undertake the job himself. Maybe—most unlikely—he would charge her brothers with such a task of family honor.

But it was unthinkable that he would commission strangers—she was now quite sure—regardless of his wrath. And certainly he would not delegate such men as these. In fact, men like Tonratu and Odlerk would not be tolerated long by any village that she had ever known or could imagine. Very likely, both were banished Inuit who happened by chance to meet on the trail, merge their teams and supplies. Two together on a winter trail could travel more safely. This explanation of casual meeting accounted for their lack of agreement on practically everything. And miscreants like these were never welcomed anywhere.

No wonder Odlerk decided to bestow personally a great favor on Narluk. Such a powerful *angakok* could perform large service, and Odlerk meant to obligate him. But no, she could not picture Narluk entering alliance with either of these scoundrels.

After lifting Nuna up and onto the sled, Kiti hovered over her gingerly not only to observe the dog but also to assess Kiti's own condition. The cage of bones protecting her chest was sending out sharp signals. Don't lift. . . . Don't draw breath deeply.

She placed her eyelid above the dog's nostrils. Nothing. Kiti removed her left mitt, touched with her warm hand the dog's cold nose, then the closed eyes. Spasms jerked the long legs suddenly. Nuna was not dead, not yet.

"Only breathe, take air in deeply, then push it out." Kiti in sympathy inhaled slowly, long and painfully. Breathe. At last she perceived the slightest increase in movement of the dog's chest. Shallow respiration, one ragged breath drawn and then released.

"Now another," she urged as she herself forced herself to make a long inhalation.

The girl got up, replaced her mittens. She had devised a plan that must be executed quickly. Hidden behind some ice ridge or hummock nearby, Tonratu might be watching the camp at this very moment. First she went into the new snowhouse and there cut an empty bladder into strips. Why had she not thought of this before? Then she removed her clothing and wrapped the bands tightly, tucking in the ends. Drawing breath still hurt, but the supporting bands let her move more easily.

Now she went outside to organize and pack and lash her sled. She would bring out more food packets if time allowed— including Odlerk's share. She built up a new, secure *upluk*, a big nest near the antler hand-grips so that she could keep watch over Nuna on the trail. On this circling of robes she managed with great struggle to drag up once again the fur hides containing the gravely injured dog. Should Tonratu suddenly appear, the sled could now go. A warning moan or howl from even one dog, and she would bolt.

Now for her plan, Kiti's Plan—this time not Pichikut's—one remaining all-important set of tasks. She hurried back into the snowhouse and searched through every bag and pouch, collected all the harness and sled strapping, every heavy sinew—anything that could be tied or knotted. She emptied out one of the sturdy hide bags containing Tonratu's food. Into this, she stuffed every thong collected. Now she dragged the bag outside, stopping only to replace the ice block door. Tonratu—if he returned—would have great need for what remained inside.

She left the bag with straps and harness open on the ice while she dashed over to the strangers' team. Out from a parka pocket came her sharp skinning knife. Moving from dog to dog, she cut away the neck strap and released each beast. She hauled all the lines over to the open bag, then dragged that bag out to the lead.

"Eh, Sedna—see what someone offers!" She upended the bag and dropped all contents into the black water.

Several among the freed dogs had by now bounded off to disappear inland. Most milled aimlessly about, and these she ordered away—chased them and shouted, threatened them with her whip. Confused, they scattered reluctantly. It happens that *kringmerk* know food comes only from those they serve, she reflected. They will return.

At her own sled, she stroked Nuna's head and spoke to her while she checked the injuries once more. No fresh blood came from the webbed wounds. She would not move the dog from these warm robes unless necessary. Nuna must, however, endure the jouncing of the moving sled. The dog still did not respond to Kiti's touch or tone. The breaths were more frequent now, seemed regular but still too shallow, and the dog felt warmer to the touch of a bare hand, even seemed more relaxed. Or are Kiti's hopes becoming palpable in false perceptions?

At last, the girl looked around her. Spirit lights rippled softly, a bright violet strip surging and fading at the base. Did she have time to drag out and tie on more food? One or two of the men's robes would not be amiss, she decided. Odlerk had no further need for robes. And it was Odlerk's knife which caused Nuna to require separate space and extra warmth.

Kiti remembered the tense words and black glances exchanged so often between the two men. She wondered once again if Tonratu were even still alive. She decided that he was not likely to be spying on the camp. If so, he would have intervened when she destroyed the trace lines.

He would have to walk from wherever he was in order to get here. And if or when he returned, he would find Odlerk dead—at least missing, if a sea bear had come. Until he arrived here, the man had no means for transportation. Ah! Should she take time also to drag the sled out to drop for Sedna? But Tonratu could go nowhere without harness. She would make one more retrieval trip into the igloo, then move out slowly on the trail to give Nuna as much ease as possible.

At last, she crawled up through the tunnel dragging behind her two robes wrapped around a little more food. Here in this place were food, shelter, and warmth enough for Tonratu. He had tools and weapons. He could remain until just before the ice broke up in spring. For now, his dogs were scattered. But most—those that did not starve or fall prey to predators—would surely return. Still, without team harness, Tonratu would have no way to follow and harass Kiti, at least not anytime soon. His trailing her on foot would be futile. He was cruel but not stupid.

Her own team became restless. They peered off to the south, in the direction from which Odlerk had arrived. Did new travelers approach? Not likely, for whoever or whatever came this way did not move rapidly or the dogs would show alarm. Tonratu? Yes, perhaps a man walking.

Kiti signaled, and they started smoothly. Arajik had fallen back into the deep hood long ago, was silent in the warm little nest of his *amaut* . . . Arajik. . . .

Kiti's breath caught in her throat. Ai-ee-ee . . . Nuna must not die. How could she have overlooked something so important? Arajik still depended on the dog for milk—had to have Nuna's milk, did he not? The girl fought the trembling which jolted her suddenly. She set her jaw, drew herself up, coiled the whip, forced both hands down to grasp the antlers. Was this baby old enough to live on solid food?

Probably not, at fewer than three moons. He had enjoyed the fatty mash of *oomingmak* she warmed for him while Tuk was in her camp—but perhaps more for the warmth and mess than any bits he swallowed. Then Kiti consoled herself. Pichikut would surely help him adapt to what they had. And Arajik's mother was fortunate in the hunt!

Chapter 28.
Terminus

They hissed north on sea ice with no actual sleep times, only short rest breaks. The tight bands had relieved some pain from motion, and Kiti had learned to inhale slowly and with care. Twice, she had stopped to start a fire so that she could offer Arajik a warmed gruel of pounded flesh and fat. The first time, he had accepted a few bites, then howled to join Nuna. The second, he had turned away utterly. Perhaps he would eat when he became sufficiently hungry. . . .

But he did not. Even if Nuna lived, Kiti realized now, her milk would be gone. And if Kiti was forced to stop to find food for the team—and even if she had good fortune in the hunt—they still must find a village soon. Someplace with a woman—or even with another gentle bitch, she supposed—one lactating for pups. Kiti must move steadily, not taking time to hunt unless they became truly desperate—for Arajik must have milk. . . .

As they skimmed a trail on sea ice, the young woman set priorities. For now and until they found people, Kiti herself must become strong or all was lost. She did not, however, require great amounts of food. Nuna must have steady provision to speed her recovery. Arajik was paramount, of course. Could Kiti masticate and liquefy solid food for the baby? Feed him like a small wolf? Would he accept such an offering?

It was after five nearly sleepless nights on the trail that the impact of what she had done finally filtered through her anxiety about Arajik, her distress over Ajak, her continuing worry about Nuna . . . and her own abiding pain. Kiti realized gradually that she had left more than small Ajak back on the ice. For she had now, with Nuna, deliberately destroyed a living creature, a human—at least, that had been her intent; probably the fact, she together with Nuna—and done the deed for reasons other than to capture food.

So where was the horror she should feel? Where the terror of his dispossessed and angry spirits wandering on the ice? Instead, she felt so . . . very . . . blank. Like a fog-filled spring day when sky and land on every side were blended grey and featureless.

But yes, she would do it again. Given the same circumstance, she would take a human life without regard. Indeed yes. . . . She would sleep as well at night as ever. Her present insomnia was connected to physical pain and anxiety about the future, not about her recent deed. . . How could this be? She raised her face high to the rippling spirit lights and shrieked. "Ai-ee-ee-ee!! And then again, long and quavering, "Ai-ai-ai-ee-EE-ee-EE!"

The howl bounced off nearby pressure ridges, off hummocks and coastal rocks. Coming to her ears as echoes, the sound was of a solitary seabird. A powerful, predatory creature that kills to keep its family and itself alive.

The blackness overhead reflected Kiti's prospects. The sled hissed north and slightly east. Nuna lay unconscious but alive. Kiti forced food into her each day by opening the dog's mouth and placing seal fat and then chewed meat far back on her tongue, then softly rubbing her throat to get the swallowing response. At the very first, Nuna still had a little milk. Kiti found that she could take it from her nipples gently, then give it to Arajik. But now the dog had nothing in those glands which had been generous for so long.

If Nuna regained health, she would be able to offer Arajik only affection and protection. The baby rejected solid food, even though Kiti carefully pre-chewed the bits of muskox and seal she tried to feed him. He drank more than usual of the melted ice and saliva she had previously given him to cut the richness of canine milk.

But nothing satisfied the little one; and although he seemed always to be hungry, he consumed very little. His eyes sank back into his head and lost their luster. The pads on his cheeks dissolved. He no longer shouted and laughed or—lately—made any sound at all except sometimes a hopeless hiccup that wounded Kiti's soul.

She rested the dogs every few hours, then continued north . . . north . . . north to Pichikut's people? She traveled on the smoother sea ice, on *tuwak*, for Nuna's sake and for speed and to save the dogs' feet as well as her sled runners. But she kept as close to shore as possible and peered until her eyes ached—always inland through eternal darkness to sight a village.

She must find some friendly snowhouse glow. But she had seen not even one village on the long trip since she left home except for that silent Dead Village on the ice. Not that she had been looking for one until now. Not that she would not have gone out of her way in order to avoid a village—until now.

For the first time since seeing Narluk and her brothers and calling up the storm, Kiti was haunted by doubt about the wisdom of her travel. Would she ever find her mother's islands? Did they still exist? Where were the villages she should be seeing along the coast? How far north had she gone? How much of "north" remained? Perhaps no one lived at the top of the world anymore.

She realized that, going along the coast this way, she would see snowhouses—if at all—only if people had not built on the far side of a rise protecting them from sea winds and seasonal tides . . . only if lamps were lit . . . only if air were sufficiently free of fog and mist . . . and of course, only if the village were there. . . . Or was she blindly passing all the people?

Owka! No. Her mother's Coastal Inupiat were somewhere still to the north and east. She had to believe that, or she would cease to struggle.

Except for what little remained of food saved back for Arajik and Nuna, her provision was gone. Desperate at last, she stopped her journey to hunt. But she found no *aglu*. No fish came to her line. If Pichikut's people—some people—did not soon appear, her trip would be ended.

Sometimes, while she rested her ribs and mustered energy to think beyond the moment, she remembered the pride-filled young woman of a moon ago who, after a few successes on the trail, was certain that she was now independent. Was positive that she needed no one's help. True, two or three could starve as easily as one where no food was to be found. Also true, decisions were made faster with one alone and no need to discuss or compromise.

Quicker decisions—yes, but not necessarily better ones. The spirits within, Kiti realized now, grow dreary in their own company sleep after sleep and moon after moon in solitude.

She drove right through most storms. Or if winds were too fierce, all including Kiti herself would dig into some drift on the lee side of a hummock and wait until the violence was spent. On one run, a ferocious northerly swept in a layer of frozen fog that burned the face and scoured the eyes, peeling back the lids. She lost all sense of direction. Progress was impossible. She could easily drive her team and herself into the sea.

Kiti veered to land and had the great luck of finding a fair-sized cave. It was so large that she brought the team in, too, before she ice-blocked the opening. They slept—all of them together. She remembered awakening only once, aware that the air was warm but stale. She got up to plunge her snow knife through chinking at the opening to give the cave a nostril. She remembered satisfaction with the *whoo-oo-oosh* of air exchange. Then, because it was so quiet and because she was so weary and ached so badly, she returned to her robes. She did not remember covering herself.

When she awoke much later, the team was refreshed and ready for the trail. Nuna breathed more easily after rest without motion. But Arajik's eyes were even more deeply settled into his small face. Kiti tried a warm mash of herbs and water, but the boy abandoned it after one taste. How long they had slept in the cave, she did not know.

Outdoors once again, and into the darkness of another winter day. Mud and ice the runners. Return to the smoother sea trail. Run north by northeast, parallel to what now passed for the coast. Stop. Food for Nuna. Create something appetizing to offer Arajik. Liquid. Rest briefly. Hunt . . . unsuccessfully . . . always unsuccessfully.

North again—north by northeast. Darkness. Stop. Food for the two fortunate ones. Try, try to get Arajik to eat. Darkness, always and abiding darkness. The roiling spirit lights no longer provided comfort, seemed bleak and impersonal, far removed from her world of cold and hunger, everlasting dark and uncertainty.

She loped ahead of the team to break trail on new snowfall, and she tried to remember the sun. A great burning ball—yes, and she must imagine it above her, lighting this unbroken trail. When the real sun returned near the end of the season, where would she be? And where Arajik? No, she must think of something else.

Hunt—hunt. Capture something, anything . . . at least some fish for the team. But nothing, nothing. . . . Move on.

North by northeast, as the coast moved. The food saved back for her brother and Nuna was finally finished. She could try those honored two on seal oil—she still had plenty of that golden fuel, largely because she seldom lit the lamp. She would happily give over her bladders of oil for one frozen fish right now. . . . A single char would keep Nuna alive for a long time—and Arajik, too, if he would swallow it. Neither the dogs nor she had eaten for more sleeps than she could remember. Was it important? She had no appetite, anymore, but chill was in the very juices of her bone.

And in this second time of great hunger in her short life, she noticed growing lethargy, found herself caring about nothing much, doing automatically whatever must be done—and later doubting its necessity.

Should she stop and stay until hunting became successful? But what if no food existed in this place and at this time—then what? Every moment spent on anything other than discovering a village—any village!—gave fading Arajik that much less opportunity for survival and put all the rest of them at ever greater risk. So no, don't stop, not yet. Not until the dogs began to die? Or until she herself expired. Here was surely one of those decisions better made by several people.

The time for dying arrived in less than half another moon. How could she have been so foolish as to think that her team and its driver could go forever without nourishment? She tried to find shelter on land. But wind had scoured the plains clear of snow, and she could not take the sled across permafrost to find a cave. So she stayed on sea ice. There, on the side of a pressure ridge, she found snow right for building a snowhouse and energy to help each dog dig in separately. She staked them well apart, for they were so ravenous by now that they could no longer be trusted near each other unless harnessed, pulling and supervised.

Nuna was finally conscious but weak as hoarfrost, unable to so much as lift her head. Certainly she had no milk for Arajik. And Arajik—increasingly fragile and listless, existing on water and a gruel warmed in Kiti's mouth—steadfastly turned away when Kiti spoke to him.

The girl barricaded Nuna inside the igloo whenever she left to hunt, for the dog was helpless to protect herself if a predator came by or even if one of the starving sled dogs slipped a collar and attacked. Nuna was, in fact, totally inactive—and therefore the only creature in the camp, animal or human, still in good flesh.

Kiti stayed on ice to hunt. She took Iyarpok first, then two other dogs one by one, to search out seal holes, *aglu*. They dragged along beside her—hungry, resentful, dispirited. How could she explain to them that finding a seal hole might mean an end to the gnawing in their bellies?

At last, she abandoned the idea of taking dogs. She would rest a few hours, then go out with the baby in her *amaut*. Repeat the process. She fished through ice, later tried to bait them while she tottered directly at the lead; but nothing found her hook. She walked in an aching crouch to locate a seal hole. The dogs could smell them, if they would. But they refused to try, and her own nose revealed nothing.

Now, as hours and sleeps passed endlessly, she once again began to see odd things. A wolverine peered at her around an ice hummock, and she grasped her spear and automatically moved toward him. She would by now savor his flesh, as would the dogs—stink and all. Out he came, but not to attack. Rather, he was harnessed with two more of his kind to a splendid sled all carved of ice and glistening in moonlight, the spirit lights reflected in dazzling colors.

Kiti's brain told her that what she saw did not exist. But her eyes and ears and nose told her that this was real. When she smelled the odor—with that very nose which gave no help in finding *aglu*—she actually perceived the rank scent given off and had a difficult time accepting that nothing at all was there.

On another hunt, a gigantic white bear came from nowhere to tower above her. He was so large that her spear thrust upward from where she stood would not even reach his stomach. She stared at him, awed by his size and stunned to silence. Then as she stared at the furry white mountain overshadowing her, its head suddenly elongated and was drawn up into the sky, the body swooshing after, like a deflating bladder. She laughed, and the sound of her laughter frightened her as the bear had not.

The time came when she could do no more. Kiti's energy was gone. She expended monumental effort to bring the ice block into her snowhouse doorway one last time. She uncovered Arajik's face from the robe and looked down at him. Would he have been better served if left on the hillside where Narluk placed him? But she remembered his laughter, his new joy following each sleep.

"Owka, that was not the time for a babe to die," she told him. "It happens that this is his finish, and Kiti's as well."

Perhaps it was another strange vision among those which had her seeing *kapvik* harnessed to grand sleds and the great white sea bear *nanuk* turned to liquid draining into the sky. But there in the dim snowhouse, using her seal oil in volume for the first time since fleeing Tonratu, her small brother's eyes seemed to hold more vitality than she had seen for days.

"Eh, a daughter has done what she can, and Pichikut knows this to be so," she told the bright spirit peering from Arajik's face.

Then the girl patted Nuna and made sure that all the robes were tucked in snugly. Next, she poured into the travel lamp as much seal oil as it would hold. "Ee-ee, we shall close our eyes to a friendly glow," she announced. Then she lay down and clutched Arajik to her, brought the remaining robes around them, put her right arm up to rest at the notch of her ear. She closed her eyes. Here was a finish, then, to this last block in the igloo of their lives.

Chapter 29.
Epiphany

Kiti choked on a thick, warm liquid that dribbled down her throat. She coughed to bring it up, then swallowed. Somewhat salty, but delicious. Too weary to open her eyes, she nevertheless heard unfamiliar voices chattering familiar words. The sound filled her with a leisurely, disconnected sense of well-being. Again liquid touched her lips, and this time she sipped with enthusiasm. Laughter, more sound. She floated in a cozy broth of contentment.

Gradually, after many sips of the thick soup, she began to track meaning in the words floating about her. When she heard baby, she came alert.

She heard a pleasant female voice ask, "Arajik? The child?!"

She tried to look about her, but a great rock rested on her head and kept it pressed with disobedient eyes against the furs within which she lay. How could someone know her brother's name?

Laughter, chuckles of delight. "The woman awakens!" echoed around her in different voices. Here were the good people sounds that she had yearned to hear and now remembered from the past. Where was she? Someplace comfortable and warm. Finally, a village!? Or perhaps another waking dream? Let it continue, then.

Suddenly, someone's face came close to Kiti's, for she could feel the warmth. "The babe is well. That little one is a ravenous wolf cub!" A woman laughed.

"Arajik," Kiti told the voice without opening her heavy eyelids. "The baby is Arajik."

"Indeed, we know!" The same woman, her voice gentle but filled with laughter, too.

"Nuna? What of Nuna and the team?"

"Eh, *Kringmerk* . . . Dogs . . . And the wounded white bitch?"

"Yes!" Still her eyes would not open. With mighty effort, she brought her right hand up to touch her ear.

"A treasured creature. All have seen her strong spirit. It happens that a village son has taken her to nurse to health. Already, she walks."

Kiti sighed in relief. She wondered if she herself could walk—not likely, not with this boulder lying on her head. "The other dogs?"

"—Are well . . . nine?"

With effort, Kiti raised her eyebrows, Yes. Incredibly, her team had survived!

"—And all becoming fat on walrus meat."

Walrus. . . . Kiti's mouth watered. She had eaten walrus flesh but once before, and remembered it as rivaling even whale *muktuk*. The blubber and ocean meats were usually not available to people inland; but her brothers traded on the trail for those thick walrus hides that they could split for making harness and sled lashing, could twist and braid for whips. Sometimes, a bit of meat was included in the exchange.

"The broth that someone served," Kiti said later, "so good. . . . What?"

No hesitation. "Blood."

Kiti came alert. Narluk always said that blood was best to bring back any Inuit near death. And Pichikut always boasted that her people kept it frozen all winter for emergencies.

With great labor, Kiti gradually opened her eyes enough to be half-blinded by the lamplit walls that arched above her. It was a relief to let the lids fall back. Others were in the igloo, for she heard the talk and enjoyed the cadence of her mother's Coastal Inupiaq. But no one had been standing nearby.

"Please? Someone?!" The woman who had been feeding her returned, for the girl recognized her smell. "How long has Kiti been in this place?"

Laughter. Rapid talk to others. "She wants to know how long she's been with us!"

"Tell her our children have all grown and learned to hunt since she arrived!"

More laughter. Warm, caring . . . comforting.

Then the woman's voice came from directly above her. "Ten sleeps—"

"—Ten!"

A chuckle. "Ten for villagers, but all one sleep time for the starved, exhausted visitor who lies here."

More merriment from others in the snowhouse. Kiti tried to rise but fell back feebly.

"Hoo-oo!" the woman chided. "Someone must give her spirits time to gather."

Near tears, Kiti slowly raised her eyebrows, Yes. "Arajik? Where?"

"Here!" The boy's face was brought down close to hers, and she heard his laughter and delight as he recognized her. She opened her eyes to slits once more. His cheek pads were back, and the glimmer was in his eyes. Held upended as he was, he dripped saliva on her face. He jabbered at her, and the sound was music.

She smiled, felt the corners of her mouth turn up before she surrendered once again to the weight that pressed her head and pushed against her eyelids.

"Someone is awake?" The broth woman introduced herself as Pusik. "Three young women, here, have babies of their own."

Kiti smiled. Here was good news, but she could not remember why.

"Continually, they argue over which among them is to feed this new child."

"Hoo-oo!" Arajik. Arguing was not good news. Were the mothers short of milk, then? Kiti's mind was misting.

"Each wants him at her breast many times each day!"

Good news after all. Kiti smiled. Good news . . . good news . . . good. . . .

Later, she awoke and drank more of the warm soup, even swallowed a few more bites of flesh offered. This time, her eyes would open and her mind felt clear, although her arm was too heavy when she tried to lift it. She looked over, and Arajik lay asleep on it. She heard an argument among women somewhere in the snowhouse. Not bitter, for they were laughing, and their tones were low.

She listened. Yes, the words were those of all Inupiat, but the tongue was exceptionally far back in the throat like . . . Tuk's . . . and similar to her mother!

She opened her eyes. "We are on ice islands?"

The woman Pusik was still nearby. "Owka, No. The edge of land, but not yet the thick ice that floats."

Kiti let herself sink back. At least, Arajik, she and even Nuna were somewhere—and in the care of compassionate people. For now, only those facts were important.

Again, she raised her brows. "Nakorami," Thank you. "The people of this village are kind." She closed her eyes, drifted off once again.

Later, "A son from our village told us, Kiti is precious." Pusik laughed. "That's why he took us out on ice to search for her when she did not appear."

"This same village son who has Nuna," said an unfamiliar voice.

"Yes," several agreed.

"And it was he who brought the people to rescue those dying on the ice."

"Yes . . . the brave young traveler named Tuk."

But Kiti was asleep.

Pusik stood looking at the dry, sunken face of her patient. She wondered if she with the others could feed and love this skeleton of a female back to the grace and dignity Tuk said she once possessed.

Chapter 30.
Walrus

Kiti dipped her paddle timidly, then again. For several summers, she had used kayaks to seek out likely fishing spots on inland waterways. This ocean water seemed more resistant than the familiar fresh water, so that she went farther with each stroke, but that appeared to be the main difference. That and knowledge that she was paddling on top of Sedna's nearly bottomless salt sea.

This small craft she'd taken from the silent village fit her still-emaciated body especially well. She had wrapped a soft fur inside, around her feet and legs. Her hunting bag, she had thrust down into the stern of the hide-covered boat.

Low fog layered above the water in moonlight, but—so long as she stayed close—she had no trouble following the others in the swirling afterpath. She had no intention of being left behind.

She experimented to see how quickly her little boat responded, found it obedient as a friendly, half-bright dog. She had insisted on going out with the village hunters for walrus, the giant *aiverk* of the floes. Some suggested that she ride with her harpoon in the *umiak*, the rounded, larger and more stable boat that the broad-chested harpooners used. A sturdy boat without a rudder which would be used later to tow the walrus catch to ice.

But she was indignant. The men patronized her, indulged her as if she were fragile. But she was strong and healthy, these days, rapidly regaining lost padding—and bustling with her old energy. Even the troublesome ribs had eased. And she was restless, too, from so much time spent in the village.

She had built her own snowhouse and made it comfortable for Arajik and herself. And for Nuna when she might finally be returned. But Kiti had practiced quite enough of household chores. Most of the time, she even managed to keep a lamp going. In fact, she had done for far too long the woman things with which she still had small patience.

Nuna? People said she remained with Tuk and was recuperating. Him, she heard of frequently but had not seen until today on this hunt and at a distance. She was distressed that he had not come to speak.

In the argument about her going on the hunt, Pusik spoke up for her. "Two other women, as well, take part in this hunt. And both in kayaks!"

Grumbling by a few men. Old Anjuk, the self-proclaimed village expert on *aiverk* capture, declared that women—any women—would make the whole hunt futile. "Spirits of the big bulls are insulted to be sought by a female," he declared loudly. And annoyingly, Kiti thought, even though the smooth-jawed, toothless fellow had been nothing but kind to her on other matters.

Fortunately, Anjuk was the accepted authority on walrus but not on spirits. So thanks to Pusik and the two widows customarily permitted to hunt with the men, Kiti was here. She wouldn't be, if anyone knew she had never before dipped a paddle in salt water. The people assumed that because she carried a kayak by the sea, she possessed the skill to use it there.

A half-inflated seal skin was fastened to her harpoon line and rested on the back of the craft. The harpoon itself lay on top along one side, at the ready, her spear along the other side. Except that her kayak was smaller, it looked like the others. Her hood was empty, for once. Arajik was at the village in the care of his milk mothers. He was the friendly favorite in the village, partial to Kiti but welcoming to all.

Kiti expected to be equal to whatever must be done during this hunt. And so long as she managed not to disgrace herself, she would at last be earning some of the vast amounts of food given so generously to her and her dogs. For more than a moon, now, she chafed at being dependent when she was capable of securing her own food if creatures were available.

And may the clever daughter be successful in the hunt . . . Eh, spirits of Pichikut, come near to help Kiti now. . . .

The paddlers closed on a cluster of floes in an unusually broad portion of lead northeast of the village. Anjuk with two other hunters reported last night before the sleep that these low ice ledges were floating in together. And that the men had heard conversational barks of *aiverk* bulls echoing back and forth among the islets.

"That means the sun will soon return," Pusik assured Kiti when they heard about the walruses. And for Kiti, that meant she might not make it to the ice islands before the village had moved inland.

Kiti did not know what the presence of walrus had to do with the end of winter, but she was certain to enjoy both. As so often before, she tried to remember that bright globe in the sky, not only the look of it and its brightness on land and water and the sharp shadows it engendered—but also the smell and feel of its warmth on her nose and cheeks and chin, its heat on the fur of her parka.

And now once again, Kiti had strong arms which could use the double-blade bone oar on first one side, then the other, to make her kayak dance lightly on surface ripples. Moonlight filtered through light cloud cover to brighten the mist that swirled in the lead. It dazzled her eyes as she peered through the churning paths to stay with other hunters.

She swiveled her head to pick out craft around her, then suddenly bumped to a stop. The bow of her kayak had come against a floe. And peering at her wild-eyed was its walrus inhabitant. The two stared at each other in mutual astonishment. Then the huge beast bellowed, and Kiti back-paddled to get clearance for a turn. As she pivoted, she saw the creature lunge into water and come for her. She dug her paddle in deeply, trying to keep her eyes on the walrus behind as well as the water ahead. He was gaining.

Terror brought vast power to her strokes, but the animal pursuing her was better fitted for the sea—and angry besides, as evident. He was but half a kayak's length behind when Kiti made a decision and veered to another floe nearby. Just before her bow rammed it, she jerked back with all her weight and gave a mighty pull on the paddle. The small craft leapt up onto ice and slid fully from the water before it tipped sideways on its rounded hull. She looked back in time to see the walrus swerve away and start back to his fellows, evidently satisfied with merely chasing the interloper from the water. Then she spilled from the hatch.

She stood up and looked around. Well, here she was—high and dry and oh so very safe. . . . Her first walrus hunt, and did she lift her harpoon? Did she thrust out with even the smaller spear? Oh no, she merely managed to irritate one of the huge beasts, then race away like a *kussuyok*, a coward. She hoped that she could refloat her craft without anyone knowing she'd paddled herself right out of the sea.

She saw no kayak in water nearby. But through the bright mist swirling, as she looked in the direction of sudden sound, she saw that she was sharing this much larger floe with a clustered colony of *aiverk*. Gradually, she made out the dark forms huddled well across from her, barely visible in the fog, at least ten kayak lengths away.

They appeared to be disturbed by action in the lead nearest them. They complained with grunts and neighs, an occasional fierce bellow. Perhaps they as well were vexed about her presence. They must have felt the bump through the ice as she bounced up into their territory.

Then, while she watched, some person walked among them. An upright figure, a hunter from the village. The grumbles and bellows increased. And then she heard a sharp howl, and the figure went down. Kiti grasped her spear in one hand, her harpoon in the other, and raced toward the herd. The seal float attached by a long line to the head of her harpoon trailed after her, snagging and bouncing along the ice.

She took a moment to find the hunter before she waded into the herd. The animals were pressed together so closely that she finally jumped onto one broad back and then another, dropped down to ice in a clear place, then leapt back onto another beast. The creatures grumbled, but a walrus is cumbersome. She moved so fast that their angry twists and lunges occurred after she was gone.

Now she stood in the middle of the herd with one *kamik* atop the back of one beast, the other on the haunch of another, and both animals packed so tightly together with their companions that they could do nothing in protest but grunt and cough.

Before her was a huge bull. And in front of him—down on the ice—rolled the hunter she had seen.

Kiti lifted her harpoon as high as she could. "Grandfather, help!" Then she jumped onto the beast and thrust the stone head into the killing spot, following through on the plunge with her whole body. The tip imbedded deeply, separated as it was meant to do, and Kiti scrambled to get clear of the great bellowing creature as it pushed past the downed hunter to flop to the water in agitation. The bull dived and swam. The attached sealskin float, snagging and popping across walrus backs, followed wildly until it bounced down to zag along the surface of the sea.

Kiti looked to the hunter fallen on ice. A young bull with red eyes rolling was making for him now, and she raised her killing spear and struck him behind and slightly above the right flipper. Blood bloomed on him and then onto ice, and the beast made no more effort to reach the man.

Walruses near the lead were sliding into the sea, but perhaps thirty creatures remained in the big herd, most milling frantically and grunting with frustration while they tried to separate themselves from each other.

Kiti pulled her spear from the smaller bull, which now lay motionless. She lifted the weapon high and thrust it deep into the ice, so that it stood upright. The harpoon shaft lay behind her. She bent to the groaning hunter. He managed to stand when Kiti pulled his left arm across her shoulders and stood up. He was not safe here among the disturbed herd. She half-dragged him rapidly as possible through and around and occasionally across the shifting beasts.

When they were clear, she lowered him to sit on ice. Then she looked for damage. His right arm hung useless within a torn parka sleeve—a mortal accident, had he been alone, for he would freeze.

"Cold. . . . So cold!" he quaked.

"Yes . . . wait here," she told him. He'd be cold not only from wind coming through his ripped furs but also from the shock of being wounded and in pain. Back at her kayak, she snatched the lap robe from the hull, raced back. She tucked the big fur under and around him snugly.

"Someone will come," she promised him, then loped toward the herd, her weapons, and the open lead. Perhaps she could hail a paddler out there in the water. At least twenty walruses remained clustered on the floe, bellowing and annoyed, all seeming to tangle themselves further as they tried to separate, their confusion blocking her path. She picked up her spear and thrust it at first one and then another of the largest and therefore most formidable of the beasts, and finally at any creature who lay with its killing spot visible.

She felt invincible, as if no hooking tusk or flailing flipper could reach her. She leaped back and forth among the creatures, thrusting and then pulling her spear, springing lightly away to thrust again.

At last, those walruses still alive were in the sea, plunging noisily but then diving down with grace to disappear. Only silence came to Kiti's ears. She walked to the edge of the lead, waited until a kayak appeared in the mist, then waved her spear high in the air.

"Please help!" she shouted, and in only moments, not one but two craft drew up to the floe. She steadied the bow of the first while the paddler pulled himself onto the ice. Then she tugged the light boat up from the sea while the first helped the other get out. She noticed a motionless walrus lashed and floating beyond the stern.

"A hunter is wounded," she explained, looking over to the place where she had left the man. But he limped toward them now, her robe wrapped closely around his tunic.

He peered at everyone. "Not badly hurt," he assured his rescuers. The two men hurried over, unwrapped the robe, examined what they could see of the bloody arm. "This clumsy *Inuk* slipped and fell," he apologized with embarrassment evident on his wry features.

Kiti raised her eyebrows as she walked up. She knew how easily someone could slip, for the ice all around was fouled with walrus feces. Besides, had she herself not managed to fall at the seal cliff where only a few creatures rested? And the mellow seal could not be compared with a worried walrus.

One of the paddlers looked here and there at motionless beasts scattered about. "Ai-ee! That Inuk gave a good account of himself before he went down!"

"Eh?" asked the wounded man. He peered around him— rapidly at first, then slowly with disbelief. He shrugged, turned to frown at Kiti, his mouth falling open.

The other paddler started back for his craft. "This man goes to find the *umiak*." The big boat would be needed for the injured hunter and also for lashing up and towing carcasses, once the large animals were hauled to water's edge.

The wounded man spoke with a deep rumble of consonants far back in his throat, each syllable coming out slowly. "It happens that someone fell even before his weapon could be used. What is visible on this ice gave itself to the woman."

Stunned silence followed his words as the two newcomers took in more carefully the scene of carnage.

Kiti grew uncomfortable, and she picked up her spear and the shaft of her harpoon to start back for her own kayak. Then she paused. "The huge bull that caused the trouble—" and she pointed with her chin to the wounded man—"is somewhere in the lead with a float attached."

Chapter 31.
Aftermath

She could feel an awkward silence surrounding her. People of the village visited in hushed tones with each other—but not with her—as they gathered around fourteen walruses laid out respectfully on the ice. Enough to feed everyone for the rest of the winter. And food to cache and for the summer journey inland, too. Hide for *kamik* soles and lashing to be used in years to come.

Even the most generous of lamp legends would not dare to describe such a feat. Anjuk gave a ceremony of thanks. He laid for a few minutes his mittened right hand on each beast, one by one, starting with the smallest cow and working up to the great bull long as any one-hatch kayak, the beast which had wounded the hunter. Before the old man removed his hand, he gave a brisk rub on the forward haunch.

"This fine creature left the water for air and for close mingling with its kind," he murmured, "then delivered itself to capture by a village which had need." When each animal in turn had received his touch, Anjuk looked up.

"We thank all the noble creatures and their ocean queen Sedna for these great gifts."

Kiti had tasted walrus meat only the one time before recently having it almost daily at the village here. She had heard, of course, but never before today seen a live one. Now she watched as the old man removed one forward flipper of each. He called out the name of the hunter who had speared the beast and gave to that person what he had cut away. Kiti decided that the right front flipper must be considered the choice portion. The remainder of each beast, save a symbolic organ or two, would probably go to families in the village according to their need.

The second name called was Tuk, and she flushed with unexpected pride as he went forward to claim the heavy prize. After a woman of the village was called to claim the fifth flipper, Kiti heard her own name. She went forward and dragged back a flipper almost as heavy as herself.

But then her name was called again. And again. When Anjuk grated out her name once more, Kiti hurried over to Pusik, begging her to come along.

"Owka," No, that woman said. "It happens that Kiti must do this thing alone." The girl thought her friend eyed her strangely.

Kiti was called nine times. She was flustered and embarrassed and exhausted when she had a mountain of walrus flippers piled around her. This ritual complete, the people of the village chattered and laughed happily among themselves while loading their sleds high with steaming meat as it was cut.

But silence surrounded Kiti. No one included her in their delight. What had she done wrong? The flippers alone were too much for her small sled, not counting flesh and blubber brought over as her share and now accumulating on the ice as the careful butchering progressed. What she had here was far too heavy for her small team, but no one offered help. The meat would go to Pusik anyway; for it was with Pusik and her husband Itok that Kiti continued to take her meals.

But those two were happily intent on getting their own walrus loaded. Kiti watched sleds leaving one by one.

She wanted to hug Tuk when he came to her after most of the heaped up sleds had hissed off across smooth *tuwak* toward the village.

He looked at her sad eyes and grinned, but she could see that he was uneasy. "The woman hunter shamed the men, today. It happens that the village has a convoluted knot to disentangle."

Kiti only stared at him, still dazed by rejection from people so friendly before. "Eh?"

"Anjuk was humiliated most of all," Tuk explained, "and yet, no one could wish to be without what was captured by the fierce woman hunter."

"Someone did not intend—" Kiti began, then broke off and tried again. "Tuk would have captured as many," she insisted, knowing it to be true, "surely even more, had he been in that place and time and circumstance."

"Perhaps . . . but Tuk was not!" he said softly, "nor was any other, only Kiti. A mysterious matter."

"Mysterious? The people think . . . " The woman's voice trailed off. She looked around. All but Tuk and she were gone and she could speak freely. "They think Kiti is some violent trail spirit? Not possible. . . . The people plucked this woman from the ice when she was close to death."

"Yes, near death. Not dead."

"And had they not brought her to their homes, had they not warmed and nourished—"

"—Eh, they do not fear Kiti. They know that she feels kindly toward them. But they are awed in the presence of what is thought to be—what they think is—!" This time, Tuk had to leave his thought unfinished.

Kiti smiled uncertainly, shook her head. "If they could know how very human is the stranger in their midst!"

Tuk studied her with no expression she could read. After silence, he continued. "A thing noticed. In Kiti's presence, five seals upon a rock were taken. By two hunters? Unusual indeed!"

"But they—" Kiti began.

"—And does someone recall a time when two inexperienced hunters could not capture the powerful musk oxen in a group? And then the creatures happened to go away?" He laughed. "And it happened that another of the creatures—only one—stood nearby and anxious to give itself."

"—But an outcast male of any grazing kind often stays near—"

Impatiently, "—Perhaps . . . Eh, *ahmi*. . . . Who can say what wonders will yet occur?"

Kiti was silent.

"Some women hunt," Tuk continued on the way back, "and the villagers accept this. Unlike some places, perhaps because of our young widows, Tuk's village allows women to use the spear."

"Truly, for none among grown women in Kiti's old village are encouraged to accompany—"

"—Allow someone to finish while the thought is on the trail. . . . Some women know the motions in the hunt, are even useful in the group. Then rarely, some one female wins the smile of fate. This one becomes the female hunter not often seen but heard about in legends."

"It happens that Kiti often enjoys success in the hunt," he added.

This she knew without his saying, had known for a long time . . . except of course when her luck ran out, as recently. . . . Hoo-oo, but a happy fate did not desert her, she thought now. Was she not rescued in the end? And with Arajik, Nuna, and all her team surviving?

"Yes, good fortune in many ways." He repeated, laughing, now more at ease simply from their exchange. "The beasts on land come to Kiti's spear, now also *puyee*, the great sea creatures. Yet this young Kiti was born of inland Inupiat. Here, surely, is another riddle with no simple resolution."

The girl stood tall, her right mitt brushing the ear within her parka. She studied the steady eyes of her friend. "Only know," she told him now, "that Kiti is no trail spirit."

He did not speak as he turned to help her heap and lash the flippers onto her small sled. He loaded separately upon his own her share of walrus hide, meat and blubber. And with no further conversation, they urged their teams forward to the village.

Chapter 32.
Feast

A special igloo was built for a feast to celebrate success in the walrus hunt. Everyone in the village attended, as did travelers invited as they passed through. A village only one sleep away to the south was also summoned to join the merriment and share the food. All would meet in a large newly-built snowhouse where five seal oil lamps cast upon the arching walls the shadows of human activity.

Outside, Kiti watched the blanket toss—youngsters in their *silipaks*, faces peering out through furry *nuilak*. The children resembled bright plovers as they tumbled and swooped gracefully above the taut, tightly sewn and hand-held skins which sent them vaulting into the sky. They shrieked with excitement as one by one they soared, competing with each other in the number and intricacy of acrobatics they could complete before gravity claimed them.

Kiti listened to the drum duel going on for so much of this special day. Two young men, antagonists from the village, worked out their differences with dance and drum and clever poetry chanted or sung—the creative breath of Inupiat. Village spectators would judge on the basis of their performances who in the ring was innocent, who guilty—to what extent and with what punishment meted to the one found culpable.

But although the process was familiar, Kiti did not know the people or the issues. She was excited and didn't want to miss anything, outdoors or in. She went over to watch the wrestlers. . . . Here were two good-natured opponents pitting speed and strength and cunning to determine which would forfeit the competition by finally losing balance, stumbling or even possibly falling. She stayed for three matches. Rapt, she finally succumbed to deepening cold, to rising wind and beguiling sounds and shadows from within the special snowhouse.

Now Kiti sat inside on a robe with Pusik and her husband Itok along with Tuk. As her body warmed and adjusted to the figures and chaotic sound, she reflected on what she had already seen. Certainly, she had attended such celebratory feasts at home.

But this was different. Unlike her own small village composed of older people, young couples with children lived in this larger hamlet so that running and shouting were a part of every moment. And the high spirits of children were infectious.

Too, drummers at the duel seemed wittier here. The wrestlers seemed stronger and more skilled as they courteously circled in the snow ring to find a single grasp to cause that one all-important misstep by the opponent. Or did Kiti imagine more vitality in this place to avoid yearning for her own home and more familiar faces?

Inside, she saw interposed between lamp and wall upon white arches all around her the outlines of fully animated creatures fashioned by agile fingers. The figures so produced swayed and gesticulated, every move attended by laughter as the hand shadows of different people interacted, the creators vocalizing spontaneous dialogue back and forth as they proceeded.

Sitting cross-legged on robes, people with other flashing fingers also manipulated intricate string figures—sometimes with accompanying words that brought "Ai-ee!" from appreciative spectators.

Mimics in the laughing games seemed funnier than those at home, somehow; their masks and those of dancers, too, more intricate than she remembered, more colorful than she had seen before.

Ah, not homesick. She realized that she was truly comfortable in this place. She felt as if she instead of Tuk had grown up here.

When he returned without parents, the village had adopted him, despite his age—and he belonged to every family, now, received their warmth and hospitality, their love.

He lived alone by his own choice, his igloo somewhat distanced from the others. He continued to be inseparable from Nuna as she slowly healed, and he reported her progress to Kiti.

But families argued over who would get to have Tuk enjoy a meal with them. Women vied with each other as to who would mend his clothing and check his *kamik* daily to be certain no seam leaked.

Young women in the village were especially affable. Kiti often saw him emerge after the sleep from one or another snow-house not his own. She still wondered what he would be like as a partner on the *iglerk*. But she always pushed the thought away.

Remember Tonratu, she would tell herself and touch her still-tender left rib cage. Would *kaoyak* ever again be other than appalling to her? So unfair, she scolded herself. Comparing Tuk to Tonratu is like comparing Nuna to a wolverine.

Pusik and then old Anjuk himself had eventually told her their versions of the reason people left her alone on the ice that day of the walrus hunt. They corroborated Tuk's guess. A newcomer, after all—who knew but that she might be not Inuit but some palpable strong spirit? It was Tuk, they informed her, who did his best to still their fears. But Kiti knew that even Tuk had been wary. Was he still?

She understood his hesitation. He remembered her emerging not only from the sea where she had fallen but also, after the storm, from the cavity of the seal. And now after the walrus hunt, he must wonder about her in his solitary musings . . . if any of his sleeps were ever solitary.

But here at the feast, half a moon after the taking of walrus, everyone was friendly. They seemed to recall only the largesse resulting from her spear.

Kiti wondered about leaving here and starting north again when Nuna could take the trail. Pusik had already suggested that she join this village permanently, and she was tempted. Arajik was well loved—and Kiti felt at home.

Now Tuk beside her at the feast jostled her elbow for attention, then pointed with his chin at two young women kneeling on heavy bearskin, arms across each other's shoulders, mouths fitted against each other.

"*Katajak*," he told Kiti. Throat throb.

By ignoring crowd noise, Kiti was able to pick out snatches of the gasping, bubbly sound they emitted. Produced were percussive, tuneless wind songs when each used her own breath to play upon the voice box of the other. Kiti had heard from her mother about this kind of music created in the high northeast. Pichikut had tried to describe it, but how?

Now Kiti found herself mesmerized by the pulsing sound unlike any she had ever heard before. No wonder Pichikut had difficulty explaining, for the timbre and the tones were alien and hypnotic.

"They practice for the woman-changing game to come," Tuk told her.

She knew this game; for her own village finished off a feast in the same way. Gatherings like this followed a hugely successful hunt. Truly large feasts might even last for several days and sleeps. But few adults slept. At the very end, late or soon, all village lamps would finally be extinguished as ongoing Great Sound commenced.

The sustained background at home was drum beat or an oldster's wailing chant.

Here, this haunting *katajak*. Always a continuing and repeated cadence pounding rhythm into the life-blood of all who heard it. By contrast and used often here in Pichikut's northeast, so *Ananak* had promised her daughter, was this wild throat throbbing Kiti saw and heard now in rehearsal.

When *katajak* started up and during the hours it continued, every married and unmarried female whose moon cycles had started—at least all those who wished to play—would be chosen and chased by some unidentified man or nubile boy. The impromptu pairs would hurry off in darkness to some *iglerk* in some snow-house—it did not matter whose.

Never knowing who the partner had been provided magic. So said the pleased participants. At home, Kiti herself had played the changing games only twice. And while she remembered the delicious mystery of a partner unknown at the time and forever unidentified, she would not participate on this night.

She planned to roll up in a robe on a far corner of her *iglerk*, as would the children here, throughout the extended time of continuing laughter and frenzy.

Kiti realized suddenly that Tuk was watching her. She stretched out her arms, yawned. "It happens that someone grows weary," she told him.

Disappointment crossed his face. Then, "A story comes soon. Kiti will wish to hear it, for it is the tale of a powerful huntress."

But Kiti was not thinking about hunting or storytelling. One day, she would need to have experience once again of a man who was not violent. Tuk? She removed her mittens, drew her hands across her face, rubbed her ear lobe. She found it to be very warm in this place.

"Ss-ss-ss!" The crowd grew silent. Everyone moved back to let the storyteller be active as necessary and visible to all. In came an old man Kiti did not recognize. Laugh furrows stretched down from the outer edge of each eye and disappeared beneath the circle of each cheek. His parka was trimmed with insets of different color, and the furs of his *silipak* rolled and draped when he walked.

"He is Kanerk," Pusik murmured aside to Kiti, "from a village nearby. His tales are cunning."

Chapter 33.
Legend

The storyteller lowered himself onto a white bear pelt, then built suspense as he took time to smooth out his parka and then his trousers, looking around and flashing droll expressions at the audience. A helper handed him a small drum, a moon of tautly-stretched hide well stained with oils from use.

He put the beater on his lap and started with his strong bare fingers a tentative rhythm on the rim, soon settling into a regular cadence. The snowhouse went silent as the *katajak* ceased. He gave no word or look to signify his commencing, seemed to be talking to himself. But his voice rose up deep as storm gale pounding waves against cliffs. . . .

"Chikut, for that name was spoken at the moment of her birth, entered this world as the scrawny, half-starved child of an old mother and even older father. This baby was for them the only glory in their miserable lives. The mother was a friendly crone but never clever in the ways of sustenance. Her lamp wick always flickered. The robes she cured shed pelt-hair handfuls at a time. The fur boots she sewed lapped up water like a sled dog under summer sun.

"Oh, she worked hard enough. But what she did hardly ever worked!

"Yet, she was a miracle of success when compared with her husband. Old Munkut was a hunter, of course, and he did indeed hunt like the others—but alas, he did not find. Seals in winter abandoned their breathing holes forever when they saw his shadow on the ice. Whales postponed their spring trip south if Munkut awaited them. Caribou at summer's end changed migration patterns when they learned the man was present."

"Hoo-oo. . . . Ai-ee-ee!" breathed the listeners, as if the story were new to them. Kiti knew she hadn't heard this tale before. But a strange restlessness grew in her as Kanerk continued.

"Chikut was a gaunt little girl with dark eyes and a runny nose. At eleven winters, she decided that she had listened to her belly groan for long enough. She spied upon the village hunters. She watched them handle dogs, observed the ways they captured food.

"Using the weapons Munkut made so beautifully and used so poorly, she went out alone to hunt with a small bone-and-sinew sled and a ragtag team of outcast *kringmerk*. She found herself successful."

With as many bends and lateral wanderings as a child lost on trackless tundra, the tale centered around a hot spring beneath a prairie sinkhole. And around Koloki, the water serpent which the spring contained. Chikut drank from this pool each day before she started on her solitary search for food.

She even washed herself in the aromatic liquid which spit steam into the cold air . . . water warmed by the fiery center of the earth. Here was a phenomenon Kiti had heard talked about but which no one professed ever to have seen.

"Villagers were curious. One who followed her reported. 'This has someone witnessed. . . . Before each hunt and after, the child goes to a strange smoking pool, removes her clothing–'

"'—Takes off her furs!'—the listeners interrupted—'in winter?!'

—And there she steps into the steaming pool!' the speaker finished.

"'She . . . no! Deliberately moistens her body?'

"—Not moistens—wets. . . . The child immerses herself from head to foot--

"'In water!?' The one to report such a spectacle must have been undergoing raptures of the trail. 'Immerses!?'"

Thus went the dozen voices as they gossiped. For none listening to the storyteller had ever had a bath beyond the time of birth—nor known of anyone who had. Hand fishing streams in summertime—walking into hip-high depths—they would get dampened in the process. But deliberately to remove the rich oils from the skin—and especially in the winter. . . . How could someone stay warm?"

The story continued with Kiti now listening closely. Chikut. Pichikut. This youngster, Kanerk said, fascinated from the start the hot spring serpent named Koloki.

"As years passed, the scrawny child hunter became a graceful maiden. The village men grew too old to hunt and perhaps a little lazy. They depended more and more on Chikut, each dark winter, to supply food and also hides to make robes and clothing.

"Throughout this time, the serpent took many forms and did great deeds first to protect the youngster and then as a young woman to attract her. In the end, the serpent spirit chose to take human form permanently—for this shape once chosen could not be reversed.

"He wooed and won her when he became a handsome and mysterious *angakok*. Together, the mystic huntress and the sorcerer left the ice islands at the top of the world to go south inland for their new life. Neither was heard from again."

Kanerk the storyteller looked around at people and flicked his eyebrows. The tale was told. He got to his feet, folded the white bear skin with dignity—and left the feasting house. Only as he got down to crawl out through the tunnel did people free themselves from his spell to stamp their feet and clap their hands and shout his name, "Kanerk . . . Kanerk!"

Astonished since halfway through the story, Kiti turned to Tuk. She had trouble keeping her voice steady. "Where would

Kanerk learn this tale?" Tuk must forgive her asking so directly.

The young man shrugged. "Where does any storyteller? 'On the wind,' or so it's said." Then silence. Soon now would come the songs with woman-changing, Kiti knew.

She turned to Pusik. "Does it happen that someone knows where a storyteller got the tale he told?"

"Most times, no. They come from the fogs of distant days. But this one Kanerk related is not so old. It is said to have started in a village to the north."

"How far north?!" Kiti demanded, exasperated, then remembered herself. "Someone would like to know the trail time."

The older woman's eyes narrowed as she turned her face to Kiti. "Too far to visit easily. The legend comes from ice isles which float upon the sea."

"Can it happen that someone here will instruct Kiti on how to reach this place?"

"Perhaps some other from further to the north and east." Pusik shrugged. "Only a tale—" she laughed, "—for who could possibly believe such a strange account?"

Kiti startled both companions when she stood up abruptly. *"Nakorami,"* Thank You, she smiled and abruptly left the feast.

Chapter 34.
North

Later, her hands trembled as she trimmed now-frozen permafrost spread across her sled runners. The only child of older parents? A lucky hunter? Later married to *angakok*? A combination of facts . . . surely more than mere coincidence. Plus of course the remnant of a name . . . Chikut.

The snowhouse lamps went out and the *katajak*, the wind song, throbbed and burned in the dry air, sweeping out across the snow and up to join and pulse with flowing spirit lights overhead. Kiti tensed when she saw Tuk approach, his eyes narrowing at what she was doing.

"Can it be that someone plans to travel?" he asked as she started the layer of ice.

"Ee-ee." Yes. She spat and then rubbed vigorously with the furry tail of a white fox. Here was the perfect rub, presented to her by Anjuk as a peace offering after the walrus hunt.

"A village wishes to have Kiti stay with them," Tuk told her. Then, softly, "Tuk wishes her to stay, as well."

Kiti sensed a new note in his voice, and she felt a warm response within herself. Perhaps it was the rush and blow of the wind song pervading all. The girl stopped her work and turned to him.

"It happens that Arajik can take flesh for his meals, now," she told him. Arajik was weaned, thriving on a mushy version of Kiti's own daily fare. "A woman must take the baby and go north to find a certain village," she told him. Tears sprang to her eyes and strangled her voice.

Tuk waited silently and without expression until she could speak further.

She dropped the water bladder and the fox tail, let the sled slide to the snow. Then she put an arm on each of Tuk's shoulders. She swallowed, found her throat constricted, swallowed once again.

"Kiti's mother was named Pichikut," she was finally able to say. "Perhaps Chikut? A hunter woman from ice islands far north who left her home to marry *angakok*." She paused, bit her lip. "Kanerk's story is surely about her."

Tuk brought additional food for her sled, Nuna limping behind him. "Twice has Kiti known deep hunger on the trail. It is not good to tempt the hunger-beast too often."

The girl looked longingly at Nuna, then harnessed Iyarpok as lead. Her big white dog would have to stay. When villagers rescued them, that dog was near death. Too far gone to worry about, they thought. But Tuk had quietly taken her to his own igloo. At first, he used his intuition and the simple remedies of his people. Later, with Kiti's help, he ministered to the dog from the girl's supply of herbs and what seemed to him her amazing knowledge of shaman lore.

Knowledge which he now and suddenly understood. And although Nuna was recovering from the grave wounds made by Odlerk's knife, she was not yet fit for the trail.

Certainly not strong enough to pull a sled. Now that maternal responsibilities were past, she would be content on the trail as nothing less than leader. Her heart was ready, but not her body. She could not yet thrash Iyarpok. He would kill her. Besides, the valiant white dog looked as if she might be readying herself to produce a new family.

Her voice nearly a whisper, "Is it possible that Tuk can keep the white dog safe until he comes north to visit or until Kiti returns?"

His face split into a broad grin. "Ee-ee, and someone will take this for an invitation."

Kiti smiled. "Naturally."

Kiti said brief but warm farewell and *"Nakorami,"* Thank you, to the villagers, then started north that very night, with Arajik and the team. Soon, the sun would actually begin to show rather than send the moments of pale glow they now welcomed daily on the south horizon. No one she asked could say how long her trail would take. Smiling, humming, running along without effort as if born by the hefty south wind *Nigituk*, Tuk with his own sled dogs and Nuna accompanied Kiti for two sleeps.

"Remember—if someone allows it, Tuk will go north all the way," he kept reminding her.

Kiti could not invite him, for she knew this to be her journey, hers and Arajik's, as pledged to Pichikut. Who could predict what awaited them? And who knew if she would ever find the village? Who knew if the place still existed? *Ahmi.* Who can know the future?

By day, they loped along beside their sleds or when necessary took turns breaking trail for the teams. Then before the sleep time, after a meal, they sometimes talked. The ice wall that had separated them was thawing, becoming more translucent. Perhaps if the events involving Odlerk and Tonratu had not occurred, Kiti thought, she would by now be speaking freely to him. She had earlier done him grave injustice, she knew now with certainty, for Tuk would not—could not!—deliberately deceive.

Yet, here she was—and here he was—and her tongue still frozen in her mouth. Hiding behind that thawing wall were not only her own domestic situation but also the recent experience with Tonratu and with her father's self-appointed emissary. And Kiti has killed a man.

The woman reminded herself continually that Narluk had not ever sent those two to find her. But their appearance meant that her flight might be so widely known that others like them might yet appear. For all such matters were talked about if known. News was a blizzard borne by strong gales as it traveled among villages and across the tundra.

All right, Narluk would never set such violent strangers upon his daughter. But who could say what conduct others might take upon themselves?

Hoo-oo, so much had happened. . . . Now, besides her family misdeeds, she had killed a man. She found it impossible to disclose such an intensely personal matter to Tuk or to anyone. He knew the pup Ajak to be gone, but he thought she had starved. Just as he still thought Arajik was Kiti's own. If Tuk knew her truly, would he not turn his face away?

Yet Kiti's brain kept pestering, even though she trusted the man completely. Does Tuk know Narluk?! He knew of Kiti's village. How could he not know the shaman? On their last night together on the trail, she mentioned the name.

"Narluk? *Ee-ee,* it is Tuk's great pleasure to have met the great inland *angakok* and his two sons as well."

Kiti stiffened.

But Tuk's face was without guile as she studied him in camp-light, and his words were open. "When his family died," Tuk said, "the son believed his own spirits would soon flee. He built a stone cache above the bodies, then stayed by it to await the Snow-walker for himself."

"How frightened someone must have been!" Kiti sympathized. No one feared death, of course; but only the very old might wish to die alone.

"Tuk fed the dogs and starved himself," he laughed. "No reason to waste food on someone who is soon to perish. Then after several sleeps, it was evident that Tuk's spirits were in no hurry to depart. By then, little food remained. So someone searched the tundra but without success."

"The man was distracted," Kiti observed aloud, "and mostly it is small creatures that are easily found inland after winter comes."

"It happened that the family of Tuk had been waiting for hard snowfall so that their teams could take them home. When snow cover came, finally, the winter season was well advanced. But now only Tuk remained, and he dared not go to any village. He sought out and spoke only to hunters he met upon the trail—and even so kept distance from them, always downwind."

"When Tuk found a village," Kiti asked curiously, "he dared not enter?"

"He must not take illness to them, and it was not possible to keep the friendly people from coming close."

"Yes." Kiti understood.

"But by inquiring of hunters near villages, Tuk was able to find the shaman Narluk."

The girl shuddered. Why had he never before admitted that he saw her father?

Hoo-oo-oo. . . . How was he to know that Narluk was her father? Nor did he know now.

Tuk did not sense her uneasiness. "The great *angakok*." Tuk chuckled. "Imagine. . . . Here is this young stranger on the trail. He walks up—but not too close—to the huge shaman others extol. He asks—artfully, of course—'How long must someone wait to die?'" Tuk laughed.

Kiti smiled in courtesy, although she was too preoccupied to grasp the humor, then waited for him to collect himself. "And Narluk responded."

"He said, 'A person waits throughout his life for death.' Truly, this was his answer, for he knew nothing of the circumstance." Tuk was still chuckling.

That sounded like her father. Kiti's lips twitched. "And then someone explained."

Tuk shrugged, raised his eyebrows, Yes. "Then the great *angakok* asked how many sleeps since someone had buried his family."

"And Tuk knew." Kiti herself knew something about sickness brought to Inuk from Sedna's strange dog-people who sailed in their huge *kamik* to take whales from the sunrise sea.

"Sixteen," Tuk remembered.

"Narluk used this information." Kiti was pleased with herself for getting answers without asking questions. She was improving.

"He said he did not know. But he suggested Tuk avoid breath contact with any other person for one full moon more."

"And Tuk did this."

"Yes, but small choice. Someone traveled east by northeast to the coast, a trail never overburdened with people—or with anything else, as it happened. The hunt for food along the way was not successful until this hunter reached the sea . . . captured some seals . . . and found Kiti that first time. Eh, a woman always fortunate in the hunt. Like the girl in Kanerk's story." Then, "A girl who it may happen is like her *ananak*?"

A shiver racked Kiti as she once again heard Pichikut's refrain: "And may the clever girl be successful in the hunt." To Tuk, she said, "And so the meeting with Narluk was before the meeting with Kiti."

Tuk raised his brows for affirmative, then hesitated. "He had observed the woman on one night, true, but not met her, never spoken."

Kiti clenched her jaw. Let him speak of that night once again. She would listen for discrepancies.

Tuk explained. Every hunter he met on the trail directed him to find Narluk for an answer to his question about contagion. At last, he approached the shaman's village deep in the sleep time. Two or perhaps three shadowy rises before he got there, he spied in moonlight a beautiful maiden suckling her child. The woman was accompanied by her guardian spirit, as he then interpreted the scene . . . a huge, ghost-white dog. He chuckled with embarrassment. Nuna, he knew now.

He laughed as he continued his tale. "As someone knows, the view beneath spirit lights can easily mislead. Still, Tuk followed the young mother to the village, saw her harness a team to a sled already loaded, watched her silent departure."

Blustering with a whole new set of questions, Kiti forced herself to wait. Someone may at last be learning patience.

Tuk continued. He had slept all too well that night, awakened tardily. When he got back to the rise overlooking the cluster of igloos, whole family groups—the entire village, as it turned out—were taking the trail. He stopped one sled and then another to inquire of Narluk. All said the same. The village was moving because of death in an unsealed snowhouse. Angakok with his family, though, must have left earlier, south and east, perhaps late in the sleep.

Thus, the young man must go off in search of Narluk once again for information about bad spirits he might carry.

"Following six days of tracking," Tuk continued, "and two of wandering after a storm swept away the tracks—Tuk found first what turned out to be Narluk's sons Oojulit and Pajuk. Finally, the great man himself."

The girl considered. "So it happens, Tuk never did follow Kiti."

Tuk responded to her tacit interrogative. "No. His focus was on *angakok*."

And thus, it was coincidence that he came upon Kiti's camp. She once again wondered if she could believe entirely these earnest assertions.

She wanted to. Her spirit said "Yes!"

But her brain remembered Odlerk and Tonratu. The great white tundra stretched in all directions from her old village. Here on the coast was endless prairie to the west. Saltwater ice swept up and down the shore, stretching far out east to an invisible sea where in some places no lead cut toward shore. Happening to find anyone seemed so unlikely—unless one followed tracks or knew the person's destination in advance.

"After that first meeting, though, her camp became his ultimate goal," Tuk confessed. Then he smiled and lay back in his coverings, pulling the furs up to his nose.

Kiti was pleased. "When sleep time is over on this night, the two great hunters have long but separate trails to follow," she murmured as she curled herself around Arajik in the warm robes.

But still they talked. Quite sure about Nuna's gravid condition, they agreed that the dog should definitely stay with Tuk. Could the new pups be healthy? "Never mind, Nuna has earned her right to have a litter without human intrusion. Kiti will someday collect her."

"And collect Tuk as well, someone wonders," he murmured softly and with great hesitation, as if he feared the response. Kiti rubbed her ear lobe invisibly beneath the covers, smiled, pretended not to hear. He did not repeat his thinly veiled query.

After long silence, giving Tuk plenty of time to have drifted off in slumber, Kiti spoke aloud to the still night and to the spirit of Tuk within it to tell about her mother's death and of the daughter's own responsibility. Voice tight and low, she described The Plan. She did not describe the extent or status of her family, certainly did not mention her brothers or Narluk by name, did not allude to her father's vocation, although she had already laid claim to Kanerk's feast tale.

After even more silence following her saga, a period so long that the girl was certain her companion had slept throughout, he spoke. "Then it happens that Kiti must find the village of her *ananak*." Any promise to someone dying became a sacred pledge from which, of course, no release is possible.

"And does Tuk agree that Arajik is now Kiti's own son?"

"As if the babe emerged from her very loins," Tuk assured her. "*Ee-ma*, absolutely."

Chapter 35.
New Faces

The trail north. Thanks to the walrus hunt and then Tuk, Kiti need not spend her time hunting. Sled runners sizzled on smooth sea ice that cra-acked and groa-n-n-ned nearby and in the distance. The great percussive concert of ice and water were pressure adjustments between tide and land, Kiti knew now—not a result of her presence with team and heavily burdened sled. Over and around ridges they swept, up and across occasional hummocks of hard drift. When clouds or flickering spirit lights permitted the sight, a watery crescent of sun showed on the south horizon for an increasing number of moments in the middle of each day.

Kiti awoke after one sleep to the sound of her staked dogs wailing and the sight of a white sea bear in moonlit silhouette atop the next ridge. The creature stood on all four legs, nose weaving slowly on sinuous neck to test the air. The camp contained a large quantity of food.

The girl rapidly packed and iced her runners, loaded up. Before they left, she put down onto ice the walrus meat and blubber from one big bag. She hoped that Nanuk would know this to be fair. Kiti possessed food and perhaps he did not, right now. But he had far greater ability to secure provision.

Near the end of another day's run north by northeast, Kiti saw the glow of lamplights coming from inside a dozen snowhouses. The village was far, for air was crisp and clear. She decided to feed and rest the dogs. She and they would go in fresh after the sleep.

The next morning, remembering the tale of Chikut and wanting to appear her mother's child, she melted a little snow above the lamp and washed her face and hands. Brr-rr-rr. But in this way had *Ananak* met the world. Such personal cleansing was not something to be done with frequency.

Then she drove into the new village. People crowded around, for hunters had not yet left on their day of foraging, and the rare visitor was a welcome novelty, even or perhaps especially a woman. After introductions, Kiti spoke privately to an old woman hovering nearby.

"It is possible that the people here know the legend of Chikut."

The woman frowned at first, then brightened. "Yes! a visitor means Pich-i-kut!"

"Oh yes!" Kiti breathed.

"The tale is enjoyed—especially because it came originally from a village not so far north."

Always, always north, Kiti thought wearily. "And it may happen, someone in this place will know the trail." A *soospuk* statement, a silly one. For if people knew the village to be not so far north, then certainly someone had been there. And an Inupiat who has ever once been to a place will forever know that location.

The woman laughed, and people gathered. Someone located clean snow and squatted to draw a map. Others made suggestions. In short time, Kiti had the direction clearly in mind.

"A young woman will need to hurry," remarked someone in the group. "People on those ice islands go inland early. It happens that they must cross frozen sea before ice rots."

"—Then return late in the season to be sure *tuwak* is thick," added someone else.

Excited, Kiti took the trail without staying even for a meal. She promised the friendly people that she would stay with them for several sleeps when next they met. Up the coast she went and onto ice that stretched beyond the sight of land, stopping briefly at this village and another, getting reassurance in each place that her destination was not far.

Two hunters came to meet her as she approached a sparkling set of igloos in the still-brief but now dazzling light of mid-day.

"People here may know the legend of Pichikut," Kiti said.

"Ee-ee" with pride. "And of Koloki the frost serpent, as well, for Pichikut was of this place."

The girl grinned with pleasure. "It may happen that this visitor can add some more to the tale." She explained her relationship to the heroine of their people.

The villagers welcomed her and Arajik as highly valued citizens misplaced temporarily and now found. Perhaps we are, Kiti reflected as she used her *ulu* to cut away at her lips a mouthful of *muktuk*. Eh, and—hard to believe!—a welcome change from walrus!

All was flurry in the village as people absorbed the traveler's news while they prepared to go southwest for summer camp. Kiti tried to trade her ubiquitous walrus for seal and whale meat. The whole idea of exchange was alien here, although the concept of giving was strong. So the girl arranged to give walrus meat and split hide, both prized here at the top of the world so late in the season . . . to some who would give her seal meat and *muktuk*.

One woman who exchanged gifts generously was Ertok. Wrinkled and tattooed, a withered little bunny in dirty white fur, she was nevertheless spry as any adolescent, could pace the lead in a fast team. She remembered and was anxious to describe Pichikut as a child. Ertok and her husband Pomakut appointed themselves to accompany Kiti and Arajik with the village on the long trip when it began after two more sleeps. It was on this trail that Kiti had a chance to hear about her mother.

"One remembers that tiny, half-starved child," Ertok told her. "*Ai-ee,* and all who lived then can recall how readily that child found food!"

Pomakut was not so wizened as his wife, and the two were probably not as old as they looked, Kiti suspected. Across the man's head, bare in the snowhouse, were a few strands of what looked like smoke-blackened sinew. His jaw was smooth, and his pleasant face a plump, rosy pad.

He too recalled the remarkable child who finally left the village. "This man who speaks was but a youth," he told her, "a *nukapiak*. At seventeen winters, perhaps fewer than Kiti's age now, he was practicing to become a great hunter. Naturally, he observed the little girl.

"But that tiny Pichikut discouraged everyone. The child would come back with her sled piled high even when the fathers and grandfathers found nothing at all!"

His naked brows rose high as he laughed, then shrugged. "A marvel it was that all the men did not give up entirely!"

"It was said that food creatures flocked to give themselves to her," Ertok added, "and that a tame spirit on the trail made magic only for her."

"Some few uncharitable men blamed her and this spirit helper for their own lack of luck," Pomakut put in, "and said that she took all that was available and left nothing for the rest."

"Still," Ertok said, "no one ever refused what she generously provided to the village."

"Yes, enjoyed their share—and most were properly grateful." Pomakut frowned. Then he added, "Men find it difficult to thank a woman who exceeds them on the trail."

Kiti nodded, remembering the walrus hunt. She understood completely.

"Some tried to accompany her," Ertok remembered, "but she permitted no one to join—"

"—Perhaps she knew, the mighty hunters of the village would be embarrassed," Pomakut went on, "by the amount of game which gave itself over to her spear—"

"—And perhaps she truly did possess a helping spirit," Ertok concluded, "a creature which could be dangerous for others."

"But whether or not a spirit was used, the girl was most fortunate in the hunt!"

Kiti stared at the man. A tremor that started at the neck and shoulders jolted through to her toes. Here again was her *ananak's* assertion expressed so often.

After an awkward silence, Pomakut cleared his throat politely. "Someone wonders if it happens that Kiti—eh . . . hunts?"

"Not successfully enough to stay alive on a recent trip," she replied.

Both Ertok and her husband stared at her and waited for an explanation that Kiti did not supply. She was still trying for herself to piece together what had happened.

"Ye-es, then. She hunts," Pomakut said thoughtfully. "And could someone say that the daughter of Pichikut is fortunate on the trail?"

Another shiver went through Kiti. "*Ee-ee*," Yes, she answered softly, "someone might say that she possesses far more luck than skill."

Pomakut chuckled. He asked Ertok, "Can this be Pichikut's child?" Then he shouted with laughter, so that others looked over and several joined them at their travel lamp. But they spoke no more of Pichikut that night.

On the trail inland to make summer camp, Ertok saw Arajik and a small village boy named Isumak playing with the muskox carved by Tuk. When they abandoned the stone figure, she picked it up and inspected it closely. Smiling, she turned to Kiti. "Pomakut, too, is expert with releasing that which hides within a stone."

And later in the evening, Ertok told her husband, "The *oomingmak* carried by a young woman is done by someone having patience and great skill. . . . Permit an old woman to guess—Kiti's father?"

"*Owka*," No. Kiti could not imagine Narluk even searching for a creature within material someone might give to him—let alone spending time with a knife to release whatever it might be. And his digging at inland stream beds or searching along coastal gravel to find likely minerals was impossible to picture. Patience of this sort was reserved by Narluk for finding special herbs and cuttings with medicinal qualities.

"A brother, then. . . . Does Kiti have brothers?" Personal questions. But Ertok was old enough and Kiti young enough that the woman had certain prerogatives.

Kiti laughed. "The only one who seemed to have such skill—Palunga—is now gone."

"Ah, Kiti does have brothers, then." Ertok was understandably curious about the family of her old acquaintance as well as this new friend. The family beyond Pichikut regarding which Kiti had spoken nothing until now.

The newcomer must not seem to be unfriendly, Kiti chided herself. Slowly, "It happens that someone has had—!" and she hesitated. Should she count Arajik? No, he was now her son. "—five brothers. But only that young one took time to carve."

Ertok frowned. "Someone has had brothers in the past but not—eh. . . . All are left behind her on the barren grounds!"

Why did coastal people—even Tuk—seem to think of inland tundra as grim and hostile—barren? Kiti shrugged. True, she supposed, that all of her brothers were gone. . . . Except for

Arajik . . . and because of Arajik—her family was lost to her. Loss of Pichikut still made her especially sad, and she tried not to think too deeply on that subject. Loss of the three who had disappeared was also painful—particularly, always, the loss of Palunga. This topic of Kiti's family Ertok steered toward repeatedly—while Kiti wished to paddle past without stopping.

To change direction in the conversation, she reached deeply into her parka pocket to draw out the bag of green stones and hand them to the woman.

Ertok peered into the leather pouch, then poured two pieces into her hand. She smiled broadly. "These must come from inland."

"Some are from a place near the stone in which the carved *oomingmak* hid—a steep stream bed where inland tundra meets with coastal plains. Does it happen that a wise woman knows what they are?"

Ertok held the two closer to the travel lamp, and Kiti could see their glow. The promise of a tundra summer lay within each. Hard, dry and sterile, yet green as prairie grass.

"One cannot be certain until a scrape is made in sunlight," Ertok told her, "but they appear to be what the whalers call jade."

"Jade." The girl repeated the unfamiliar word. Was it truly stone or did it only seem so? Kiti was reminded of the partially digested green matter often found in the stomach of captured *tuktu*, caribou. Like that, this material looked delicious, and her mouth watered. Eh, ice island Inupiat like these must rarely taste the long-legged deer, might not know of the belly delicacy.

Yet, Ertok seemed to know about this jade.

"Can one somehow eat it?" Otherwise, it held small value. Far too heavy to make a sled, even if one could find it in such bulk.

Ertok laughed. "*Owka*, only mineral. But strong and beautiful in sunlight. Somewhat hard, useful to make light tools. Often, small but elegant creatures conceal themselves within."

"It happens that Pomakut would like these." Kiti's question was implied.

Slowly, "Ye-es, yes he would. But so would whoever released that muskox."

Ertok was probing, and Kiti chuckled. She tried to think back. Tuk knew nothing of her find at the Silent Village. But had he seen her pick these up on the day they took *oomingmak*? Eh, he was always absorbed in finding likely bits of stone.

The older woman laughed. "And Kiti will not reveal the art-ist? Hoo-oo. . . . *Ungayok!* She must love him!"

Kiti reached up to finger her right ear lobe as she felt her face grow warm. She said no more.

"These stones," and Ertok gently replaced those she held and handed back the soft hide bag, "have value in the making of strong harpoon heads. Also fine amulets, since the stone carves well."

None of those items interested Kiti. But she did retrieve from the pouch two of the largest pieces and hand them over. "For Pomakut," she said.

"*Owka,* No. The gift must come directly from the giver." Ertok smiled. "A girl will give them to him from her hand—perhaps sometime when his spirit is dark and restless."

So went time pleasantly as the village moved off the ice and onto land. Soon they arrived at a place where a decision must be reached. Melting snow cover meant that they must either set up here for summer camp or carry on their backs what they had to have, then cache their sleds along with extra provision for the trip back home at summer's end. Much discussion.

Kiti was amused. When her village looked for straggling caribou in summer, Narluk as shaman told people where to stop. And she as Narluk's daughter knew—but never, ever said, of course—that whatever reason he might give for his decision, camp was always made in places likely to produce the healing herbs he needed.

Following hours of high poetic drama and eloquent sarcasm, the favored methods for discussion, people agreed to stay where they found themselves. An old caribou hide was discovered, and some caves lay above a thawing lake. Were these not auspicious omens? Was this not a hospitable place?

Chapter 36.
Summering

Days turned light and long, some few with brilliant sunshine, many more with cloud cover and slow, drenching rain. All days had wind, soon or late. The black of night got ever shorter until no darkness came at all. Insects swarmed—biting, stinging, each trying to live a full life within its short breeding season. Berries ripened on the blooming, buzzing tundra, and these were gathered mostly by women and children.

Kiti and Ertok turned for home one dazzling afternoon. Young Isumak was with them, a chattering child of three winters who liked to play with Arajik. Kiti's boy, by this time, was asleep in her *amaut* bouncing along on her back. The women's skin bags were stuffed with bearberries and sourberries, and Isumak's broad face was smeared with evidence of liberal sampling.

"Look!" Ertok pointed with nose and chin into a nearby valley they had avoided for fear of deep bog.

Kiti followed the point. An upright figure was there, tall but far too slender for a brown bear. As she watched, the creature took several steps toward them. *Inuk*, human. A head looked in their direction, and arms waved in the air.

"Eh, perhaps a spirit," Ertok muttered.

"Spirit man!" Isumak proclaimed loudly.

Kiti wasn't certain she believed the hunters' tales about walking, talking, visible spirits on the trail. She knew about hallucinations, yes. And she knew from her experience, and certainly from Tuk's, that days and nights of solitude could produce unpredictable raptures within the lonely soul.

But Pichikut always laughed at spirit tales—said they were a man's creation to boast of his bravery. Trail dreams to fill the long, eventless hours and days of isolated hunting in a broad and featureless land.

Such spirit persons, Kiti would have to see for herself in order to believe.

"Someone from the village who left early?" she asked now.

"Owka. Who would go on treacherous marsh alone?"

Kiti knew no one so foolish.

"Spirit, spirit, spirit man, see the spirit man!" Isumak chanted.

The women left the boy with the bags and an enticing pile of berries to eat. Then they walked out toward the stranger. He fell, lay still for a few moments. But as they approached him, he raised himself to hands and knees. Now he staggered up once more to lurch forward.

The women picked a way carefully through the valley marsh. A misstep could mean sinking into deepening muck above permafrost—a cold, messy ooze even in summer. The man had fallen again by the time they reached him. Kiti squatted to turn him so that he did not lie face down in wet ground cover. Ertok helped place him in a sitting position.

"Ergh . . . eh!" said the man, and the women looked at each other. He was long but lean as a clean-picked caribou leg. Stringy, matted hair hung across a broad face covered with scratches and running sores. An angry crimson gash came down the left side of his face from hairline to jaw. His beard was splotchy, louse-infected. His body stank. He wore underfurs only, *illupak*, at least the filthy and torn remains of rabbit and fox skins.

Kiti could see, though, that the cut and arrangement of hide were similar to that which her tundra people made for wearing at all times, under *silipak* and within the igloo and under sleep robes at night. Here was no animal or spirit of the trail—but a human, an *inuk*, and an inland man. . . .

Kiti put one of his arms across her shoulder, waited for

Ertok to do the same. Slowly, the stranger's limp feet dragging and bouncing along the ground between them, they picked their way through the slough to go back for Isumak and the berries.

Then they returned to camp. The man's mouth made strange noises all the while. Sometimes, his legs moved in effort to support the long body. Mostly, they dragged.

After some several days of care, it seemed that the newcomer might live. Since he did not supply a name, they called him Adla, the Stranger. Kiti applied herbs to the sores, and they gradually scabbed and healed. She privately thought, however, that Ertok's thick red soup made the vital difference. The man's eyes cleared. The crust which had encircled them was wiped away and did not return.

But the snowy mist fogging the eyeballs was replaced by a hard, reflecting glare. Adla's eyes rarely blinked. Nor did understandable words pass through the healing lips.

One sunny afternoon, Kiti put Arajik down to sleep on a fur in the shade of the cave mouth. She stayed nearby to brush away mosquitoes and the triangle flies which stung so painfully. Everyone in the village was gone except for her, Arajik and Adla the Stranger. Some hunters were out to search for caribou. Most children and women looked for berries. All others hand fished at a stream which fed the lake.

The baby dozed, and Kiti herself was half asleep in sunshine.

Suddenly, something sharp poked her back, and she sat up, instantly vigilant.

"Agh-rr-rr!" said the Stranger, lurching around her. He was completely naked. "See the wild one!" he said then, in perfectly understandable Inupiaq. Familiar speech . . . in a familiar voice? She shook her head to clear the odd illusion. Of course his pronunciation was familiar; for unlike the others here, other than she herself, he was of the inland tundra.

His eyes glared as he waved what Kiti recognized to be her own spear. She gazed at him sternly, since the jab had hurt. It had certainly torn her light *illupak*, and the small wound was probably bleeding. His eyes seemed to bounce when they left her—to sky and cave entrance, to the lake below.

Finally, they fell upon the baby. He raised the spear, and Kiti shot up.

"See the savage stranger capture food!" he told her, and he drew the weapon higher.

Kiti crashed against him, easily knocking him down. She pulled her spear from his weak grasp, then forced herself to speak soothingly. "The man must be gentle with a child," she told him. "And he must let Kiti help him back to his robes."

He was limp and listless as she hoisted his slight weight. Tears flowed from his eyes. "*Issumariyungnaerpok,*" Forgive . . . forgive, he murmured all the way back to the cave where he had been. He slept for the rest of the day and through the night, not rousing for a meal.

"He must be washed," Kiti declared to Ertok and Pomakut. The two women had fashioned for Adla a complete new set of underwear, *illupak* prepared and recently constructed from hare and weasel trapped inland. They were now planning *silipak* and *kamik*, outer garments and boots, so that Adla could strongly meet the coming snows. Summer was passing. Although sunshine remained generous, a chill haunted the air. Cold rains came more frequently, and only last night did sleet ride the wind.

Ertok finally agreed that Adla should not put on even his new *illupak* until he looked and smelled better.

"But how can he get clean?" Ertok wondered aloud. "He is asked to accompany the villagers for fishing, but he ignores the invitation."

Kiti dug into her hunting bag for certain herbs. Some, she had collected this summer from tundra soils and grasses. "It happens that this can go into his food," she said as she used her pestle in Arajik's bowl to crush fleshy stems.

Ertok watched with interest, then awe, finally with fear. "Kiti is *angakok*?"

The girl laughed. "Kiti is a dabbler, a cook," she told her friend. "This will go into some of Ertok's good soup heating in the sun. Adla will sleep well on this day."

That late afternoon, people returned from fishing and hung their gutted catch on bone drying racks. Adla lay in the sun at the opening to his small cave, asleep and snoring raggedly. Ertok and Kiti stripped the rags from his frail body and bathed him with warm water. Kiti saw on his chest and thigh more of the puckered red scars, these also on his left side. She rubbed a frothing herb on the man's face, and Pomakut used his sharpest knife to shave away the thin, vermin-infested beard. He did such a good job that Kiti begged him to trim and comb out the man's head and pubic hair, as well.

"Perhaps the biting creatures will leave if their nests are disturbed."

"He's young!" Pomakut exclaimed as he finished. For everyone had thought the stranger to be wizened with age. Dirt and matted hair removed, only scars and unhealed wounds remained on face and body.

"Hardly more than a boy," Ertok agreed. "Surely not more than twenty-five winters."

"Such serious injuries," Pomakut remarked, "might be from struggle with a bear."

Kiti said nothing, but she stared at the man with foreboding. Here was no hoary elder having confused thoughts. When healthy and strong, this man could wreak damage. She had never spoken of the spear attack from half a moon ago. Something else. Something about this Adla was familiar. She tried to imagine him without sores and scars.

The three of them—with Isumak and even small Arajik helping—plucked and snapped remaining lice from the scant hair upon the body. At last, the light new clothing was pulled over the bony limbs and rib-lined torso. They laid him on a clean robe. The other robe, they scraped and brushed and then hung out beyond the reach of dogs on a rack to bake in sunshine. Adla would surely be astonished when he awakened in the morning. He smelled much better, and no great number of flies swarmed around him.

But if Adla noticed the change, he gave no indication. From the day after his cleaning, though, the man's appetite improved as did his physical health. He ate ravenously, and flesh began to pad his skin. Strength developed. He spoke Inupiaq clearly and distinctly but not sensibly.

Sometimes he smiled. Those who saw the smile looked around to find a reason. The expression itself was more grimace, as if the corners of his mouth were attached by sinew which was lifted or lowered by some alien whim. The strange glare in Adla's eyes did not fade. Nor did he seem to notice anything or anyone in particular.

He responded only to what he saw as obstacles to progress when he walked through the camp. With no word of displeasure, he would kick out viciously at anyone or anything in his path. He showed no interest in going out with hunters, although he ate with gusto the good freshwater fish and occasional caribou that everyone contributed.

Sagak was the wise one of the village. He was not very old, being still a vigorous hunter. But he was a thoughtful *Inuk* from youth, so Ertok explained, and people tended to listen when he spoke. "We shall give this youth our food and time, also tender care," Sagak said. "One has observed this illness in the past—always by solitary Inuit found wandering on ice or tundra. His enraptured spirits are starved and frozen. Let them feed and thaw."

Others were content to feed the stranger, to smile and try to talk with him. Still, as sleep times passed and then another moon, they grew discouraged and might have given up.

"Nothing is lonelier than a human spirit encircled by a season of empty horizons," Sagak reassured everyone. "His soul is badly bruised, and time is required to blot the discolor."

Chapter 37.
Reunion

For Tuk, an odd summer followed a peculiar spring. Food creatures were generous that year, especially those of the sea, so that his village stayed not far from the coast. Small herds of caribou drifted north and—never completely predictable—actually moved east for calving.

People erected furry tents, often to extend a cave dug into a hill, always high on rolling prairie, to stay above the streams and rivulets that appeared above the permafrost during frequent and sometimes heavy rains of this season. People and their dogs tried to avoid the soggy inland tundra and bottomless bogs.

Tuk and a few others settled inland with Nuna and his dogs, but only far enough from the ocean to escape the mighty summer tides. Yet, they could easily tramp to shore—since sleds and teams were useless without snow and ice—and search out seal or walrus. These big mammals love to sunbathe in summer and let warm beams scour saltwater lice from their hides. On shore, they also enjoy safety from the insatiable black-and-white whales that cooperate in packs to tumble them from floes.

During low tide, kayaks went out day and night in endless light for fish to fatten new caches that for once could be conveniently located. Sometimes in the sea, someone spied a solitary tusked narwhal or even a mighty bowhead tardy in migration. Then came great excitement, and if the tide were right a launching of *umiaks*—the slow but sturdy, rudderless boats of thick hide.

Rarely was one of the huge mammals captured, in fact none

that summer, but anticipation and imagination lent magic to each sighting.

From a high coastal rock, Tuk watched a broad lead nearby where a herd of twelve spotted white narwhal dived. Their graceful, wraithlike forms danced down to disappear in clear green water. Much later, when he thought he had somehow missed their return, he saw a great cloud of ocean cod come boiling up ahead of the narwhals.

The fish leaped clear before flopping back motionless to the surface. Cod lose consciousness when herded rapidly from great depths. Not only the herding spear-toothed narwhals but also seals and birds—jaegers and shrieking gulls—fed greedily on the fish before sense returned and survivors could dive to safety.

Tuk was restless. Energy crackled through his body, and he seldom slept. When the summer village first appeared, the bachelor hut he built backed onto a shallow, broad-mouthed cave. From this base careened hides draped on whalebone. Space enough for half a dozen people, or so the others teased him.

Much rain fell in summer. How was the young man to keep collected water from collapsing his roof?

"Hoo-oo. . . . Someone plans to hold a drum-feast day and night."

"Does it happen that this Tuk will surprise the village with a family previously hidden?! Much tittering followed that question, for people believed Tuk and Kiti with Arajik to be a likely unit.

He laughed with his friends good-naturedly and looked at the vast shelter. Yes, he realized suddenly. A family was badly needed here.

"Eh, Nuna," he told the dog where others could hear, "come live with Tuk a while. Actually, she bore six pups soon after the camp was established. And she did bring her litter inside. There, with this trusted temporary master, the little ones were dry during downpours and swirling gray mists, then at other times protected from relentless, endless blinding sun.

Food was easy now—berries, fish, small creatures from the prairie, all in addition to what came from the sea. Tuk went out with village hunters and was successful. So successful that on most days he did not hunt. Fish swarmed the rivers, and everyone waded in to spear them, ate the smaller ones or fed them to the dogs, then helped with drying the largest fish as a buffer against the long winter to come.

But nothing truly satisfied Tuk. Extra energy continued to course through him. He knew that Kiti for some unknown reason kept and prized the carved muskox he had freed from rock. Therefore, his seal oil lamp, every manner of bowl, certainly each weapon and utensil he owned became enhanced by his art. The crudely-stitched rawhides of his lean-to carried outline pictures from the hunt, and these were much admired.

Even so, as spring passed and summer moved to its zenith, the ground all around his hut was strewn with finished, useless and therefore discarded separate carvings of stone or bone.

And he remembered how much Kiti liked those slitted spectacles made of soft, what she called "friendly" wood, those *idjak*. He would spy otherwise useless bits of driftwood as he walked along the shore, dry it in sunshine, then if large enough would turn it into cunningly decorated *idjak*.

"What manner of beast is this that Sedna has rejected?" Kiti always asked when she admired Tuk's sled or some tool made from driftwood. Neither Inuit of course had ever seen a tree, and no summer berry bush was supported by more than a spindly stem or vine. Kiti thought the material most beautiful when carved. Both she and Tuk agreed that *idjak* made from driftwood instead of bone fit more comfortably on the face. But the source of this mysterious substance was just one more of many secrets guarded by Queen Sedna and the sea.

If the bit of precious wood retrieved was too small for practical use—as a spear, a runner, a crossbar, a harpoon—then Tuk was secretly pleased. He would turn the piece in his grasp slowly, study it from every angle, then easily and once again free from bark and pith whatever hid inside—often some sea mammal, some *puyee.*

From one, though, emerged a kittiwake—the slender, gull-like bird he often saw attacking cod brought up by narwhal. He charred the legs and wingtips to make those parts black as raven quills. Finished, he discarded the piece—or as he thought, released it.

On side-hills along the shore, he would find shiny soapstone uncovered by fierce tide. During the bright night while others slept, he worked this material with knives and mallet. He labored long over his carvings, whether wood or mineral . . . and he thought.

The aching pain from loss of family had subsided. But anxiety and restlessness dwelt within him just as this form or that one dwelt uneasily within the materials on which he worked. He could liberate the creatures, but who could release the tension in Tuk's own muscles and tight belly, the stiffening of his neck, the dull pain across his shoulders?

With Nuna, when she could leave her new litter so long, the young man walked out on isolated prairie. One day he heard a distant hail and looked about. Even the dog was mystified. On a hill to the south he finally made out two figures walking, unaccompanied by dogs. Tuk watched as they appeared on the next rise. One was tall and slender, taking long strides. The other was shorter, broad, quick-paced, a hurrier.

Each carried a bulging pack high on his back and braced with a strap across the forehead. As the two came closer, their tempo increased. Did they know him? No one would shout out a name, for no Inupiat would tempt malignant spirits hovering in the air.

But something about the visitors tugged a cord linked to his memory.

Ah, Narluk's sons! . . . He trotted forward to meet them.

Pajuk arrived before his brother, but was overwhelmed by a leaping, licking Nuna. Tuk watched in awe as the normally stand-offish bitch rose up to put her paws on Pajuk's shoulders. She whined and gave high, joyous yelps. Her tail became a blur of rapid movement. Clearly, the two knew each other.

Then Oojulit was there, laughing, undergoing the same treatment. Nuna dashed back and forth between them as Tuk observed with open mouth.

"Nuna, drop!" Pajuk commanded, grinning happily.

Hoo-oo. . . . They knew her name—eh, of the same village, so naturally they recognized each other?

"It happens that two young men have trailed far north inquiring of the coastal boy named Tuk," Oojulit said.

"—But then to find as well the pride of one's own family team!" Pajuk stooped to caress the wriggling form.

"It happens that a long search may now be finished." Oojulit smiled.

Tuk did not respond. Narluk's sons were looking for Nuna? Surely not for Tuk alone, as they professed. . . . But how unlikely that anyone would come so far—and limit oneself to travel afoot—to locate a mere *kringmerk*, however magnificent that dog might be.

Pajuk looked up, shining dark eyes fastened on Tuk's face. "Where is she?"

"She?" Tuk stammered. Nuna was right here before them. How did they know her so well? And how did Nuna know them—far better than merely coming from the same village, he decided. These three had shared more than that.

Oojulit prompted him. "The sister of these two brothers who stand before you."

"Sister," Tuk repeated in confusion.

"Sukitilan, of course," Oojulit said.

Tuk echoed, "Sukitilan."

Oojulit finally read the bewilderment on Tuk's features. His face darkened. "This Nuna dog was found where?"

A ray of light came into Tuk's mind—one slash of brilliance surrounded by murky fog. Details came to mind. His early observation of Kiti's exodus from the village while others slept. Her present name. Such unreasoning anger as comes only from fear when he had said he planned to return Arajik to that very village she had left. And always—the distance she maintained in conversation with him and with others, the careful weighing of what little she revealed about herself.

"We took the dog off the ice, near-dead of wounds and hunger," Tuk responded slowly. His stomach roiled with the discomfort all Inupiat feel about being less than fully honest.

Oojulit looked at Pajuk, and despair was exchanged in that grim glance.

"She was alone in her anguish," Oojulit said softly.

"True," Tuk agreed, but now more confused than ever. Such compassion and sorrow for a dog seemed unlikely. But then, these were Inupiat of the inland caribou. He must try to console them. "Still, she has had someone with her and caring for her at all times ever since her rescue."

"Not the dog!" Pajuk told him. "The daughter of Narluk, the small sister of these worthless brothers who stand before you."

"Small sister," Tuk repeated.

"Practically still a child," Oojulit said, "and very timid. "

"A timid child." If the Kiti he knew was this Sukitilan they sought—and considering Nuna, how could she not be?—then the young woman they described must have been away from home for longer than the one full season he presumed. Perhaps she only passed through on that night when he saw—no! She was accepted by the dogs. She had collected a team there. But the daughter of Narluk? These two surely spoke of someone else.

Chapter 38.
Contact

The mystified young man changed the subject. "It happens that the village of Tuk is not far away," he said, "and a man has space and food—poor though it is!—for these most welcome travelers."

He turned back to take the brothers to his people. He did not worry that villagers would reveal anything. Neither Oojulit nor Pajuk was likely to ask total strangers about their sister Sukitilan, now that Tuk was found. These two evidently believed her dead, with only Nuna remaining. As might truly be the situation by now, Tuk told himself, for all anyone here could know. . . .

Except, he was certain that he would somehow discern her finish just as he had picked up on her distress before he went with villagers to search for her on ice. No, Kiti was alive and healthy. Somewhere inland by now. And although he held these two and their father—Narluk was Kiti's father?!—in high esteem, he respected Kiti's reasons for leaving her family, whatever they might be, and resolved not to disclose her presence among ice islanders inland for the summer.

In the next days of never-ending light, sunshine broken by frequent rain and wind but never darkness, the three walked out together. Gradually, Tuk understood that these were indeed brothers to Kiti, and that they were genuinely saddened by her disappearance. Mighty Narluk was her father. She had deliberately hidden this fact from Tuk. He wondered why.

"The male parent has never been the same," Oojulit told him gravely, "since those two sweet females departed his igloo and his life."

Two abandoned his igloo? Perhaps the father and his sons were not as pleasant when nested in the family unit as they seemed upon the trail. Or did they mean Kiti and the dog—unlikely. Or if their Sukitilan had an older sister Kiti—

"—A mother died," Oojulit explained. "A young sister found it necessary to take the trail."

"Was pushed to do it," Pajuk agreed with such bitterness of tone that Tuk stared and Oojulit cleared his throat uncomfortably. Pajuk continued. "A child forced onto a black winter trail by a family that lacked compassion."

After walking a long time in silence, Oojulit spoke. "It happens that someone so young could not possibly get this far—"

"—Yet, a family's chants went out to many spirits for a miracle," Pajuk said.

"—Only a child," Oojulit resumed, "a pampered female who had never needed to endure hardship."

"Helpless and ignorant alone on a trail," Pajuk said with an air of finality.

Tuk spoke no more. Even if the brothers did ask villagers, this child they described as their Sukitilan could not easily be linked to the fierce and confident huntress Kiti. Through Nuna? Still, so far as people here could know, Nuna had been picked up along the trail and added to Kiti's team. They did not know the dog had nursed Arajik. In their view, two inlander friends of Tuk would be visiting to learn from coastal people the skills of harvesting an iceless sea. People here would be delighted to show these affable visitors ways to stalk seal and capture walrus. And to avoid catastrophe from the high tides. . . .

Still sleepless at night, Tuk pondered. Neither Oojulit nor Pajuk had asked about a baby. Yet, Arajik was born before Kiti left her people. Still another mystery.

After five long nights of continued deception with his guests, Tuk could no longer digest the food he forced himself to eat. His belly ached. He felt dizzy. Nothing seemed real. He watched and listened, even spoke, with a growing sense of detachment—he was the useless flapping strap on a stranger's sled. He felt himself to be present but no longer part of what went on around him.

The time had come, he decided late one sleepless night, to go find Kiti. She would summer with her mother's people if she had found them. And she must have done so, for she had agreed to return to his village if the trail northeast concluded without success. Therefore, she must be with one or another of the ice villagers.

But on what pretext could he go? He could not track her down and suddenly appear, saying only that his soul had become restless. Nor was it credible to contend that their paths just happened to cross.

Hoo-oo. . . . He had his reason for seeking her out—a reason far more important than that Nuna was ready to be returned to her. Kiti must be informed that her brothers were nearby—that they in fact thought her dead. Then she could herself decide whether to make her existence known to them. But somehow, someway—for curiosity chewed him without mercy—he must find out why she had left her family.

At the end of his sleep time without sleep, he made a backpack by using thongs to bundle some robes wrapped around food for a walking trail. His spear lay beside the burden he would carry. When the brothers awoke, he spoke softly to them. "Someone makes a journey."

"Let Tuk add the company of two brothers," Pajuk suggested, "two who have nothing to do until winter trails can be followed." The young men had been making gifts to villagers of caribou they captured so deftly here with experienced skill on inland forays.

In reciprocation, village folk had promised them this extra dog and that one in order to make up a team when ice and snow arrived. The brothers would be using sinew on bones from a beached whale for runners and sun-dried antlers from caribou as cross-pieces to make ready a magnificent sled for their return. Meantime, villagers were enjoying the extended stay of these vigorous and pleasant aliens from inland.

Tuk said, "It happens that this travel must be made alone." Would Nuna be permitted to go with him? Her pups were weaned. Their mother was in his care, after all, and he was responsible for her safe return to Kiti. But Kiti being absent, the dog obviously belonged to the two young men.

The brothers made no protest when their host insisted on making his trip unaccompanied—for they were still weary of travel and enjoyed the hospitality of the village. Oojulit shrugged when Tuk said he wanted to take Nuna with him. Although the two quietly claimed her, they agreed to let her stretch her legs after confinement first with wounds and then a litter now independent and distributed.

Tuk was careful not to say he would bring the big dog back— and Kiti's brothers did not think to ask. Why would they? After all, their friend promised to return well before the snow. Meantime, the two could stay here and care for Tuk's team. They could continue to learn from enthusiastic villagers the ways of finding provision in the sea. And they could try to stockpile food against their long return journey.

So Tuk with Nuna set out to the northwest. A rising wind *Nigituk* hastened him on his way.

Chapter 39.
Justice

Kiti's early thought about the identity of Adla, after his cleaning, was based entirely on his appearance. His healing and weight gain strengthened her earlier notion. She had no doubt but that Adla was—well, had been—her brother Palunga. As the days passed, though, anticipated joy was replaced by deepening dread. The wit and humor of the brother she once loved best had vanished with no trace.

Yes, of course she recognized this now strong and physically healthy man. But the essence of her youngest brother was confused by raptures on a trail too long solitary and by grim events no one would ever know. Was his condition permanent? This question haunted her. At least, he was no longer Adla the stranger, not to her.

In the sunshine of night during sleep, she awakened to his shadow crossing her face as he walked alone. She checked to see that Arajik slept soundly before she herself got up and padded outside after the man. He sat on the lake shore embankment. She touched his shoulder and spoke only to let him know that she was there, then sat beside him. For a time, both watched the water.

Kiti finally cleared her throat. She turned to watch his face. She tried to ignore the ugly silver scar. "Palunga," she said softly, "a sister welcomes her brother back."

Not so much as a narrowing of eyes betrayed his hearing let alone his understanding of her words. He continued to stare straight ahead at the riffling lake surface while Kiti waited.

At last, she chanted in a low voice, "Palunga . . . Palunga . . . PALUNGA!" She continued to watch the face for response of any kind, but nothing happened. "Fifth son of Narluk and Pichikut . . . brother to Sukitilan . . . and named Palunga."

The mouth of the man beside her began to work, twisting and opening several times before words would come. "This one is Adla the stranger, the Wild One. Then he turned to look at her and a grin sliced his face below glowering eyes. Suddenly, he grabbed her, forcing her shoulders to the gravel. He stared down at her, then fumbled with her *illupak*. She tore herself away and stood over him higher on the bank.

"Kiti is someone's sister!" she scolded. Every Inuit knew that such coupling is prohibited.
He lurched up from the ground to grasp her wrists.
"Palunga!" Again she twisted away and ran fully up the bank. There she stood with hands on hips. "Someone forgets himself!" she told him, her eyes flashing anger and her feet ready to run. How strong he had become with his healing.
He blundered up toward her, then stopped, mouth open. His head cocked, then jerked to another angle. His eyes narrowed, a single line of concentration deepening between his brows. And Kiti watched as tears collected and trickled down his cheeks.
"Forgive, forgive, *issumariyungnaerpok*," he told her as he turned, slid hurriedly down the bank, dropped once more onto pebbles beside the lake.

Back in the lean-to and rolled into light robes with Arajik, Kiti trembled for a long time before sleep would come again. Not fear, but a vestige of anger and mostly something else . . . hopelessness finally admitted.

The next morning in a gloomy drizzle, Adla walked away from camp. A rumor that he had made himself a knife alarmed

Kiti. Ertok told her that the man had gone toward the place where *kringmerk* were staked. He has been with the village long enough to have the smell of the camp on him, she thought, and the dogs will not bother him. Still . . . "*Ahmi*, who can say what is to happen?"

Kiti armed herself and followed at a cautious distance, Arajik in her *amaut*.

She arrived to see Palunga standing perfectly still and looking around at the dogs.

"Iyarpok?" he asked. Kiti remembered once again that her own team's Laughing One had once been Palunga's lead dog. Of course he knew that name even if not his sister's.

The dog looked up when his name was called, wagged his tail tentatively as Adla hurried to him. The big creature was in a far better mood, these days, now that Nuna was not around.

"Iyarpok!" The man got onto his knees before the staked dog, put an arm around his neck. Kiti saw movement at her brother's side, one flash of motion, no more. But the creature fell to the ground when Palunga raised his arm. Kiti hurried forward, then stopped.

"Iyarpok? Iyarpok?!" The man lifted one of the dog's legs, watched it fall back limply when he let go. The other hand held a bone knife with blood dripping from its point. Palunga stood up. "IYARPOK!?!" He kicked at the body. No response.

Then he dropped his head and Kiti heard his gasps for breath. She knew that tears were falling once again. "Forgive!" sobbed this Palunga who was not Palunga. "*Issumar-iyungnaerpok!!*" He grasped the dog's neck, raised the body to hug the creature with both arms.

Kiti felt tears dampening her own eyes as she walked up, and she knew that she did not grieve for Iyarpok. Together, Adla and she removed the dead dog's neckstrap. They helped each other carry the creature to a hillock above the lake. And together, wordless, they dug down to permafrost, then afterward laid rocks over the husk of what had been The Laughing One.

The sun now hid for hours in the middle of each sleep-time. This was a cold night with wind moaning outside the lean-to. Already, a few flurries had come to auger winter. The village was ready to move back to the sea as soon as hard freeze and snow cover promised a base for sled runners. Everyone yearned for home. Two dozen caribou hides stretched and cured on high bone racks.

Kiti had helped with strategy for capturing these long-legged *tuktu* who had dared to lag on green tundra behind their migrating companions. Countless firm-fleshed whitefish were sun dried and cached ready for lashing onto sleds. Handsome pelts from small game, too, awaited final processing to be used for *illupak* and clothing trim. Stacked ready to load beside individual sleds were bladders and pouches stuffed with dried berries, herbs and mosses, and sturdy bags of permafrost as well.

On the day Iyarpok died, Kiti and Arajik ate their meal before the sleep as usual with Ertok and Pomakut. After, Kiti stared into the lamp flicker as she revealed to these friends the truth about Adla and the dog, then about the earlier scene at the lake and finally about the spear threat to Arajik more than a moon ago.

"Hoo-oo!" Ertok breathed, and Pomakut echoed that response.

They decided to consult Sagak, and that man once again advised patience. "In summer can come madness from unending sunlight," he told them. "Soon will arrive the cold for which Inupiat was made. The useless *kringmerk* will work again and our own legs will stretch beside the sleds. Displaced spirits will settle into place. Let the people watch and be wary but tolerant."

Kiti tried to stay alert, but most days she went out, Arajik in her hood, to search for stragglers among end-of-season caribou. The great southern migration of these beasts had ended. Or Kiti went to fish with sinew at the edge of the lake, where hard ice was beginning to form and where the water was too cold for wading and hand fishing. Adla's new parka, trousers and boots were ready long since because village women all helped with the curing and careful assembly.

One day while most of the village was gone, Adla raped an old widow who had remained in her tent because, as she explained that morning, her bones creaked with the change of season. Kiti when she heard of this on coming home found herself sick at the stomach. She left the group to retch over and again, cold shivers wracking her and birdflesh rising on her skin. Part of what she felt was fear.

She remembered Tonratu. On top of the terror she felt guilt. Adla had displayed before now the strange predilection for violence so unlike his former self. And although Kiti had ultimately described those events to Sagak and her friends, she had warned no one. That late afternoon, when she had finally relieved herself and soothed her roiling stomach, she went immediately to the victim.

The sweet old grandmother was not injured, she told Kiti. Not hurt at all. Her reaction was, in fact, a combination of surprise and amusement. "He was gentle but persistent," she said. The language Inupiaq has no word for sex against the will because it does not ordinarily happen. Among people who enjoy the pleasure of each other's bodies from childhood, the idea of taking someone sexually by force is unthinkable. As was Tonratu's action, Kiti remembers.

The woman's eyes glittered as she gave a dramatic account. "And afterward, the boy called Adla cried true tears and said, 'Forgive, forgive!' A strange happening."

Later, the people turned to Sagak.

He wrinkled his small nose to show disapproval. Most of the villagers did not know of Adla's earlier transgressions. "It happens that this is not a good thing," Sagak told them. "A savage specter remains within the young man's healthy body."

"Yet, he asked forgiveness," the old woman reminded him. "Is this not honorable?"

Sagak looked at Kiti, and she dropped her eyelids down for a long time: No. Asking forgiveness is not honorable when someone fails to change behavior.

"Now everyone knows of the tortured person in our midst, this Adla," Sagak said at last. "He shall continue to receive tender regard, but all must be vigilant. No one should be alone at any time."

Good snow finally fell. Temperatures plummeted. Planning to leave for the coast within the next few days, villagers became intent on preparing sleds, packing for the journey home. Arajik bounced up and down in Kiti's hood and amused himself as she filled the last bladders with dried fish and arranged bags and pouches for her sled. No one paid attention to Isumak, the only youngster in the village permanently out of the *amaut*, a boy who seemed to be everywhere, chatting and laughing and asking questions. But people paid attention when the evening meal time came and Isumak did not appear.

The question went around the camp, "Does it happen Isumak is in someone's igloo?"

"No? Then where must he be?"

They found his body beyond a rise, near a frozen streamlet that dropped into the lake. He had been strangled. Pomakut went to find Adla, who came willingly enough.

When he saw the child, he cried. Great, aching sobs tore from his throat. "Forgive, forgive!" he said. Over and again.

The people turned away. Isumak, this time on earth, had drawn breath for a mere chink in the snowhouse of his lives. All went to comfort his parents.

That night brought howling wind with ice particles that swept parallel to the ground, intense wet cold. Every villager assembled in the larger of the two big caves, one several openings from where Adla had slept since late summer among other unmarried men and boys. He himself was invited to attend, but his was not among the solemn faces gathered around the seal oil lamps.

"If he were *kringmerk*," said Pomakut, "we could bind his limbs until good spirits returned."

"Hoo-oo!" the people disapproved. A shocking thought unworthy of consideration for an *inuk*.

Sagak cleared his throat for attention. "And everyone knows that Inupiat cannot live in a condition of restraint."

"It becomes necessary now to say," Kiti announced clearly, "that the stranger is Kiti's brother."

"Ai-ee . . . Ai-ee-ee. Hoo-oo!" Surprise and dismay.

"His name is Palunga. He is the fifth son of Pichikut. He disappeared two seasons past from tundra far south and west of here."

"Ee-ee," sadly. That explained it—a whole winter of solitude added to the summer before. How did he survive at all? Silence and gloom were in the group, sympathy, no sound. Based on long experience as well as the recent actions of a physically healthy Adla-Palunga, villagers agreed that no hope remained. Such a man was not Inuk, now, but rather Paija's Person, violent at the core, a danger to all and to himself. He would, most likely, be forever feral and frenzied, would never be predictable.

At last, Sagak spoke up once more, his eyes on Kiti. "The body is Palunga's, but the spirits within will ever be *adlait*, always strangers in battle with each other and the world."

Kiti's hand found the notch at her ear, tugged it unconsciously. Now she sucked in a long breath to show that she heard and accepted Sagak's words . . . and also that she reluctantly agreed. She stood up, as did Ertok and the other women. She was grateful not to be involved in what would come next.

As she pushed past the baffle to enter her own lean-to, carrying Arajik, she heard the village males file past to go down the embankment to the lakeshore. There, she knew, they would select fourteen small smooth pebbles and one larger, uneven one. They would station themselves well apart and privately near water's edge. There in the stormy night, Sagak would pass each man to drop a rock at random to sink into the shallow snow before him. Whoever then retrieved the larger and uneven stone would do the deed, and

269

only that one man would ever know. Responsibility for the act rested with every member of the group. Her brother Palunga—but now again Adla the stranger—would not live through this night. *Pirtok.* One cannot ever, ever change what has occurred.

A little later, she came awake in darkness to feel a hand on her shoulder. She sat up, clasping the robe to herself tightly, for the cold on this stormy night was intense.

"Come out," whispered the familiar voice. Kiti checked Arajik, arranged one furry robe around her shoulders and took time to pluck up her sharpest skinning knife.

She had no words when finally she got out and braced herself against the fierce wind. Sleet whirled everywhere and stung her face as she looked at the dim shadow close by. She could not see the features of that once-loved face, and she was glad.

Palunga too clutched a robe. He bent over her to speak into her ear and be heard above the gale. She clung tightly to the handle of her knife, had it outside the robe but hidden in a fold.

"Sometimes comes a moment's memory," he hissed, "of dear family and good times before the loneliness."

His recollections were returning. Was this not a healthy sign?

"Palunga!" she groaned. "Come, the brother and sister with her child will go together from this place. They will leave tonight! Her mind was racing. Here might be hope for him . . . but not so much that she could endanger Arajik. So leave the baby? Ertok would take him—but where? Of course, to Tuk!—all she need do was tell her. Then she heard her brother's voice once again in her ear.

"Owka—No, for strong evil lies within the man who stands here . . . a burning presence churned at the hot center of the earth. . . . Sukitilan, forgive!"

He flung away his blanket, stepped from his *kamik* and flung away his warm new furs, then stripped away his underwear. With no sound or backward glance, he raced naked away from camp to the heart of Ooangniktuk, the powerful north wind.

Chapter 40.
Encounter

Kiti was numb for the first days of travel on the return to ice islands. She grieved silently, even knowing that her doomed brother had made a sensible choice at the end. Ever since Palunga left the family and their village so many moons ago and then did not return, his fate had been to her a strip of pelt that flapped upon the drying rack but never tempered. His tale was now a seasoned hide—true, not her choice in outcome but at least a painful event concluded.

She wondered if spirits of enraptured Inuit would heal in the sky and then return as protectors. Palunga's would if any could, she decided; for the brother she remembered had once possessed a graceful manner and a loving heart.

The weather was terrible for their return, day and night producing cold blasts which carried sleet and frozen fog. The hours of darkness increased—a result of storm-saturated overcast and portent of black winter to come. Whiteouts and shrieking blizzards forced frequent stops. Wind picked up snow previously fallen, coated it with sharp new frost, then churned it like a thousand tiny knives into the face and eyes. Frigid gale carried gusts that whipped the nose and mouth, rimed the lining of the lung.

Overland toward the coast contained rough terrain with sharp rocks jutting through still insubstantial ground cover. Many stops were necessary to pack and re-ice runners. To keep it malleable, a bag of permafrost was fastened inside every *silipak*. And here on the rock-savage *felsenmeer*, jagged edges were insufficiently ice-glazed and snow-covered. Thus, every driver had to fit hide bags around the bleeding pads of *kringmerk*, slip-string each canine *kamik* tight with sinew. Kiti kept unfrozen in her tunic pocket an herb paste she used to treat wounds on paws of all the suffering dogs. On whim, Kiti placed at the sole of each dog *kamik* a bit of *qiviut,* muskox fur to soften the trail.

Where is Tuk right now? She hoped that he would not go alone for dangerous *oomingmak*. . . . Tuk and Kiti hunted well together, did they not?

And Nuna—where is she? Kiti needed the great white bitch. With Iyarpok gone, her team which had previously performed as one creature of one mind was now confused. She kept testing different dogs in lead position, but without success. Individually, all had proven themselves valiant and hard-working; but none so far had the necessary strength of will overlaid with intelligent sensibility. Yes, Nuna is needed, here. As is Tuk.

Kiti shuddered as she ran beside her sled. Tuk? Why would she think he should share the suffering? Nuna, yes. Much needed. But if Tuk wanted to be here, he would have come. And when he did not, then he was not needed!

So cold. . . . So very cold. . . . She must turn her thoughts to overcoming the Snow Walker in this first severe storm of the season. Here was a circumstance during which each Inuk must tighten *nuilak* so that only the tiniest peep-hole remained, and that obscured by hide hairs. Those fortunate ones with *kapvik* on their parkas—with rich, frost-free wolverine pelt—need not forever slap away accumulating ice. Much as Kiti missed and yearned for Nuna, she had to admit relief that her still-fragile white dog was absent during this painful trek.

The villagers fussed over Kiti, especially Ertok and Pomakut. They worried, she knew, that she suffered greatly from the shock of losing Palunga. Sagak one night came to her tiny trail igloo just before the sleep. He coughed courteously before crawling through the baffle. Suspecting that she chewed interminably on this last occurrence as well as other events unknown to him—for she must have endured hardship to come alone to search out their village—he spoke to her directly about the recent tragedy, something no other villager would invade her grief to do.

"Even the great disasters in our puny lives are small ones," he told her, "when someone looks to the circling horizon with all its pain and joy. And that ring itself is trivial within a sky that may peer down on countless horizons under myriad suns and moons, each sharing as many seasons as there are sand granules on the coast of the Sunrise Sea."

Inupiat have always known that the earth circles the sun while the moon circles the earth. Have in fact always taken pleasure in the roundness of it all. For several moments, Kiti envisioned herself as a single hair on an *iglerk* full of fur. The fantasy helped, and she summoned that very perspective often in days to come.

The sadness of this puny woman will pass.

At last, and after many sleeps, her grief could be managed. She had six brothers. Three were surely dead, and one was now her son. Therefore she had two brothers. To continue her inventory, the old Sukitilan had two parents. The mother was gone, but her spirit was nearby. Nearby to Arajik and to Kiti, that would be. So then, did Kiti have two parents?

The father. Hoo-oo. Here was a matter for study at a later time, when Kiti's own soul was not so troubled. Perhaps, as sleep times with their moons and seasons passed, she would understand. Or might Narluk someday comprehend the thinking of his wife and daughter?

Meantime, Kiti had proven herself to herself, in making the long trip from family and village. In being independent. In fulfilling the pledge to Pichikut. So now once again, back to her mother's village . . . to Kiti's village. . . . To the rest of her life and of Arajik's? *Ahmi.* Who can know the future?

She came awake suddenly in the tiny trail igloo she had built the night before. Someone—something—fumbled at the robes where she and Arajik lay. She jerked up, Tonratu uppermost in her blurred consciousness. She had the sharp knife in her hand and was trying to focus on shadow visible from the low lamp wick and in the pale flicker of spirit lights on the arc of snow overhead.

Her team was staked just outside the entry. Why had they made no sound? Even now, her dogs were quiet, unalarmed. Unless they were dead? She raised her knife high over the shaggy creature beside her—then felt a wet lick on her cheek. Another. She lowered the knife slowly.

"Nuna?" Kiti asked.

Awakened, and even from his robes in near-darkness, Arajik shouted with joy as he recognized first the name and then the touch and smell of his foster mother.

Then the young woman saw the hide baffle at her doorway push up, recognized Tuk crawling through. In hot confusion, she reached out to raise the sinew in the lamp. She felt a chaos of conflict. Her first impulse had been to raise her arms and clasp this man to her tightly and forever, take solace and strength from his presence. Why?

Her second impulse? To dismiss him, just order him away. Again, why?

Ah, Nuna. How she had missed the dog—and Arajik longing for her even more. The small boy was tangled and half out of the robes, his bare arms and fists pummeling the creature. Nuna put down a paw to anchor him, then nosed and bathed him excitedly.

Still muddled, trembling, frowning, Kiti turned back to Tuk. Had they not agreed that she was to make this journey alone?

"It happens," he told her with a slow, uncertain smile spreading across his face, "that someone brings news."

Nuna leading joyously, her old position no longer contested, Tuk and Kiti shared her sled to go north and east with her village.

"Hoo-oo!" Ertok teased at first. "Here is a fine young man whose existence Kiti hid away!" Others also tried to joke with her about him while Tuk was out with the men to find provision for the trail. But banter gradually ceased when the girl did not respond.

She showed no anger or embarrassment over their friendly jibes, but no particular pleasure, either. People noticed that although the two spent trail time together and ate their meals with Ertok and Pomakut, they continued to build separate little igloos for the night.

Kiti could not talk of her visitor even to Ertok, because the girl herself was in a drift of confusion. She tried not to let herself think about Tuk, for he only complicated the quandary in which his news had placed her. Should she make her existence known to Oojulit and Pajuk? What of Arajik, if she did? Should she let them know of his survival? And if so—for it would be hard to hide him if she herself appeared—might she then somehow endanger him?

No. She remembered the threats of Odlerk, and she recalled her automatic and violent response to those threats. Nothing would happen to Arajik. She would not let harm come to him. Nor would Nuna. Whatever was necessary for his safety, she could do. Both of them. . . .

Narluk was not here with his sons, Tuk said. Surely her brothers would not have walked all this way simply to harm a child they believed died long ago. . . . So why had they come? Hoo-oo, yet another question. To compel her to return? But she would never again live with Narluk and her old village. . . . And should she tell her brothers about Palunga?

No. Why cause new pain needlessly?

As she made her way with Tuk and villagers to the east, she devised a plan and discussed it with Tuk. When they finally reached the coast, he was to take her team with Nuna southeast to his village, she continuing north and east, sharing sled and provision with willing Ertok and Pomakut. Tuk would tell Oojulit and Pajuk that their sister was alive. Then—if they wished to see her—he would see to it that they went to the ice islands or else found her on the trail. She wanted to meet with them—if at all—in the company of her new people, those from Pichikut's original home.

The child in her, the frightened young woman who had started this long, uncertain trip almost a dozen moons ago, wanted someone else to take responsibility for that first encounter. But the mostly confident person she had become was grateful to Tuk. Not only had he protected the secret of her existence and of Arajik's. He had also left to her those decisions that affected her, since it was she who must live with the results.

What an unusual man, this Tuk—somehow intuitive. Perceptive of her situation, even when he understood only part of it.

She realized at last that her long-standing resentment over what she thought to be his many mysteries stemmed mostly from her own unwillingness to talk. Her own unfounded suspicion and lack of trust. Her fear of Narluk and of the unknown future. Unjustified as she gradually knew her caution over Tuk to be, she had continued to closely screen her speech.

Now, though, without restraint, she told him everything about her family circumstance as they moved along the trail. All the pieces he had heard before—and all that he had surmised from observation—now were lashed tightly with the sturdy sinew of truth. Pichikut. Narluk. The Dead Village. Yes, Tonratu. Even Odlerk. All, all, all. . . .

The young man followed closely her words and her countenance. His own features betrayed no surprise or chagrin or pleasure. He was the perfect listener as Kiti shared her secrets of fact and even fancy.

Ertok had been first to mention Tuk's special qualities. "The

277

person who released *oomingmak* from the stone," she said of the carving Kiti kept, "possesses not only skill but great patience as well! Skill and patience with carving, yes, Kiti thought, and with Nuna. And with people. Especially with Arajik. And with Kiti herself—even when she was angry and unreasonable. Hoo-oo. . . . Such thoughts made her restless.

Later, they agreed that Tuk should not mention the baby to Oojulit and Pajuk. If they came north to see their sister, Arajik would be with her, and they would then of course see him and deduce his origin.

"It is fully agreed, then," she said once more to Tuk before he left, "that Arajik is none but Kiti's son?"

"Yes, as said before. No mother could care more."

Snow fell and drifted. At the last sleeptime before Tuk left the group to return to his own village, the two by tacit agreement built but one small trail snowhouse. Kiti cut extra blocks while Tuk layered from the center. When the woman crawled inside, her head bumped the sleeping shelf, the *iglerk*. The ice ledge claimed four-fifths of the tiny igloo.

"Hoo-oo! It may be that half the village will join us tonight in the robes!" She rubbed the top of her head.

Tuk grinned. "And it may also be that they will not!" He plumped and then smoothed the many robes piled on the shelf.

This, then, was what *nuliakpok* could be. The coming together of a man and woman who cared deeply for each other. Kiti felt Tuk's nose nuzzle the hollow between her own nose and cheek. The patient man with the delicate touch. An artist whose medium was his body on this night. What did his artistry see in Kiti? What would he release? Here within the furs was something unique and of great value among her life experiences. Here was more than joy. Throbbing, she pulled him close to make every bit of this man a part of her.

Chapter 41.
Parity

In the short light of early winter midday, two sleds came up the trail behind the moving villagers. All stopped and waited. Pajuk with a ragged fan of obviously still unfamiliar dogs pulled around the lead to approach first and start the process of staking his team well behind the barking, snarling village dogs.

Next came Nuna jauntily leading Kiti's own team—and with Oojulit driving them. Anxiously, the girl scanned the trail behind the sleds. Where was Tuk?

Kiti took her hunting bag off Pomakut's sled, set it in the snow after grasping the spear. The meeting would be cordial, she decided, quite formal on her part at least. What is their true reason for coming so far? After one last search for Tuk along the back trail, Kiti walked over to release Nuna from the team. The big white dog beside her and the spear clutched in her right hand but pointed to the ice on which she stood, she turned to meet her brothers.

Ertok had been carrying the baby, and she padded behind, dragging Kiti's hunting bag. Now the older woman brought Arajik from her own makeshift *amaut*, stood him on the ground. A vigorous toddler, these days, he broke away and half-crawled, half-ran to meet an enthusiastic Nuna.

Ertok followed the boy to the small group collected near the teams. Kiti had told her that her brothers might be visiting, although she had not explained the circumstance. The woman introduced herself.

"It will be better," Kiti told her friend, "for the village to keep moving and use wisely the gift of such good weather."

Ertok caught her eye sharply, and the younger woman smiled. "As can be seen, Nuna and the team have arrived. These two hulking men—" she glanced at Oojulit and Pajuk—"are also testing dogs to make a team which will take them back inland and home."

Anyone could see that the *kringmerk* of Pajuk's team were motley and mismatched. Where had the brothers found such creatures? Pajuk was the better trainer, Kiti knew. But both had much work in front of them before this bunch could become a unit to break a tundra trail south and west.

Ertok gave Kiti a slow smile, then went forward to confer with others in the village. She returned almost immediately. "It happens that Kiti's people—" and she looked soberly at the brothers—"will continue slowly along the trail." Then the woman reached down to collect Arajik.

"The child needs to stay," Kiti told her friend softly.

Ertok hesitated, then seemed to sense the need for privacy, so wheeled and trotted up to join the others. In a moment, the ice villagers moved on north and east to break a trail. Kiti swung a protesting Arajik into her hood.

Oojulit and Pajuk stood before her, watching mutely. Nor did Kiti speak, for she could not think of what to say first. Questions lay crowded on her tongue like red-billed terns on a cliff face—but she was determined to contain them.

She lowered herself onto the familiar robes that Oojulit had strapped to her tidy sled. Palunga's sled. It would be good to have her own coverings at sleep time. She had wondered at night how much time would pass before she could reclaim the sled and tested team—and of course Nuna. As she lowered herself, Arajik scrambled nimbly from the *amaut*, dropped down to join the big white dog once more.

Oojulit and Pajuk also chose to sit, one on each side of their sister. The villagers probably thought it odd that Kiti sat unresponsive, clinging to her spear, impassively watching the antics of the child and dog before her.

No one spoke. In fact, the brothers too watched closely as Nuna and Arajik tussled on the ice, rolling and diving at each other with canine yips and childish crows of merriment. Over and again, Arajik tried to climb onto Nuna's back. They romped for a long time before the action mellowed and finally ceased as dog and child crawled into the sled robes together, curled up and closed their eyes contentedly.

Now what, the girl wondered.

The brothers shifted their attention to Kiti, and Pajuk finally spoke. "It happens that a snowhouse is needed here to contain the three talkers."

Kiti looked for the first time at his face and caught mischief in his eyes. With no responding smile, she added, "And for the smaller two who love deeply without words."

"A cozy igloo," Oojulit added as he stood up and took his own hunting bag from the sled, pulling out the broad snow knife, "because it is likely going to take some time for these great talkers to begin."

Relieved to have activity replace the uneasy silence, Kiti found clear freshwater ice in a draw, cut a rough circle of it and carried it to her brothers for use in making an eye for the top of the trail igloo. Then, while she waited to chink the blocks, she unloaded from her sled all that Oojulit had packed. She was relieved to see that he had brought food. With the villagers gone, she had no provision.

After a silent meal, Kiti sat on the *iglerk* to mend her left *kamik* snagged on a sharp rock by the pool where she got ice. She chewed the hide patch to soften it so that it would fit smoothly into the repair. She had to consciously hold back from inquiring whether her brothers had damage that required a woman's attention.

Then she had to bite back a giggle. She would and did

regularly sew and patch—like any Inupiat woman—for any villager whose clothing or *kamik* needed maintenance, also for Tuk, even for a stranger on the trail who had no one else to do the task. She did it not because it was a woman's job, but rather because only a woman had been trained from childhood to do it properly. A poor patch on clothing and especially on *kamik* could mean death to the wearer if he or she were on the trail. And yet—Kiti would not on this day offer aid to her two brothers?

Eh, and not tomorrow, either. First they must ask!

Oojulit and Pajuk sat watching Kiti from their seats on folded robes in the middle of the snowhouse floor. The two men traded bewildered glances from time to time, but Kiti had no sense of secrets or signals being exchanged. Clearly, they had arrived upon a situation they did not expect.

Now Kiti lay down her mending and turned to her hunting bag. From it she finally found and withdrew the mortar and small pestle she needed to prepare Arajik's food. She used her knife to slice off layers of seal from the split Oojulit had brought in. Now she mashed the flesh and blubber for warming it in the stone bowl that heated above the lamp. Arajik must have his final meal before the sleep.

Kiti kept her features serene. She ignored her guests except, of course, in wildly churning thought. She would not ask, must not ask, absolutely refused to ask any of the questions seething in her.

She amused herself by imagining ways to phrase them elegantly so that they were not questions but rather comments that did not absolutely require response. And she fastened her upper teeth along her lower lip to keep from blurting out a likely phrase. She would not so much as clear her throat. They must speak first, these two, for they had sought her out, not the reverse.

Kiti got up, went outside to retrieve Arajik from Nuna and the sled.

Oojulit and Pajuk looked at each other. Where was the fragile sister they remembered? They did not doubt but that this woman crawling in with the child was Sukitilan. Yet the person they saw held her head high, moved with certainty, possessed a thick hide of independence which was hard if not impossible to pierce. Kiti sensed their thoughts, drew herself up even more strongly, placed Arajik in her *amaut*, and busied herself on several tasks not absolutely necessary.

"Pichikut's child." Oojulit finally punctured the silence.

"Yes, the child who died on ice now lives." Their sister gazed at them with unwavering eyes. "And is son to the woman called Kiti."

"Hoo-oo. . . . Kiti!" both breathed out softly, nodding, their eyes fastened on her.

After another uncomfortable pause, Kiti allowed herself one word. "Narluk."

Oojulit's face clouded. "Angakok has become a feeble man."

"Skin hangs in wrinkled folds across his shrinking bones," Pajuk added.

"Yes, and a frozen fog sits silent in his eyes," Oojulit told her, "ever since he lost his two sweet women."

"Hoo-oo!" Kiti flared. "One lost, the other pushed away."

Had they come to retrieve her, then? And did they think to force her return by filling her with pity for her father? Eh, she could speak her thoughts now, she decided.

In a few bitter words, she described what she had seen as they passed her on the trail eleven moons before. "Narluk was strong and vital then. He was determined to do as he thought he must. So intent on slaughter that he ran before the sled, pacing the lead team."

"No." Oojulit spoke softly. "Until this very day, all thought the babe had perished on the ice where Narluk left him."

Pajuk stood. "Yes, and so the search seen by Sukitilan was for a young woman, Narluk's only daughter." He took a step toward Kiti, reached out with both arms.

Kiti stood still, eyes narrowed and cold. She would not retreat, but her stony stare stopped his advance. Eh, Koloki. . . . And at the end, does a frost serpent regret mortality? Perhaps.

Her unspoken words echoed in her ears. "It happens, then, that a father has sent his sons," she said. Would the brothers take her words as the question they were meant to be? Had Narluk sent them to find her?

Rebuffed, Pajuk walked over to sit on the sleep ledge. He placed his hand softly upon the boy's head, and Kiti eyed her hunting bag against the wall. Never mind, Nuna had come in through the buffer, now, and would not permit harm to her foster son—not even by other members of the family she loved. Probably not even by Kiti. The dog's head went up, alert, her muzzle busily nosing Pajuk's hand away.

"It may be that a father and two brothers were wrong, Sukitilan—"

"—Kiti! Remember that this woman before you is Kiti." She drew out the two syllables with equal strong emphasis on each. "And Narluk is father to Sukitilan, not to Kiti."

"The boy—"

"—Arajik."

Silence. Pajuk studied his sister, his hand once more resting soft upon the child's form beneath the robes. Then he looked over at Oojulit before returning his gaze to his sister.

"The dog, though—" and Pajuk lifted his fingers to scratch one of Nuna's furry ears "—is Nuna still?"

Kiti glared at him, then softened when she saw the twinkle in his eyes.

It was Oojulit who responded to her earlier statement. "Narluk has asked his sons to find his only daughter, if she is still alive—and to request her forgiveness."

Kiti did not respond other than to search their faces for a

measure of their sincerity.

"Each night before the sleep," Oojulit continued, "he tells his two worthless sons how wrong it is to do a thing blindly and for no good reason other than that it has been done so in the past."

"'*Peeusinga* is not infallible'—Over and again, he tells those brothers," Pajuk said, "until his sons would have taken the trail anyway, just to be away from him." He sighed. Like his father, Pajuk exercised patience with difficulty.

"Yet, he himself put a son on ice to die," Kiti said harshly.

"Yes," Oojulit said, "and he tells his sons about it so often because he cannot accept the revulsion of his having performed that very deed."

"He learned late in life, he says, and at great cost." Pajuk sighed.

Chapter 42.
Quest

Her brothers went foraging with her in the stormy, darkening days that followed. Two teams must be fed, and four people. They hunted following the sleep, then took the trail northeast for some hours before building a single trail igloo to share. Now they traveled coastal prairie ridges and finally *tuwak*, a safely frozen sea. Kiti saw her brothers become increasingly comfortable.

Not meaning to, she daily exhibited her skill in coastal searches. And her luck revealed itself. As winter settled in, the ratio of grounded sea ice expanded. The three of them used trail time and leisurely evenings to visit, to let Kiti rebuild trust slowly, watchfully. The pressure ridge of fear and resentment she had nurtured now for nearly twelve moons gradually subsided.

Neither brother questioned her leadership in this setting, but rather remained in awe of it, despite their recent instruction and practice at Tuk's village. But it was Kiti and not they who readily found sea and even coastal game in this place.

It was she who could approach and capture it. What had been an observation evoking mirth and banter at home—that their younger sister saw prey faster and more frequently—was now a demonstrated fact. Her speed and expertise dazzled them.

Nor did any remnant remain of her old hesitation to strike when opportunity came. She did not seem to take pleasure in killing, but she got much satisfaction from harvesting their surroundings for food.

And she did by now know marine creature uses never dreamed of by the two inlanders.

These days of hunting were for Kiti a balance of anxiety and routine. She fought the growing warmth for her brothers by reminding herself of how they ignored her distress when Narluk took the baby, of how they followed their father to track her on the trail. In fact, after a dozen sleeps—her new village by now far ahead and perhaps even settling for the winter on their island—she wished that the brothers would move on. The three of them had made peace, but all knew by now that the fabric of family was torn irreparably.

Oojulit and Pajuk accepted that she would not return to Narluk with them, never live at her former home permanently. They could observe daily how much at ease she was, how self-reliant, here at the top of the world. Nothing was to be gained by their lingering, and they had far to go.

Besides, Kiti awaited Tuk without admitting this fact to the brothers or even to herself. At first, she was sure he would soon arrive. Each passing day, to her thinking, made it all the more certain that his return was imminent. She scanned the south and west whenever she could do so without notice.

And as time passed, she tried to contain her disappointment. After all, she warned herself, he did have his own team—and she had hers, along with Nuna. There was no particular need for him to seek her out, was there?

She had learned that her brothers had been with Tuk throughout much of the past summer. That they had packed and carried on their backs from inland their hunting gear, their winter clothing, only a little food, and a few small items for trade. And satisfying her great curiosity, she had learned that her brothers' second sled—the one handled by Pajuk; certainly not her own, with Oojulit on the lines and Nuna at the head—was drawn by *kringmerk* put together from gifts and trades made in Tuk's village—very young dogs or quite old ones, and some few troublesome creatures as well—all now being taught to work together under Pajuk's firm control.

Two of Nuna's last litter scampered loose with the working team, and these were especially prized by the men.

At last, Kiti accepted that Tuk was not going to come. He knew that her brothers would find her. Perhaps he thought that all of them together might wish to return to their tundra home and to Narluk for a cohesive family unit. The woman sighed. Not possible.

Those in Tuk's village know of no Sukitilan," Oojulit told her one night before the sleep. That day had been unusually successful, with three seals taken while basking on a flow, two of these by Kiti. She would happily lash all three to their sled if only the brothers would go back now.

"Tuk, though, must have known." Her eldest brother was asking a question.

"He heard that name first when two brothers inquired," she assured him.

Pajuk spoke up. "The villagers there did say that a woman called Kiti is valiant in the quest for provision."

"—And lucky," Oojulit added. "It is said of a village to the south that she is known to have captured more walrus than all the others together—"

Pajuk broke in. "—That she is extremely fortunate in the hunt."

Those words again. . . . "Someone's helping spirit—" Kiti began, then ceased. The stronger and more independent they thought her, the more likely that they would leave soon and peaceably without her.

As if to read her thought, Oojulit continued. "Following this sleep, it happens that two brothers must take the trail for their own village inland," he said. "It may be that Kiti will wish to go as well."

Like a sunbeam descending from the sky, the girl suddenly saw her future—not events so much as circumstance. The ice island here was to be her home, the people here surely hers, unless . . . until. . . .

"*Owka*," No, she told her brothers, "for it happens that Kiti has something she must do."

She watched both faces darken with sadness but not anger or even surprise.

"A father promised not to seal his igloo before his sons returned with news," Pajuk muttered.

The girl smiled. No Narluk she recalled would die so passively. She did not doubt but that he might have threatened such a thing. "The sons may tell their father—"

"—Not Sukitilan's father also?" Pajuk prompted.

"—Sukitilan no longer exists. But the sons may tell their father that Kiti with her child will come to visit—"

Oojulit smiled. "—Soon?"

The woman lifted her eyebrows, Yes. "Before the snow of this coming season is gone," she promised.

Oojulit and Pajuk took their sled south and slightly west on sea ice to make a final provisioning at Tuk's village. A direct path with a team on smooth ice would mean an easier trip than the one coming north to find their sister.

On that same day, Kiti with Arajik started due south with the team led by Nuna. She had decided not to follow the clear trail northeast left by the villagers. Not yet. Instead, the young woman embarked on the most important journey of her life. Nor did she care how long it might take.

Just now starting her eighteenth winter, Kiti knew what she wanted. Not the where or the when or even the how, exactly. But she had a clear quest and determined focus. She would find Tuk and let him know how she felt.

Eh, Pichikut? Eh? Smile on Kiti to insure that a daughter has great good fortune in the hunt!

Epilogue

The villagers sat rapt as the storyteller continued his tale

> Kitilan lay upon the surface of the sea.
> Sedna saw her there. "This one, we will take," she decided.

But *Ooangniktuk*, the north wind, was in a temper. He was, as usual, warring with *Nigituk* from the south about—also as usual—who was stronger.

"No!" he blared, just to be contrary. Then he blasted a breath beneath Kitilan that flung her looping high into the air and onto the icy ledge from which she had fallen.

The girl snatched breath in the clashing gales and looked about for shelter, but saw only the five seals captured before she fell.

She shivered. Ooangniktuk swept frozen fog along the ground. *Nigitook* answered his power with a blizzard having frozen flakes so tightly packed as to be blowing drifts.

Kitilan drew from her icy parka the jagged tooth of a Greenland shark. Fighting the gale, she lurched to the biggest seal, sliced open his belly and hauled out still-steaming intestines, then crawled inside.

"Now shriek, thou windy two!" she muttered before she pulled in close to her the cut flap of skin with its heavy blubber. She curled down into the warmth of her well-insulated refuge.

"Let them rage," she murmured once again before she slept.

Glossary

aa-gii-ii!: no (emphatic)

adlait: strange

aglu: seal breathing hole on ice

ahmi: no one can predict the future

ai-ee-ee! (or similar): exclamation of surprise or horror

aiverk: WALRUS

alertik: furred house shoes/slippers or stockings

amaut: woman's extra hood for carrying baby

amoutik: women's parka built to accommodate *amaut*

ananak: mother

angakok: shaman; healer, sorceror, philosopher; spiritual leader

ee-ee: eyes

ee-ma!: yes absolutely! (emphatic)

Hoo-oo!: interjection to express disapproval

idjak: slitted spectacles for snow (to prevent snow blindness)

iglerk: sleep ledge in igloo

igloo: any shelter: lean-to, hide hut, snow blocks, wood, reinforced concrete–whatever

illupak: light undergarments kept on to wear inside shelter

ingminekone's: self alone

inueruttyok: the people are (all) gone

Inuit: general term for native Arctic people (formerly Eskimos)

Inuk: general term for native Arctic person (formerly Eskimo)

Inupiaq: language spoken by Inupiat

Inupiat: Inuit of northernmost Canada, Greenland, certain parts of Alaska, Siberia

issumariyungnaerpok: forgive

kalunait: "heavy-eyebrowed" people (from everywhere "south")

kamik: custom-fitted, warm, waterproof boots for winter wear

kaoyok: to copulate
kapvik: WOLVERINE
kargolarpok: what a great smacking of lips (good manners)
katajak: the "wind songs" of wind witches; throat music
kayak: small, enclosed canoe
kinaowit?: What's your name?
kringmerk: SLED DOG(s)
kussuyok: coward
nakorami: thank you
nanuk: POLAR BEAR
nathek: true (earless) SEAL
Nigituk: The South Wind
nipjarnok!: Shh! Be silent! (command)
nuilak: any fur trim on parka
nukapiak: male youth
nuliakpok: copulates
Ooangniktuk: The North Wind
oomingmak: MUSKOX
owka: no
Paija: spirit/goddess who incites evil deeds
peeusinga: culturally "correct"; the way of the people
perlerornaq: how very wearisome is life
permafrost: permanently frozen earth which in Arctic may go down many meters
pinnak!: don't!
pirtok: no one can change what has already occurred
puyee: (big) sea creatures
qiviut: soft muskox underfur
sog?: why?
siku: nomadic (ungrounded) sea ice
silipak: outer (fur) garment, often just trousers
soospuk: nitwit
suwit?: What do you want?
tokoyok: dead people/village
tuktu: CARIBOU
tullimak: rib/rib cage
tuwak: grounded sea ice

ulu: sharp, circular knife used for eating
umiak: sturdy, relatively large, rudderless "women's boat" or "
    whale boat" (rounded)
ungayok: love
upluk: nest (a small shelter of fur or snow)
ussuk: penis
uttuk: vulva

[eyebrows raised] yes (nonverbal)
[sucking in breath] yes and agreement (nonverbal)

Acknowledgments

I am indebted most deeply to Dr. Olav Oftedal at the Smithsonian for so graciously sharing his expertise on lactation. My thanks go also to the visionary Dr. Anwar Dil, who dispatched me to the Arctic; and to Dr. Edmund Carpenter, who made me feel at home there; and to Barry Lopez who explained so thoroughly what I saw at that time and feel now.

And of course kudos go to the usual great gals and guys who read, grimace, suggest, applaud, and doubtless weep in private. Jenny Kay forever, who has read this and my other belles-lettres for so many years. Walter Mayes who long ago heard my plan on Kiti and said: "Wow! A quest adventure with a female protagonist! DO it!" Daughter Karol Sarıtaş, who got me through a multitude of technological vicissitudes. Son Kent Brisby, who provided assistance with advice and by examining possibilities. To Chicki Mallan for tough and knowledgeable criticism and some well-placed kicks.

And to the geniuses in 6Meet (Gary Briley, Clidean Dunn, Willa Perrine, Mike Sajben, Jim Smith) and T.A.T. (Uncle Bob Ingram, "Rotten" Richard Rasmussen, amazing Nancy DeMarco, supportive Doug Bratten, and faithful Joan Tuttle), all of whom (sigh) listened to the foregoing along with the O.L.L.I. members from Chico State, and the Monday Group of writers in Paradise under Claire Braz-Valentine, including (again!) Gary Briley and Chicki Mallan, George McClendon, the late Bob Clark, Cindy McCusker, Jenifer Bliss, Chris Wood, Gloria Shogrun. . . . so California to New Hampshire, "♪...from sea ♪ to shining sea.... ♫"

A very special thank you goes to Doug Bratten for unfailing and sustained support and encouragement and to Pam

Marin-Kingsley who is probably responsible for this 2nd edition*
of my first book ever AND for continuing encouragement along
with her cover design (here) and oh-so-necessary but time-consuming computer expertise.

Phyl Manning

Comments and Annotations

[1] The muskox is a "misnamed" creature. First of all, it possesses NO musk glands. Second, with no "ox" or bovine ancestry of any kind, it belongs to the goat-antelope family. The Inupiaq word for this creature—*oomingmak*—means "animal with skin like a beard." Built to withstand the extreme cold of their habitat, the ventral hairs of a muskox may be two feet long covering a dense underfur wool about two inches long. Eight times warmer than wool, *Quviut* is cloth made from this fur, and is considered the warmest cloth on the planet.

[2] A first edition of this book was published in 2004 as *Kiti on Ice.*

About the Author

Phyl Manning

Author Phyl Manning has lived and worked within a variety of cultures. Focused on the traditional Inupiat in conjunction with doctoral studies in anthropology, she was determined to give these remarkable people literary breath, thought and action after her scholarly writing was concluded. Mrs. Manning divides time with family in New Hampshire and Northern California.

www.ingramcontent.com/pod-product-compliance
Lightning Source LLC
Chambersburg PA
CBHW031558240626
47153CB00002B/556